CORK CITY LIBRARY
Leabharlann Cathrach Chorcaí

J LEG.

www.corkcitylibrary.ie

Tel./Guthán (021) 4924900

This book is due for return on the last date stamped below.
Overdue fines: 5c per week plus postage.

11.

Central Adult: 4924908/9	Central Child: 4924903	Central Music: 4924919
Douglas: 4924932	Hollyhill: 4924928	Hollyhill: 4924935
St Mary's Rd Adult: 4924933	St Mary's Rd Child: 4924937	Tory Top Rd: 4924934

D0410131

◆ VOICES ◆

· VOICES ·

Ursula Le Guin

Orion
Children's Books

5437768

First published in Great Britain in 2006 by
Orion Children's Books
an imprint of the Orion Publishing Group
Orion House, 5 Upper St Martin's Lane,
London WC2H 9EA

The right of Ursula Le Guin to be identified as the author
of this work has been asserted by her in accordance
with the Copyright, Designs and Patents Act 1988.

A CIP catalogue record for this book
is available from the British Library

ISBN-10 1–84255–507–3
ISBN-13 978–1–84255–507–1

10 9 8 7 6 5 4 3 2 1

Typeset by Deltatype Ltd, Birkenhead, Merseyside
Printed in Great Britain by Clays Ltd, St Ives plc

www.orionbooks.co.uk

CASPRO'S HYMN

As in the dark of winter night
Our eyes seek dawn,
As in the bonds of bitter cold
The heart craves sun,
So blinded and so bound, the soul
Cries out to thee:
Be our light, our fire, our life,
Liberty!

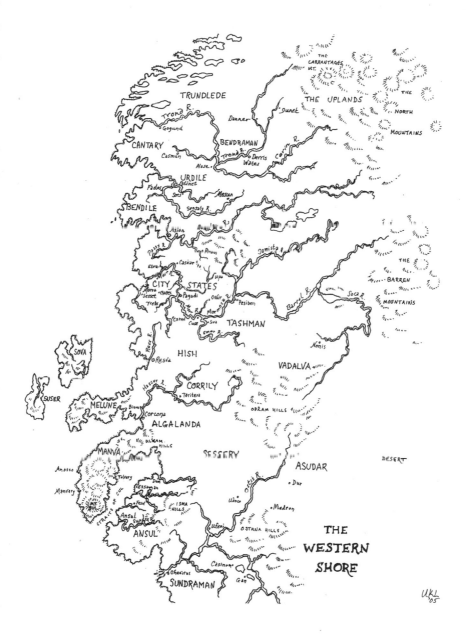

THE
WESTERN
SHORE

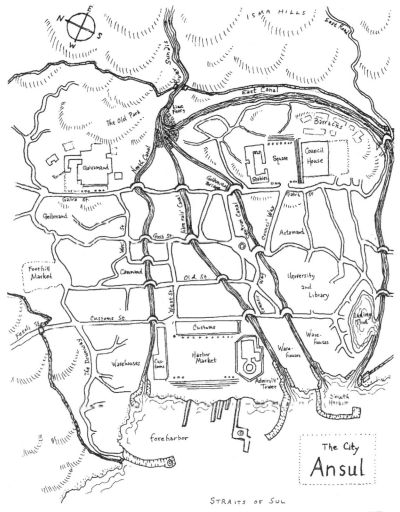

The City

Ansul

◆ 1 ◆

The first thing I can remember clearly is writing the way into the secret room.

I am so small I have to reach my arm up to make the signs in the right place on the wall of the corridor. The wall is coated with thick grey plaster, cracked and crumbling in places so the stone shows through. It's almost dark in the corridor. It smells of earth and age, and it's silent. But I'm not afraid; I'm never afraid there. I reach up and move my writing finger in the motions I know, in the right place, in the air, not quite touching the surface of the plaster. The door opens in the wall, and I go in.

The light in that room is clear and calm, falling

from many small skylights of thick glass in the high ceiling. It's a very long room, with shelves down its wall, and books on the shelves. It's my room, and I've always known it. Ista and Sosta and Gudit don't. They don't even know it's there. They never come to these corridors far in the back of the house. I pass the Waylord's door to come here, but he's sick and lame and stays in his rooms. The secret room is my secret, the place where I can be alone, and not scolded and bothered, and not afraid.

The memory isn't of one time I went there, but many. I remember how big the reading table looked to me then, and how high the bookshelves were. I liked to get under the table and build a kind of wall or shelter with some of the books. I pretended to be a bear cub in its den. I felt safe there. I always put the books back exactly where they belonged on the shelves; that was important. I stayed in the lighter part of the room, near the door that's not a door. I didn't like the farther end, where it grows dark and the ceiling comes down lower. In my mind I called that the shadow end, and I almost always stayed away from it. But even my fear of the shadow end was part of my secret, my kingdom of solitude. And it was mine alone, until one day when I was nine.

Sosta had been scolding me for some stupid thing that wasn't my fault, and when I was rude back to her she called me 'sheep hair', which put me in a fury. I couldn't hit her because her arms were longer and she could hold me off, so I bit her hand. Then her mother, my bymother Ista, scolded me and cuffed me. Furious, I ran to the back part of the house, to the dark corridor, and opened the door and went into the secret room. I was going to stay there till Ista and Sosta thought I'd run away and been taken as a slave and was gone forever, and then they'd be sorry for scolding unjustly and cuffing and calling me names. I rushed into the secret room all hot and full of tears and rage – and there, in the strange clear light of that place, stood the Waylord with a book in his hands.

He was startled, too. He came at me, fierce, his arm raised as if to strike. I stood like a stone. I could not breathe.

He stopped short. 'Memer! How did you come here?'

He looked at the place where the door is when it's open, but of course nothing was there but the wall.

I still couldn't breathe, or speak.

'I left it open,' he said, without believing what he said.

I shook my head.

Finally I was able to whisper, 'I know how.'

His face was shocked and amazed, but after a while it changed, and he said, 'Decalo.'

I nodded.

My mother's name was Decalo Galva.

I want to tell of her, but I can't remember her. Or I do but the memory won't go into words. Being held tight, jostling, a good smell in the darkness of the bed, a rough red cloth, a voice which I can't hear but it's only just out of hearing. I used to think if I could hold still and listen hard enough, I'd hear her voice.

She was a Galva by blood and by house. She was head housekeeper for Sulter Galva, Waylord of Ansul, an honorable and responsible position. In Ansul there were no serfs or slaves then: we were citizens, householders, free people. My mother Decalo was in charge of all the people who worked in Galvamand. My bymother Ista, the cook, liked to tell us about how big the household used to be, back then, how many people Decalo had to look after. Ista herself had two kitchen assistants every day, and three helpers for the big dinners for visiting notables; there were four housecleaners, and the handyman, and a groom and stableboy for the horses, eight horses in the stable, some to ride and some to drive. There were quite a few relatives and old people living in the house. Ista's mother lived up over the kitchens; the Waylord's mother lived in the Master's rooms upstairs. The Waylord himself was always travelling up and down the Ansul Coast from town to town to meet with the other Waylords, sometimes in the saddle, sometimes in a carriage with a retinue. There was a smithy in the west court in those days, and the driver and postboy lived on the top floor of the carriage house, always ready to go out with the Waylord on his rounds. 'Oh it was all busy and a-bustle,' Ista says. 'The old days! The good days!'

When I ran through the silent corridors past the ruined rooms, I used to try to imagine those days, the good days. I used to pretend, when I swept the doorways, that I was making ready for guests who'd come through them wearing fine clothes and shoes. I used to go up to the Master's rooms and imagine how they'd looked clean and warm and furnished. I'd kneel in the windowseat there to look out through the clear, small-paned window over the roofs of the city to the mountain.

The name of my city and all the coast north of it, Ansul, means 'Looking at Sul' – the great mountain, last and highest of the five peaks of Manva, the land across the straits. From the seafront and from all the western windows of the city you can see white Sul above the water, and the clouds it gathers round it as if they were its dreams.

I knew the city had been called Ansul the Wise and Beautiful for its university and library, its towers and arcaded courts, its canals and arched bridges and the thousand little marble temples of the street-gods. But the Ansul of my childhood was a broken city of ruins, hunger, and fear.

Ansul was a protectorate of Sundraman, but that great nation was busy fighting over its border with Loaman and kept no troops here to defend us. Though rich in goods and farmland, Ansul had long fought no wars. Our well-armed merchant fleet kept pirates from the south from harrying the coast, and since Sundraman enforced an alliance with us long ago, we had had no enemies by land. So when an army of Alds, the people of the deserts of Asudar, invaded us, they swept over the hills of Ansul like wildfire. Their army broke into the city and went through the streets murdering, looting, and raping. My mother Decalo, caught in the street coming from the market, was taken by soldiers and raped. Then the soldiers who had her were attacked by citizens, and in the fighting she managed to get away and get home to Galvamand.

The people of my city fought the invaders street by street and drove them out. The army camped outside the walls. For a year Ansul was besieged. I was born in that year of the siege. Then another, greater army came out of the eastern deserts, assaulted the city, and conquered it.

Priests led the soldiers to this house, which they called the Demon House. They took the Waylord away as a prisoner. They killed any people of the household who resisted them, and the old people. Ista managed to get away and hide at a neighbor's house with her mother and daughter, but the Waylord's mother was killed and her body thrown into the canal. Younger women were taken as slaves for the soldiers to use. My mother escaped by hiding with me in the secret room.

I am writing this story in that room.

I don't know how long she hid here. She must have had some food with her, and there's water here. The Alds ransacked the house, looting, burning what would burn. Soldiers and priests kept coming back day after day, wrecking the rooms, looking for books or loot or demonry. She had to come out at last. She crept out at night, and found refuge with other women in the basements of Cammand. And she kept herself and me alive, I don't know where or how, until the Alds ceased looting and wrecking and settled down as masters of the city. Then she came back to her house, to Galvamand.

All the wooden outbuildings had been burned, the furnishings broken or stolen, even the wooden floors torn out in places; but the main part of the house is stone with tile roofs, and it was not much harmed. Though Galvamand is the greatest house in the city, no Ald would live in it, considering it to be full of

demons and evil spirits. Little by little Decalo put
things in order again as well as she could. Ista came
back from hiding, with her daughter Sosta, and the
old hunchback handyman Gudit turned up. This
was their household, and they were loyal to it and to
one another. Their gods were here, their ancestors
who gave them their dreams were here, their blessing
was here.

After a year had passed the Waylord was released
from the Gand's prison. The Alds put him out into
the street naked. He could not walk, because their
torture had broken his legs. He tried to crawl down
Galva Street from the Council House to Galvamand.
People of the city helped him, carried him here,
carried him home. And there were people of his
household to care for him.

They were very poor. Every citizen of Ansul was
poor, stripped bare by the Alds. They lived somehow, and under my mother's care the Waylord
began to regain his strength. But in the cold and
hunger of the third winter after the siege, Decalo
took ill of a fever, and there was no medicine to cure
it. So she died.

Ista declared herself my bymother and looked

after my needs. She has heavy hands and a hot temper, but she loved my mother and did her best for me. I learned early to help with the work of the house and liked it well enough. In those years the Waylord was ill much of the time, in pain from the broken limbs and the tortures which had crippled him, and I was proud to be able to wait on him. Even when I was a very young child he'd rather have me wait on him than Sosta, who hated any kind of work, and spilled things.

I knew it was because of the secret room that I was alive, for it saved me and my mother from the enemy. She must have told me that, and she must have shown me the way to open the door; or I saw her do it and remembered. That's how it seemed to me: I could see the shapes of the letters being written on the air, though I couldn't see the hand that wrote them. My hand followed those shapes, and so I would open the door, and come here, where I thought only I ever came.

Until that day when I faced the Waylord, and we stood staring at each other, he with his fist raised to strike.

He lowered his arm.

'You've been here before?' he asked.

I was quite terrified. I managed a nod.

He wasn't angry – he had raised his arm to strike an intruder, an enemy, not me. He'd never shown me anger or impatience, even when he was in pain and I was clumsy and stupid. I trusted him utterly and had never been afraid of him before, but I did hold him in awe. And at this moment he was fierce. His eyes had a fire in them as they did when he spoke the Praise of Sampa the Destroyer. They were dark, but that fire would come into them like the smoulder of opal in dark rock. He stared at me.

'Does anybody know you come here?'

Shake head.

'Have you ever spoken of this room?'

Shake head.

'Do you know you must never speak of this room?'

Nod.

He waited.

I saw that I had to say it aloud. I took a breath and said, 'I will never speak of this room. Witness my vow all you gods of this house, and you gods of this city, and my mother's soul and all souls who have dwelt in the House of the Oracle.'

At that he looked startled again. After a moment he came forward and reached out to touch my lips with his fingers. 'I bear witness that this vow was made with a true heart,' he said, and turned to touch his fingers to the threshold of the little god-niche between the shelves of books. So I did the same. Then he put his hand lightly on my shoulder, looking down at me. 'Where did you learn such a vow?'

'I made it up,' I said. 'For when I swear that I will always hate the Alds, and I will drive them out of Ansul, and kill them all if I can.'

When I had told him that, my own most secret vow, my heart's wish and promise that I had never told to anyone, I burst into tears – not fury tears, but sudden, huge, awful sobs that seemed to pick me up and shake me to pieces.

The Waylord got down somehow on his broken knees so that he could put his arms around me. I wept against his chest. He said nothing, but held me in a strong embrace until at last I could stop sobbing.

I was so tired and ashamed then that I turned

away and sat on the floor with my face hidden against my knees.

I heard him haul himself up and go limping down towards the shadow end of the room. He came back with his handkerchief wet with water from the spring that runs there in the darkness. He put the wet cloth in my hand, and I held it to my hot blubbery face. It was lovely and cool. I held it against my eyes for a while and then scrubbed my face with it.

'I'm very sorry, Waylord,' I said. I was ashamed to have troubled him with my being there and my tears. I loved and honored him with all my heart and wanted to show my love by helping and serving him, not by worrying and disturbing him.

'There's a good deal to weep about, Memer,' he said in his quiet voice. Looking at him then I saw that he had cried, too, when I did. Tears change people's eyes and mouth. I was abashed to see that I had made him weep, and yet it eased my shame, somehow.

After a while he said, 'This is a good place for it.'

'Mostly I don't cry, here,' I said.

'Mostly you don't cry,' he said.

I was proud he'd noticed that.

'What do you do in this room?' he asked.

It was hard to answer. 'I just come when I can't bear things,' I said. 'And I like to look at the books. Is it all right if I look at them? If I look inside them?'

He answered gravely, after a pause, 'Yes. What do you find in them?'

'I look for the things I do to make the door open.'

I didn't know the word 'letters'.

'Show me,' he said.

I could have drawn the shapes in the air with my finger as I did when I opened the door, but instead I got up and took the big dark-brown leather-bound book from the bottom shelf, the book I called the Bear. I opened it to the first page with words on it. (I think I did know they were words, but maybe not.) I pointed to the shapes that were the same as the ones that opened the door.

'This one, and this one,' I said, whispering. I had laid the book on the table, very carefully, as I always did with the books when I looked inside them. He stood beside me and watched me point at the letters I recognised, though I didn't know their names or how they sounded.

'What are they, Memer?'

'Writing.'

'So it's writing that opens the door?'

'I think so. Only for the door you do it in the air, in the special place.'

'Do you know what the words are?'

I didn't entirely understand what he was asking. I don't think I knew then that the words in writing are the same as the words in speaking, that writing and speaking are different ways of doing the same thing. I shook my head.

'What do you do with a book?' he asked.

I said nothing. I didn't know.

'You read it,' he said, and this time he smiled as he spoke, his face lighting up as I had seldom seen it.

Ista was always telling me how happy and hospitable and genial the Waylord was in the old days, how merry his guests in the great dining room used to be, and how he had laughed at Sosta's baby tricks. But my Waylord was a man whose knees had been broken with iron bars, his arms dislocated, his family murdered, his people defeated, a man in poverty and pain and shame.

'I don't know how to read,' I said. And then,

because his smile was fading fast, going back into the shadow, I said, 'Can I learn?'

It saved the smile for a moment. Then he looked away.

'It's dangerous, Memer,' he said, not speaking to me as to a child.

'Because the Alds are afraid of it,' I said.

He looked back at me. 'They are. They ought to be.'

'It's not demons or black magic,' I said. 'There isn't any such thing.'

He did not answer directly. He looked me in the eyes, not like a man of forty looking at a child of nine, but as one soul judging another soul.

'I'll teach you, if you like,' he said.

◆ 2 ◆

So the Waylord began to teach me, and I learned to read very quickly, as if I had been waiting and more than ready, like a starving person given dinner.

As soon as I understood what the letters were, I learned them, and began to make out the words, and I don't remember ever being puzzled or stopped for long, except once. I took down the tall red book with gold designs on its cover, which had always been a favorite of mine before I could read, when I called it Shining Red. I just wanted to find out what it was about, to taste it. But when I tried to read it, it made no sense. There were the letters, and they made

words, but meaningless words. I could not understand a single one. It was nonsense, garble, garbage. I
was furious with it and with myself when the
Waylord came in. 'What is wrong with this stupid
book!' I said.

He looked at it. 'Nothing's wrong with it. It's a
very beautiful book.' And he read some of the garble
out loud. It did sound beautiful, and as if it meant
something. I scowled. 'It's in Aritan,' he said, 'the
language spoken in the world a long time ago. Our
language grew out of it. Some of the words aren't
much changed. See, here? and here?' And I recognised parts of the words he pointed to.

'Can I learn it?' I asked.

He looked at me the way he often did, slowly:
patient, judging, approving. 'Yes,' he said.

So I began to learn the ancient language, at the
same time as I began to read the *Chamhan* in our
own language.

We couldn't take books out of the secret room, of
course. They would endanger us, and everyone in
Galvamand. The redhat priests of the Alds would
come with soldiers to a house where a book was
found. They wouldn't touch the book, because it was

demonic, but they'd have slaves take it down to the canal or the sea, bind stones to it to weight it, and throw it in to sink. And they'd do the same with the people who had owned it. They didn't burn books or people who read them. The god of the Alds is Atth, the Burning God, and death by fire is a grand thing to them. So they drowned books and people, or took them to the mudflats by the sea and pushed them in with shovels and poles and trampled them down until they suffocated, sunk in the deep wet mud.

People often brought books to Galvamand, at night, in secret. None of them knew of the hidden room – people who'd lived in the house all their life didn't know of it – but people even outside the city knew that the Waylord Sulter Galva was the man to bring books to, now that it was dangerous to own them, and that the House of the Oracle was the place to keep them safe.

None of us in the household ever entered the Waylord's rooms without knocking and waiting for his answer, and since he was no longer so ill, if he didn't answer we didn't bother him. What he did with his time and where he spent it, Ista and Sosta never inquired. They thought he was always in his apartments or the inner courtyards, I suppose, as I used to think. Galvamand is so big it's easy to lose people in it. He never left the house, being too lame to walk even a block's length, but people came to see him, many people. They'd spend hours talking with him in the back gallery or, in summer, in one of the courts. They'd come and leave quietly, any time of the day or night, attracting no notice, using the ways through the back part of the house where nobody lived and the rooms were empty and in ruin.

When he had daytime visitors, I'd serve water, or tea when we had any, and sometimes I could stay with them and listen. Some were people I'd known all my life: Desac the Sundramanian, and people of the Four Houses, like the Cams of Cammand, and Per Actamo. Per had been a boy of ten when the Alds took the city. The people of Actamand put up a hard fight, and when the soldiers took the house they killed all the men and carried off the women as slaves. Per hid from the soldiers in a dry well in a courtyard for three days. He lived now as we did, with a few people in a ruinous house. But he joked with me and was kind, and younger than most of the Waylord's visitors. I was always glad when Per came.

Desac was the only visitor who made it clear I was not welcome to stay and listen to the talk.

The people I didn't know who came to see the Waylord were mostly merchants and such from the city; some of them still had good clothes. Often men came who looked as if they'd been on the road a long time, visitors or messengers from other towns of Ansul, maybe from other Waylords. After dark, in winter, sometimes women came, though it was dangerous for women to go alone in the city. One who used to come often had long grey hair; she seemed a little mad to me, but he greeted her with respect. She always brought books. I never knew her name. Often the people from other towns had books, too, hidden in their clothing or in parcels containing food. Once he knew I could enter the secret room, the Waylord would give them to me to take there.

He mostly went to the room at night, which was why we'd never met there before. I hadn't gone often, and never at night. I shared a sleeping room in the front part of the house with Ista and Sosta, and couldn't just vanish. And the days were busy; I had my share of the housework to do, and the worship, and most of the shopping too, since I liked doing it and got better bargains than Sosta did.

Ista was always afraid Sosta would meet soldiers and be taken and raped if she went out alone. She wasn't afraid for me. The Alds wouldn't look at me, she said. She meant they wouldn't like my pale bony face and sheep hair like theirs, because they wanted Ansul girls with round brown cheeks and black sleek hair like Sosta's. 'You're lucky to look the way you do,' she always told me. And I stayed quite small and slight for a long time, which really was lucky. By order of the Gand of the Alds, women could go in the streets and marketplaces only if they had a man with them. A woman who went alone in the street was a whore, a demon of temptation, and any soldier was free to rape, enslave, or kill her. But the Alds apparently didn't consider old women to be women, and children were mostly though not always ignored. So grannies and children, many of them 'siege brats', half-breeds like me, the girls dressed as boys, did most of the shopping and bargaining in the markets.

All the money we had was what an ancestor had hidden long ago when a pirate fleet threatened Ansul; the pirates were driven off, but the family left the luck-hoard, as the Waylord called it, buried out in the woods behind the house; and that was what we lived on now. So I had to look for the best bargains I could, which took time. So did the worship and the housework. Ista got up very early in the morning to make the bread. The only time I could go regularly to the secret room without being missed and rousing a lot of curiosity and questions would be at night when the others had gone to bed. So I told Ista I wanted to move my bed to my mother's room, just down the hall from the room we all shared. That was fine with her. She and Sosta were generally snoring away not long after we'd washed up from supper; they weren't likely to notice if I wasn't in my room. So every night I'd go softly in darkness through the corridors and passages of the great house to the secret door, and go in, and read and learn with my dear teacher.

Nights when he had visitors, he couldn't come to teach me Aritan or help me with my reading, but I could get along on my own well enough. Often I stayed reading, lost in the story or the history till long after he would have sent me off to bed.

When I started growing a little taller and coming

into my womanhood, I did get terribly sleepy sometimes, not at night but in the morning. I couldn't make myself get out of bed, and felt heavy as lead and stupid as a sowbug all day. The Waylord spoke to Ista, though I begged him not to, and asked her to hire the street girl Bomi to do the sweeping and cleaning that I'd been doing. I said to him, 'I don't mind sweeping and cleaning! What takes all the time is doing all the altars. We could hire a girl for that, and I'd have lots more time.'

That was a mistake. He looked at me slowly: patient, judging, but not approving.

'Your mother's shadow dwells here, with the shadows of our ancestors,' he said. 'The gods of this house are her gods. She blessed them daily. I do them honor as a man,' and it was true, he never missed a day or an offering due, 'and you do them honor and receive their blessing as the daughter of our grandmothers.' And that was that.

I was ashamed of myself, and also cross. I'd had it in my head that I'd be able to get out of the whole hour it took sometimes to go to all the god-niches, dusting them, giving fresh leaves to Iene, and lighting incense for the Hearthkeepers, and giving and asking blessing of the souls and shadows of the former householders, and thanking Ennu and putting meal and water on her altar on her days, and stopping in the doorways to say the praise of the One Who Looks Both Ways, and remembering when to light the oil lamps for Deori, and all the rest.

We have more gods in Ansul, I think, than anybody else has anywhere. More gods, and closer to us, the gods of our earth and our days, our blood and bone. Of course I was blessed in knowing that the house was full of them, and that I was doing as my mother had done in returning their blessing, and that my own room-spirit dwelt in the little empty niche in the wall by the door and waited for me to return and watched over my sleep. When I was little, I was proud of doing worship, but I'd been doing it for a long time now. I got tired of the gods. They wanted so much looking after.

But all it took to make me do my worship cheerfully, with all my heart and soul, was to remember that the Alds called our gods evil spirits, demons, and were afraid of them.

And it was good to be reminded that my mother had done the woman's worship in the house. The

Waylord had trusted her with that, as he trusted her with the knowledge of the secret room, knowing she was of his own lineage. Thinking about this, I realised clearly for the first time that he and I were the only ones of our lineage left; the few people now in our household were Galvas by choice, not by blood. I hadn't thought much about the difference till then.

'Did my mother know how to read?' I asked him, once, at night, after my lesson in Aritan.

'Of course,' he said, and then, recollecting, 'It wasn't forbidden then.' He sat back and rubbed his eyes. The torturers had stretched and broken his fingers so that they were twisted and knotted up, but I was used to how his hands looked. I could see that they had been beautiful once.

'Did she come here to read?' I asked, looking around the room, happy to be there. I had come to love it best at night, when warm shadows stretched up and out from the lamp's yellow dome of light, and the gilt lettering on the backs of books winked like the stars you could sometimes glimpse through the small, high skylights.

'She didn't have much time for reading,' he said.

'She kept everything going here. It was a big job. A Waylord had to spend a lot of money – entertaining and all the rest of it. Her books were account books, mostly.' He looked at me as if looking back, comparing me with my mother in his mind. 'I showed her the door to this room when we first heard that the Alds had sent an army into the Isma Hills. My mother urged me: Decalo was of our blood, and had a right to the secret, she said. She could preserve it, if things went badly. And the room could be a refuge for her.'

'It was.'

He said a line from the 'The Tower', the Aritan poem we had been translating: *Hard is the mercy of the gods.*

I countered with a line from later in the poem: *True sacrifice is true heart's praise.* He liked it when I could quote back at him.

'Maybe when she was hiding here with me, when I was a baby, maybe she read some of the books,' I said. I had thought that before. When I read something that gave my soul joy and strength, I often wondered if my mother had read it, too, when she was in the secret room. I knew he had. He had read all the books.

'Maybe she did,' he said, but his face was sad.

He looked at me as if studying me with some question in his mind; finally, coming to a decision, he said, 'Tell me, Memer. When you first came here, by yourself – before you could read them, what were the books to you?'

It took me a while to answer. 'Well, I gave some of them names.' I pointed to the large, leather-bound *Annals of the Fortieth Consulate of Sundraman*. 'I called that the Bear. And *Rostan* was Shining Red. I liked it because of the gold on the cover . . . And I built houses with some of them. But I always put them back exactly where they'd been.'

He nodded.

'And then some of them—' I had not meant to say this, but the words came out of me '—I was afraid of them.'

'Afraid. Why?'

I did not want to answer, but again I spoke: 'Because they made noises.'

He made a little noise himself, at that: *ah*.

'Which books were they?' he asked.

'It was one of them. Down at . . . at the other end. It groaned.'

Why was I talking about that book? I never thought about it, I didn't want to think about it, let alone talk about it.

Dearly as I loved being in the secret room, reading with the Waylord, finding my greatest happiness in the treasure of story and poetry and history that was mine there, still I never went all the way to that end of the room where the floor became a rougher, greyer stone and the ceiling was lower, without skylights, so that the light died away slowly into the dark. I knew there was a spring or fountain there because I could hear the faint sound of it, but I'd never gone far enough to see it. Sometimes I thought the room became larger there in the shadow end, sometimes I thought it must grow smaller, like a cave or a tunnel. I had never been past the shelves where the book that groaned was.

'Can you show me which book?'

I sat still at the reading table for a minute and then said, 'I was just little. I made up things like that. I pretended the *Annals* was a bear. It was silly.'

'You have nothing to fear, Memer,' he said softly. 'Some might. Not you.'

I said nothing. I felt sick and cold. I was afraid. All I knew was that I was going to keep my mouth shut so that nothing else I didn't want to say could come out of it.

Again he sat pondering, and again came to some decision. 'Time enough for that later. Now, ten more lines, or bed?'

'Ten more lines,' I said. And we bent over 'The Tower' again.

Even now it's hard for me to admit, to write about my fear. Back then, at fourteen or fifteen, I kept my thoughts away from it, just as I kept myself away from the end of the room that went back into shadow. Wasn't the secret room the one place where I was free of fear? I wanted it to be only that. I didn't understand my fear and didn't want to know what it was. It was too much like what the Alds called devilry and evil spirits and black magic. Those were nothing but ignorant, hateful words for what they didn't understand – our gods, our books, our ways. I was certain that there were no demons and that the Waylord had no evil powers. Hadn't they tortured him for a year to make him confess his wicked arts, and let him go because he had nothing to confess?

So what was I afraid of?

I knew the book had groaned when I touched it. I was only about six years old then, but I remembered. I wanted to make myself brave. I dared myself to go all the way to the shadow end. I went, keeping my eyes on the floor right before my feet, until the tiles gave way to rough stone. Then I sidled over to a bookcase, still keeping my eyes down, seeing only that it was low and built into the rock wall, and reached out to touch a book bound in shabby brown leather. When I touched it, it groaned aloud.

I pulled back my hand and stood there. I told myself I hadn't heard anything. I wanted to be brave, so that I could kill Alds when I grew up. I had to be brave.

I walked five steps more till I came to another bookcase and glanced up quickly. I saw a shelf with one book on it. It was small and had a smooth, pearly-white cover. I clenched my right hand and reached out my left hand and took the book from the shelf, telling myself it was safe because the cover was pretty. I let the book fall open. There were drops of blood oozing from the page. They were wet. I knew what blood was. I shut it and shoved it back on the shelf and ran to hide in my bear's den under the big table.

I hadn't told the Waylord about that. I didn't want it to be true. I had never gone back down to those shelves in the shadow end.

I'm sorry, now, for that girl of fifteen who wasn't as brave as the child of six, although she longed as much as ever for courage, strength, power against what she feared. Fear breeds silence, and then the silence breeds fear, and I let it rule me. Even there, in that room, the only place in the world where I knew who I was, I wouldn't let myself guess who I might become.

◆ 3 ◆

Even ten years later, it's hard to write truly about how I lied to myself. It's as hard to write about my courage as about my cowardice. But I want this book to be as truthful as it can be, to be of use in the records of the House of the Oracle, and to honor my mother Decalo, to whom I dedicate it. I'm trying to put the memories of all those years in order, because I want to get to where I can tell about meeting Gry the first time. But there wasn't much order in my mind and heart when I was sixteen and seventeen. It was all ignorance and passionate anger and love.

What peace I had, what understanding I had, came from my love for the Waylord and his kindness to me, and from books. Books are at the heart of this book I'm writing. Books caused the danger we were in, the risks we ran, and books gave us our power. The Alds are right to fear them. If there is a god of books it's Sampa the Maker and Destroyer.

Of all the books the Waylord gave me to read, in poetry I most loved *The Transformations*, and in story *The Tales of the Lords of Manva*. I knew the *Tales* were stories, not history, but they gave me truths I needed and wanted: about courage, friendship, loyalty to the death, about fighting the enemies of your people, driving them out of your land. All the winter I was sixteen I came to the secret room and read about the friendship of the heroes Adira and Marra. I longed to have a friend and companion like Adira. To be driven with him up into the snows of Sul, and suffer with him there, and then side by side with him to strike down like eagles on the hordes of Dorven, driving them back to their ships – I read that again and again. When I read of the Old Lord of Sul I saw him like my own lord – dark, crippled, noble, fearless. All about me in my city and my life were fear and distrust. What I saw in the streets daily made my heart shrink and cower. My love for the heroes of Manva was my heart's blood. It gave me strength.

That was the year we took the street girl Bomi into the household, and the Waylord gave her the name Galva in the old ceremony at the house altars. She moved into the room down the hall from Sosta's. She worked hard and well, satisfying even Ista most of the time, and was good company too. She was about thirteen; she had no idea when she was born or who her mother was. She was hanging around our street as a beggar for a while, and old Gudit began coaxing her in, luring her like a stray cat. When he'd got her to sleep in the shed in the courtyard, he started making her earn her food by helping him clean the stables, which were full of burned lumber and wrecked furniture and trash. Gudit was determined that the Waylord was going to have horses again. 'It stands to reason,' he'd say. 'How can a Waylord travel his ways without a horse to carry him? Would you have him walk on foot? Clear to Essangan or Dom? Bad as his legs are? Like some common peddler, with no dignity? It won't do. He needs horses. It stands to reason.'

There never was much to do with Gudit but agree

with him. He was crazy, old, hunchbacked, and worked very hard, if not always at the most useful job. He had a foul mouth but a clear heart. When Ista hired Bomi to take my place housecleaning, he was furious, not at Ista but at Bomi for 'deserting' him and his precious stable. Every time he saw her for months he cursed her by the shadows of her ancestors, which didn't both Bomi much, since she didn't know any of her ancestors or where their shadows were. Then he got over it, and she went back to helping him after her housework with that terrible job of cleaning out the stable and rebuilding the stalls, because she had a clear heart too. She took in cats, just as Gudit took her in. The stableyard swarmed with kittens that summer. Ista said that Bomi ate like ten girls, but I thought she ate like one girl and twenty cats. Anyhow, the stable was finally clean, which turned out to be fortunate, even if it didn't exactly stand to reason. And we had no mice.

Ista took a long time to accept the fact that the Waylord had taken me under his particular charge and that I was being 'educated', a word she always spoke very carefully, as if it were in another language. And indeed it was a word to be spoken carefully under the dominion of the Alds, who thought reading a deliberate act of evil. Because of that danger, and because she herself had forgotten, as she said, whatever hen-scratching she was taught as a girl ('And what earthly use would all that be to a cook, I ask you? You just show me how to make a sauce with a pen and ink, will you!') Ista wasn't entirely comfortable with my becoming educated. But it would never have occurred to her to hold it against me, or to question the Waylord's judgment or his will. Maybe I loved loyalty so dearly because I knew this house was blessed with it.

Anyhow, I still helped Ista with the rough work of the kitchen, and went to the market, with Bomi if she was free to go, alone if not. I stayed short and bony, and by wearing old cut-down men's clothes I could still look fairly much like a child, or at least an unattractive boy. Street gang boys sometimes saw I was a girl and threw stones at me – boys of my race, of Ansul, acting like filthy Alds. I hated to pass them and kept away from the places they gathered. And I hated the swaggering Ald guards posted around all the marketplaces to 'keep order', which meant to bully citizens and take whatever they liked from the vendors' stalls without paying. I tried not to cringe when I passed them. I tried to walk slowly, ignoring them. They stood there puffed up in their blue cloaks and leather cuirasses, with their swords and clubs. They seldom looked as low as me.

Now I have come to the important morning.

It was late spring, four days after my seventeenth birthday. Sosta was to be married in the summer and Bomi was helping her sew for her wedding – the green gown and headdress and the groom's coat and headdress too. It was all Ista and Sosta had talked about for weeks, wedding wedding wedding, sewing sewing sewing. Even Bomi blithered about it. I'd never even tried to learn to sew, or to fall in love and want to marry, either. Someday. Someday I'd be ready to find out about that kind of love, but it wasn't time yet. I had to find out who I was, first. I had a promise to keep, and my dear lord to love, and a lot to learn. So I left them chattering, and went out to market alone that morning.

It was a bright sweet day. I went down the steps of the house to the Oracle Fountain. The broad, shallow, green basin was dry and littered, and the pipe from which the water had risen stuck up jagged from the broken, defaced central sculpture. The fountain had been dry all my lifetime and long before that, but I said the blessing to the Lord of the Springs and Waters as I stood beside it. And I wondered, not for the first time, why it was called the Oracle Fountain, and then why Galvamand itself was sometimes called the Oracle House. I should ask the Waylord, I thought.

I looked up from the dead fountain, out over the city, and saw Sul across the straits like a great white rising wave of stone and snow, one banner of mist blown northward from its crest. I thought of Adira and Marra and their ragged soldiers driven up to the icy heights, without food or fire, and how they knelt to praise the god of the mountain and the spirits of the glacier. A crow came flying to them with a spray of leaves in its beak and dropped it before Adira. They thanked the crow, offering it what little bread they had: 'In the beak of black iron, the gift of green hope.' My thoughts were always with the heroes.

I spoke praise to Sul and the Seunes, whose white manes I could see just out past the headland. I went on, speaking to the Sill Stone, and touching the street-god's niche as I passed the corner and turned left to West Street. I'd decided to go to the Harbor Market, which was farther to carry things home from but a better market than Foothill. I was glad to be outdoors, to see the sunlight strike blue-green down into the canal and the bright shadows of the carvings on the bridges.

The sunlight and the sea wind were a joy. As I walked I became quite certain that my gods were with me. I was fearless. I went past the Ald soldiers on guard at the marketplace as if they were wooden posts.

Harbor Market is a broad marble pavement, with the red arcades of the Customs House on the north and east sides and the Tower of the Sea Admirals on the south; to the west it's open to the harbor and the sea. Long, shallow marble steps with curved, carved banisters go down to the Admiralty boat-houses and the gravel beach. It was all sun and wind and white marble and blue sea that morning, and nearby were the colored awnings and umbrellas of the market stands and all the cheerful racket of the market. I passed by the market god, the round stone that represents the oldest god of the city: Lero, whose name means justice, agreement, doing right. I saluted the god openly, without even thinking of the Ald soldiers.

I had never in my life done that. When I was ten I saw soldiers beat an elderly man and leave him bloody and unconscious on the street under the empty pedestal of a god he had saluted. No one dared go to him while the soldiers were there. I ran away crying and never knew if he had been killed or not. I had not forgotten that, but it did not matter. This was a day without fear for me. A day of blessing. A holy day.

I went on across the square, looking at everything, for I loved the stalls and the goods and the coaxing, insulting vendors. I was heading for the fish market, but went a bit out of the way when I saw they were setting up a large tent in front of the Admirals' Tower. I asked a boy selling dirty rock-sugar what the tent was for.

'A great storyteller from the Uplands,' he said, 'very famous. I can hold a place for you, young master.' Market boys will turn a turd into a penny, as they say.

'I can hold my own place,' I said, and he, 'Oh, it'll be terrible crowded in no time – he's to be here all day, a terrible famous man – half a penny to hold you a good place right up close?'

I laughed at him and went on.

I was tempted to go over to the tent, though. I felt like doing something foolish, like listening to a storyteller. The Alds are crazy about makers and tellers. Every rich Ald has a storyteller in his retinue, they say, and every company of soldiers too. There hadn't been many in Ansul, the Waylord told me, before the Alds came, but there were more now that books were banned. A few men of my own people told stories for small change on street corners. I had stopped to listen a couple of times, but they mostly told Ald stories to get pennies from the soldiers. I didn't like the Ald stories, all about their wars and their warriors and their tyrant god, nothing I cared a straw for.

It was the word 'Uplands' that caught me. A man from the Uplands would not be an Ald. The Uplands were far, far to the north. I'd never even heard of them or any of those distant lands until last year, when I read Eront's *Great History*, with its maps of all the lands of the Western Shore. The market boy repeated the word as he'd heard it spoken, without any meaning for him except somewhere-very-far-away. Even to Eront, the Uplands were mostly hearsay. I didn't remember anything on that part of his map except a big mountain with a strange name I couldn't bring to mind, as I made my way on past the potmenders to the fishwives.

I bargained down a big redspot that would feed us all today, even the cats, and make fishhead soup for tomorrow. I went round the stalls and bought a fresh cheese and some coarse greens that looked good. Then before I set off home I wandered over towards the big tent to see if anything was happening yet. The crowds were thick. I saw riders above the people's heads, and horses' heads tossing up and down: two Ald officers. The Alds brought no women from their deserts, but they brought their fine, pretty horses, which they treated so well that it was a street joke to call the horses 'soldiers' wives'.

People in the crowd now were trying to get out of the horses' way, but there was some kind of commotion behind them and a good deal of confusion. Then all at once one of the horses reared up squealing and bolted, bucking stiff-legged like a colt. People in front of me pressed back to get out of

its way. It came straight at me. There were people
crowding from behind and I couldn't move. The
horse came at me – there was no rider on it, and the
flailing reins slapped my hand as if thrown at me. I
grabbed and pulled. The horse's head came down
right by my shoulder, its eye rolling wildly. That
head seemed huge; it filled the world. But the horse
had stopped. I shortened my grip on the rein up to
the bridle and stood firm, not knowing what else to
do. The horse tried to toss its head, which half lifted
me off the ground, but I hung tight out of pure
terror. The horse gave a great whuff through its
nostrils and stood still – even pushing up against me
a little as if for protection.

All around me people were shouting and screaming, and I could only think of how to keep them
from panicking the horse again. 'Be quiet, be quiet,' I
said foolishly to the shouting people. And as if they
had heard me they began to back away, leaving a
space of marble pavement empty behind the horse.
In that white, sunlit space was the Ald officer, who
had been thrown hard and was lying stunned, and a
woman standing near him, and a lion.

The woman and the lion stood side by side.

When they moved, the clear space of pavement moved with them. The crowd had gone almost silent.

I saw the top of some kind of carriage behind the woman and the lion. They turned towards it. The pavement appeared as if by magic in front of them as the crowd backed away. It was a little caravan wagon. The two horses hitched to it stood calmly, facing away from us. The woman opened the back door of the wagon, the lion leapt up into it, its tail disappearing in a lovely curve, and the woman latched the door. She came back at once, and the crowd backed away from her again, even without the lion.

She knelt by the Ald officer, who was sitting up looking dizzy. She spoke to him a little, and then stood up and came to me where I was standing, still holding the horse because I didn't dare let it go. The crowd drew back with some pushing and shoving, which scared the horse again. It jerked against my grip on the bridle, and the market basket on my arm fell open and the fish and cheese and greens all flew out, which scared the horse worse, and I could not hold it – but the woman was there. She put her hand on the horse's neck and said something to it. It shook its head, with a kind of grumble in its chest, and stood still.

She put out her hand and I gave her the reins. 'Well done,' she said to me, 'well done!' Then she said something else to the horse, close to its ear, softly, and blew a little of her breath into its nostrils. It sighed and drooped its head. I was frantically trying to pick up our food for the next two days before it was trampled on or stolen. Seeing me scrabbling on the pavement, the woman gave the horse a hard pat and bent down to help me. We tumbled the big fish and the greens into the basket, and somebody in the crowd tossed me the cheese.

'Thank you, good people of Ansul!' the woman said in a clear voice and a foreign accent. 'He deserves a reward, this boy!' And to the officer, who was now standing up shakily on the other side of his horse, she said, 'This boy caught your mare, Captain. It was my lion frightened her. I ask your pardon for that.'

'The lion, yes,' the Ald said, still dazed. He stared at her, and stared at me, and after a while dug into his belt pouch and held out something to me – a penny.

I was fastening the clasp on my basket. I ignored him and his penny.

'Oh, so generous, so generous,' people in the crowd murmured, and somebody crooned, 'A fountain of riches!' The officer glared around at them all. He finally refocused on the woman who stood in front of him holding his horse's reins.

'Get your hands off her!' he said. 'You – woman – it was you had that animal – a lion—'

The woman tossed the reins at him, slapped the mare lightly, and slipped into the crowd. This time the people closed round her. In a moment I saw the roof of the wagon moving off.

I saw the wisdom of invisibility and ducked away into the old-clothes market while the officer was still trying to remount his mare.

The old-clothes vendor called High Hat had been watching the show, standing on her stool. She clambered down. 'Used to horses, are you?' she said to me.

'No,' I said. 'Was that a lion?'

'Whatever it is, it goes with that storyteller. And

his wife. So they say. Stay to hear him. He's the prime lord of storytellers, they say.'

'I have to get my fish home.'

'Ah. Fish don't wait.' She fixed her fierce, mean little eyes on me. 'Here,' she said, and flipped me something, which I caught by reflex. It was a penny. She had already turned away.

I thanked her. I left the penny in the hollow under Lero, where people leave god-gifts and poorer people find them. I still didn't care if the guards saw me, because I knew they wouldn't. I was just starting up West Street away from the market, past the high red arcades of the Customs, when I heard a clip-clop and the clatter of wheels. There along Customs Street came the two horses and the caravan wagon. The lion woman was perched on the driver's seat.

'Lift?' she said, while the horses stopped.

I hesitated. I almost thanked her and said no. It was different, and nothing different ever happened, so I didn't know how to do it. And I was not easy with strangers. I was not easy with people. But the day was blessed, and to turn away blessing is to do ill. I thanked her and climbed up onto the seat beside her.

It seemed very high.

'Where to?'

I pointed up West Street.

She seemed to do nothing, not shaking the reins or clucking her tongue as I had seen drivers do, but the horses set right off. The taller horse was a fine red-brown color, almost as red as the cover of *Rostan*, and the smaller one was bright brown with black legs and mane and tail and a bit of a white star on her forehead. They were bigger than the Ald horses, and more peaceable-looking. Their ears went back and forth, listening constantly; it was pleasant to watch that.

We went along some blocks without speaking. It was interesting to look down the canals, to see the bridges, the facades and windows of buildings from this height, and people walking along, the way people on horseback see them, looking down on them. I found it made me feel superior.

'The lion is – back there – in the wagon?' I asked at last.

'Halflion,' she said.

'From the Asudar desert!' When she said the

word 'halflion', I remembered it and the picture from the *Great History*.

'Right,' she said, with a glance at me. 'That's probably why it spooked the mare. She knew what it was.'

'But you aren't an Ald,' I said, suddenly fearing she was, even though she was dark-skinned and dark-eyed and couldn't be.

'I'm from the Uplands.'

'In the far north!' I said, and then could have bitten my tongue in half.

She glanced at me sidelong and I waited for her to accuse me of reading books. But that was not what she had noticed.

'You aren't a boy,' she said. 'Oh, I am stupid.'

'No, I dress like a boy, because . . .' I stopped.

She nodded, meaning, no need to explain.

'So how did you learn to handle horses?' she asked.

'I didn't. I never touched a horse before.'

She whistled. She had a little, sweet whistle, like a small bird. 'Well, then you have the knack, or the luck!'

Her smile was so pleasant I wanted to tell her

that it was the luck, that Lero and Luck himself, the deaf god, were giving me a holy day, but I was afraid of saying too much.

'I thought you'd be able to take me to a good stable for these two, you see. I thought you were a stableboy. You were as quick and cool as any old hostler I ever saw.'

'Well, the horse just came at me.'

'It came to you,' she said.

We clip-clop-rattled on for another block.

'We have a stable,' I said.

She laughed. 'Aha!'

'I'd have to ask.'

'Of course.'

'There aren't any horses in it. Or feed, or anything. Not since – not for years. It's clean, though. There's some straw. For the cats.' Every time I opened my mouth I talked too much. I clenched my teeth.

'You're very kind. If it isn't convenient, never mind. We can find a place. The fact is, the Gand has offered us the use of his stables. But I'd rather not be beholden to the Gand.' And she shot me a glance.

I liked her. I'd liked her from the moment I saw

her standing beside her lion. I liked the way she talked and what she said and everything about her.

You must not refuse the blessing.

I said, 'My name is Decalo; Galva's daughter Memer of Galvamand.'

She said, 'My name is Gry Barre of Roddmant.'

Having introduced ourselves we got shy, and went on to Galva Street in silence. 'That's the house,' I said.

She said in a tone of awe, 'It is a beautiful house.'

Galvamand is very large and noble, with its wide courts and stone arches and high windows, but it's half ruined too, so it touched me that somebody come from far away, who had seen many houses, saw its beauty.

'It's the House of the Oracle,' I said. 'The Waylord's house.'

At that, the horses stopped short.

Gry looked at me blankly for a moment. 'Galva – the Waylord – Hey, wake up there!' The horses walked patiently on. 'This is a day of the greatly unexpected,' she said.

'This is a day of Lero,' I said. We were at the street gate. I slid down off the seat to touch the Sill

Stone. I led Gry in, past the dry basin of the Oracle Fountain in the great front court, and around the side of the house to the arched gates of the stable courtyard.

Gudit came out of the stable scowling. 'What by all the ghosts of your stupid ancestors do you think I'm going to do for oats?' he shouted. He came up and began to unhitch the red horse.

'Wait, wait,' I said. 'I have to talk to the Waylord.'

'Talk away, the beasts can have a drink while you talk, can't they? Here, let be, lady. I'll see to it.'

Gry let him unhitch the horses and lead them over to the trough. She watched the old man open the spigot and saw the clear water pour into the trough. She looked interested and admiring. 'Where do you get the water from?' she asked Gudit, and he started to tell her about the springs of Galvamand.

As I passed the wagon it shook a little. There was a lion in it. I wondered what Gudit would say about that.

I ran on into the house.

◆ 4 ◆

The Waylord was in the back gallery talking with Desac. Desac was not a native of Ansul but of Sundraman; he had been a soldier in their army. He never brought books, or talked of books. He stood very straight, spoke harshly, and seldom smiled. I thought he must have known much grief. He and the Waylord treated each other with respect and friendship. Their long conversations were always private. They both looked at me rather sternly, in silence, as I walked down the room to where they were sitting under the end window in a patch of sunlight. The back part of the house, the oldest part, all of stone and built right up against the hillside, is chilly, and we didn't have much firewood to warm the rooms.

I greeted them. The Waylord raised his eyebrows, waiting for my message.

'There are travellers here from the far north who need stabling for their horses. He is a storyteller and she,' I paused, 'she has a lion. A halflion. I told her I would ask if they may keep their horses here.' As I spoke I felt like a person in a tale of the Lords of Manva, bearing a request from a noble visitor to a noble host.

'Circus people,' Desac said. 'Nomads.'

Outraged at his contemptuous tone, I said, 'No!'

The Waylord's eyebrows went down at my rudeness.

'She is Gry of the Barres of Roddmant of the Uplands,' I said.

'And where are these Uplands?' said Desac, speaking to me as to a child.

'In the far north,' I said.

The Waylord said, 'Memer, a little further, please?' That was how he always asked me to go on translating a line of Aritan or explaining anything. He liked me to do it in order, making sense. I tried.

'Her husband came to tell stories in the Harbor Market. So they were there. Her lion frightened an Ald's horse. I caught the horse. Then she quieted it. Then when I was coming home I met her with her wagon and she brought me home. She was looking for stabling. The lion is in the wagon. Gudit is watering the horses.'

Only as I mentioned coming home did I realise that the market basket with a ten-pound fish and cheese and greens in it was still weighing down my arm.

There was a pause.

'You offered her use of the stables?'

'I said I'd ask you.'

'Will you ask her to come to me?'

'Yes,' I said, and got away quickly.

I left the basket in the pantry cooler – Ista and the others were all still sewing in the workroom – and ran back to the stableyard. Gry and Gudit were talking about dogs; that is, Gudit was telling her about the great followhounds of Galvamand in the old days, that ran with the horses and guarded the gates. 'Nowadays all it is is cats. Cats everywhere,' he said, spitting aside. 'No meat for dogs any more, see.

It stands to reason. It was meat they were themselves, those dogs, in the siege years.'

'Maybe it's just as well you have no followhounds just now,' she said. 'They'd be anxious about the contents of our wagon.'

I said, 'The Waylord asks if you will be pleased to come into the house. He would come himself but it's hard for him to walk far.' I wanted so badly to welcome her rightly, nobly, generously, as the Lords of Manva welcomed strangers to their houses.

'With pleasure,' she said, 'but first—'

'Leave the horses to me,' said Gudit. 'I'll put 'em both in the loose box and then be off for a bit of hay from Bossti down the way there.'

'There's a truss of hay and a barrel of oats in the wagon,' Gry said, going to show him, but he brushed her off – 'Na na na, nobody brings their own feed to the Waylord's house. Come along here, then, old lady.'

'She's Star,' said Gry, 'and he's Branty.' At their names both horses looked round at her, and the mare whuffed.

'And it would be well if you knew what else is in the wagon,' Gry said, and there was something in her voice, though she spoke low and mild, that made even Gudit turn and listen to her.

'A cat,' she said. 'Another cat. But a big one. She's trustworthy, but not to be taken by surprise. Don't open the wagon door, please. Memer, shall I leave her here in the wagon or shall she come with me into the house?'

When you're lucky, press your luck. I wanted Desac to see the 'circus' lion and be scared stiff. 'If you wish to bring her . . .'

She studied me a moment.

'Best leave her here,' she said with a smile. And thinking of Ista and Sosta screaming and screeching at the sight of a lion passing by in the corridor, I knew she was right.

She followed me through the courtyards around to the front entrance. On the threshold she stopped and murmured the invocation of the guest to the house-gods.

'Are your gods the same as ours?' I asked.

'The Uplands haven't much in the way of gods. But as a traveller I've learned to honor and ask blessing of any gods or spirits that will grant it.'

I liked that.

'The Alds spit on our gods,' I said.

'Sailors say it's unwise to spit into the wind,' she said.

I had brought her the long way round, wanting her to see the reception hall and the great court and the wide hallways leading to the old university rooms and galleries and the inner courts. It was all bare, unfurnished, the statues broken, the tapestries stolen, the floors unswept. I was half proud for her to see it and half bitterly ashamed.

She walked through it with wide, keen eyes. There was a wariness in her. She was easy and open, but self-contained and on the alert, like a brave animal in a strange place.

I knocked at the carved door of the back gallery and the Waylord bade us enter. Desac had gone. The Waylord stood to greet the visitor. They bowed their heads formally as they spoke their names. 'Be welcome to the house of my people,' he said, and she, 'My greeting to the House of Galva and its people, and my honor to the gods and ancestors of the house.'

When they looked up and at each other, I saw his

eyes full of curiosity and interest, and hers shining with excitement.

'You've come a long way to bring your greeting,' he said.

'To meet Sulter Galva the Waylord.'

His face closed, like a book shutting.

'Ansul has no lords but the Alds,' he said. 'I am a person without importance.'

Gry glanced at me as if for support, but I had none to give. She said to him, 'Your pardon if I spoke amiss. But may I tell you what brought us to Ansul, my husband Orrec Caspro and me?'

Now at that name he looked as utterly amazed as she had when I said his title to her.

'Caspro is here?' he said, 'Orrec Caspro?' He took a deep breath. He gathered himself and spoke in his stiffest, most formal tone: 'The fame of the poet runs before him. He honors our city with his presence. Memer told me that a maker is to speak in the marketplace, but I did not know who it was.'

'He will recite for the Gand of the Alds too,' said Gry. 'The Gand sent for my husband. But that's not why we came to Ansul.'

The pause was a heavy one.

'We sought this house,' Gry said. 'And to this house your daughter brought me – though I didn't know she was its daughter, and she didn't know I sought it.'

He looked at me.

'Truth,' I said. And because he still looked at me, distrustful, I said, 'The gods have been with me all day. It is a day of Lero.'

That carried weight with him. He rubbed his upper lip with the first knuckle of his left hand the way he does when he's thinking hard. Then suddenly he came to a decision, and the distrust was gone. 'As you are brought in Lero's hands, the blessing of the house is yours,' he said. 'And all in it is yours. Will you sit down, Gry Barre?'

I saw that she watched the way he moved as he showed her to the claw-foot chair, that she saw his crippled hands as he lowered himself into the armchair. I perched on the high stool by the table.

'As Caspro's fame has come to you,' she said, 'so the fame of the libraries of Ansul has come to us.'

'And your husband came here to see those libraries?'

'He seeks the nourishment of his art and his soul in books,' she said.

At that I wanted to give all my heart to her, to him.

'He must know,' the Waylord said without emotion, 'that the books of Ansul were destroyed, with many of those who read them. No libraries are permitted in the city. The written word is forbidden. The word is the breath of Atth, the only god, and only by the breath may it be spoken. To entrap it in writing is blasphemy, abominable.'

I flinched, hating to hear him speak those words. He sounded as if he believed them, as if they were his own words.

Gry was silent.

He said, 'I hope Orrec Caspro brought no books with him.'

'No,' she said, 'he came to seek them.'

'"As well seek bonfires in the sea",' he said

She came right back, '"Or milk a desert stone."'

I saw the flicker in his eyes, that almost hidden glint, when she answered with the rest of Denios' line.

'May he come here?' she asked, quite humbly.

I wanted to shout Yes! Yes! I was shocked, ashamed, when the Waylord did not at once answer inviting him warmly to come, to be welcome. He hesitated, and then all he said was, 'He is the guest of the Gand Ioratth?'

'A message came to us when we were in Urdile, saying that Ioratth, the Gand of the Alds of Ansul, would make welcome Orrec Caspro, the Gand of All Makers, if he would come and display his art. We are told that the Gand Ioratth is very fond of hearing tales and poems. As are his people. So we came. But not as his guests. He offered stabling for our horses, but not for us. His god would be offended if unbelievers came under his roof. When Orrec goes to perform for the Gand it will be outdoors, under the open sky.'

The Waylord said something in Aritan; I wasn't sure, but I thought it was about the sky having room enough for all the stars and gods. He looked at her to see if she understood the line.

She cocked her head. 'I am an ignorant woman,' she said in her mild way.

He laughed. 'Hardly!'

'No, truly. My husband has taught me a little, but

my own knowledge is not in words at all. My gift is to listen to those who don't talk.'

'You walk with a lion, Memer said.'

'I do. We travel a lot, and travelers are vulnerable. After our good dog died, I looked for another guardian companion. We met with a company of nomads, tellers and musicians, who'd trapped a halflion and her cub in the desert hills south of Vadalva. They kept the mother for their shows, but sold us the cub. She's a good companion, and trustworthy.'

'What is her name?' I asked very softly.

'Shetar.'

'Where is she now?' the Waylord asked.

'In our wagon, in your stableyard.'

'I hope to see her. As I too am unburdened with belief, I am free to offer you the shelter of my roof, Gry Barre – you and your husband, your horses and your lion.'

She thanked him for his generosity, and he said, 'The poor are rich in generosity.' Ever since she had spoken her husband's name, his face had been alight. 'Memer,' he said, 'which room—?'

I'd already decided that and was calculating

whether the fish could feed eight if Sosta made a stew with it. 'The east room,' I said.

'How about the Master's room?'

That startled me a little, for I knew his mother had lived in that beautiful, spacious apartment, upstairs from his rooms in this oldest part of the house. Long ago when Galvamand housed the university and library of Ansul, that apartment had belonged to its head, the Master. Its unbroken, small-paned windows looked over the lower roofs of the house westward to Sul. There was a bedstead in it and nothing much else, now. But I could bring a mattress from the east room, and the chair from mine.

'I'll lay a fire there,' I said, for I knew the unused room would be dank and cold.

The Waylord looked at me with great kindness. He said to Gry Barre, 'Memer is my hands and half my head. She is not the daughter of my body, but of my house and heart. Her gods and ancestors are mine.'

I knew well that I was of the blood of Galva, but it gave me a painful joy to hear him say what he said.

'In the market,' Gry said, 'a horse bolted when it

saw my cat. It threw its rider and ran straight at Memer. She caught the reins and stopped and held it.'

'I'll go get the room ready,' I said, finding praise hard to bear.

Gry excused herself and came with me, wanting to help me with the room. Once we had made up the bed and got a fire going in the hearth, it was done, and she said she'd go bring her husband here from the Harbor Market. I longed to hear him, and she saw that. 'He'll be nearly done speaking, I think,' she said, 'but I'd be glad of your company. I'll leave Shetar in the wagon. She's fine there.' As we went out she added, 'One lion is enough.'

How could I not love her?

So Gry Barre and I went afoot back down to the Harbor Market. There I first heard the maker Orrec Caspro speak.

The tent was full, and the front and sides had been raised for people to stand outside it, crowded together like trees on a mountainside, all still, listening. He was telling the tale of the Fire-tailed Bird from Denios' *Transformations*. I knew it, and older people of Ansul there knew it, but to the Ald soldiers – and there were many, all in the best places, up close to the platform in the tent – and to most of the young people, it was new, a wonder. All stood with moving lips and gazing eyes, rapt in the story-poem. Caught in it too, hearing the teller's even, resonant voice and clear northern accent, I hardly saw him himself. I listened, and saw the story happen.

When he was done, the great crowd stood in silence for a long breath's space, and then said, 'Ah!' And then they began to applaud him, the Alds by hitting their palms together loudly, and we by crying the old praise-word, 'Eho, eho!' I saw him then, a handsome, thin, straight, dark man, with a certain defiance in his stance up there on the dais, though he was most gracious with the crowd.

We could not get near him for a long time. 'I should have brought the other lion too,' Gry said as we tried in vain to pry through the massed backs of the soldiers and officers with their blue cloaks and their sheep hair and their swords and crossbows and bludgeons, all pressing round the speaker, who had come down among them.

When he leapt back up on the platform and

scanned the crowd, Gry made her bird's whistle, loud and piercing this time. At once he saw her; she nodded to our left; and a few minutes later he met us by the steps of the Customs.

Now that the soldiers had dispersed, many citizens trailed him, but they were timid, unwilling to press forward. Only one elderly man came up to him, and bowed as we bow in thanks to our gods, deeply, with open hands that hold the gift given and received. 'Praise to the maker,' he whispered. He straightened up and walked swiftly away. He was in tears. He was a man who had brought books to the Waylord more than once. I didn't know his name.

Orrec Caspro saw us and strode forward. He took both Gry's hands for a moment. 'Get me out!' he said. 'Where's Shetar?'

'At Galvamant,' she said, pronouncing the name northern-wise. 'I am with Decalo's daughter Memer of Galvamant. We're to be guests of that house.'

His eyes widened. He greeted me courteously and asked no questions, but he looked as if he had some.

'Please excuse me,' I said on the spur of the moment, 'I forgot something at the market this morning. You know the way. I'll catch up.' And I left them. It was true that Ista would need more greens for a stew for eight.

I always wondered why the makers leave house-keeping and cooking out of their tales. Isn't it what all the great wars and battles are fought for – so that at day's end a family may eat together in a peaceful house? The tale tells how the Lords of Manva hunted and gathered roots and cooked their suppers while they were camped in exile in the foothills of Sul, but it doesn't say what their wives and children were living on in their city left ruined and desolate by the enemy. They were finding food too, somehow, cleaning house and honoring the gods, the way we did in the siege and under the tyranny of the Alds. When the heroes came back from the mountain, they were welcomed with a feast. I'd like to know what the food was and how the women managed it.

I saw Gry and her husband at the top of West Street when I started up the hill from the Gelb Bridge. When I came into the kitchen, Sosta and Bomi were all agog, having met the guests, and Ista was on the very edge of a tantrum – 'How in the name of Sampa the Destroyer is a woman to feed guests on a scrap of fish and a kale stalk?' The additional greens and celery-root I brought averted disaster. She set to work grating ginger and chopping thessony and ordering Bomi and even Sosta about unmercifully. Galvamand would not scant its guests or shame its ancestors if Ista could help it. This is part of what I meant about housework. If it isn't important, what is? If it isn't done honorably, where is honor?

Ista could tell us about the banquets for forty in the great dining hall in the old days, but we always ate in what she called the pantry, a large room full of shelves and counters, between the dining hall and the kitchens. Gudit had built a table of pine scraps, and we had found a chair here and a chair there. The Waylord's longest walk in a day was often from his room, through the corridors, past the staircases and the inner courtyards, to dinner in the pantry. Tonight he came wearing the heavy, stiff, grey robe that was the only fine clothing he had left from the good days. All of us had cleaned up a bit except Gudit, who smelled very much of horse. Gry wore a long red shirt over narrow silk pants, and her husband a white shirt, black coat, and black kilt that left his legs bare below the knee. He was very good-looking in his black, and Sosta goggled at him like the fish on its slab in the market.

But the Waylord was a handsome man too for all his lameness, and when he greeted Orrec Caspro I thought of the heroes Adira and Marra. Both he and Caspro stood very straight, though it must have cost the Waylord more to do so.

We sat to table, Gry at the Waylord's right hand and Caspro at his left, Sosta next to Bomi down the table, Gudit next to me, and the place at the foot empty, because Ista would never sit with us till late in the meal. 'A cook at the table, a burnt dinner,' she said, which may have been true when there were more people to be served and more dinner to burn. She stood while my lord gave the man's blessing and I the woman's, and then she vanished while we ate her excellent bread and fish stew. I was glad for the honor of our house that the food was so good.

'You of Ansul do as we do in the Uplands,' Caspro said. His voice was the most beautiful thing about him; it was like a viol. 'The household eats at one table. It makes me feel at home.'

'Tell us something of the Uplands,' the Waylord said.

Caspro looked about at us smiling, not knowing where to begin. 'Do you know anything of the place at all?'

'It's far to the north,' I said, as no one else spoke, 'a hilly land, with a great mountain—' and the name came to me then as if I was seeing Eront's map '—the Carrantages? And the people are said to practice wizardry. But that's only what Eront says.'

Bomi and Sosta stared, the way they always did when I knew anything they didn't. I thought it very stupid – as if I should stare every time they talked about how to hem a gusset, or gusset a hem, whichever it is. I didn't always understand them, but I didn't stare at them as if they were crazy for knowing what they knew.

Caspro said to me, 'The Carrantages is our great mountain, as Sul is yours. The Uplands are all hill and stone, and the farmers poor. Some of them have powers, indeed; but wizardry is a dangerous word. We call them gifts.'

'Among the Alds, we called them nothing at all,' said Gry in her dry, slightly teasing way, 'not wishing to be stoned to death for the sin of coming from a gifted people.'

'What,' Bomi began, and then stuck. For once she was shy. Gry encouraged her, and Bomi asked, 'Do you have a gift?'

'I get along with animals, and they with me. The gift is called calling, but it's more like hearing, actually.'

'I have no gift,' Caspro said with a smile.

'I cannot believe you are so ungrateful,' the Waylord said, not joking.

Caspro accepted the reproof. 'You're right, Waylord, I was indeed given a great gift. But it was . . . It was the wrong one.' He frowned and sought almost desperately for words, as if it were the most important thing in the world that he should answer honestly. 'Not wrong for me. But for my people. So it took me from them, from the Uplands. I have great joy in my art. But there are times – times I'm sick at heart, missing the rocks and bogs and the silence of the hills.'

The Waylord looked at him patiently, unjudging, approving. 'One can be sick for home in one's own city, in one's own house, Orrec Caspro. You are an exile among exiles here.' He raised his glass. There was water in it; we had no wine. 'To our homecoming!' he said, and we all drank with him.

'If your gift is the wrong one, what would the right one have been?' asked Bomi, whose shyness once gone is gone forever.

Caspro looked at her. His face changed again. He might have given a light answer to her light question and she'd have been satisfied, but that wasn't in him to do.

'My family's gift is the unmaking,' he said, and involuntarily put both hands over his eyes for a moment – a strange moment. 'But I was given the gift of making. By mistake.' He looked up as if bewildered. I saw Gry watching him across the table, intent, concerned.

'No mistake about it,' said the Waylord with a calm, genial authority that lightened the uncanny mood. 'And all you were given you give to us in your poetry. I wish I could come and hear you.'

'Don't encourage him,' Gry said, 'he'll spout you poems till the cows come home.'

Sosta giggled. I think it was the first thing anybody said she understood, and she thought it was funny to say 'till the cows come home'.

Caspro laughed too, and told us that he could speak poetry forever. 'The only thing I like better than saying is hearing,' he said, 'or reading.' In his glance at the Waylord there was a signal or challenge, heavier than the words themselves. But then, reading was a heavy word, in our city under the Alds.

'This was a good house for poetry, once,' my lord said. 'Will you have a little more fish, Gry Barre? Ista! Are you coming or not, woman?'

Ista likes it when he raises his voice, when he orders her to sit and eat. She bustled in at once, bobbed to the guests, and, as soon as she had blessed her bread, asked, 'What's Gudit going on about, about a lion?'

'It's in the wagon,' Gudit said. 'I told you, you godless fool. Don't go meddle with that wagon, I said. You didn't, did you?'

'Of course I did nothing of the sort.' Offended by Gudit's coarseness and his loud voice, Ista became ladylike, almost mincing. 'A lion is nothing to me. Will it be staying in the wagon, then?'

'She'll be best staying with us, if it won't disturb the household,' Gry said, but seeing the sensation this caused in Sosta and Bomi and possibly Ista, she added quickly, 'But maybe it's better she sleeps in the wagon.'

'That sounds cramped. May we meet our other guest?' said the Waylord. I had never seen him like this, genial, forceful. I was seeing Ista's Waylord of the good days. 'Has she had her dinner? Please, bring her in.'

'Ohhh,' Sosta said faintly.

'"Twon't be you she eats, Sos,' Ista said. 'More likely she'd fancy a bit of fish?' She was not going to be overawed by any lion. 'I kept out the head, just for broth you know. She's more than welcome to it.'

'I thank you, Ista, but she ate early this morning,' Gry said. 'And tomorrow's her fasting day. A fat lion is a terrible thing to see.'

'I have no doubt,' said Ista primly.

Gry excused herself and presently came in with her halflion, led on a short leash. The animal was the size of a large dog but very different in shape and gait – a cat, long-bodied yet compact, lithe, smooth, long-tailed, with the short face and forward-looking, jewel eyes of a cat, and a pace between slouching and majestic. She was sand-colored, tawny. The hairs round her face were lighter, long and fine, and the short fur round the mouth and under the chin was white. The long tail ended in a little tawny plume. I was half scared half enchanted. The halflion sat down on her haunches, looked all around at us, opened her mouth to show a broad pink tongue and fearsome white teeth in a yawn, closed her mouth, closed her great topaz eyes, and purred. It was a loud, rumbling, deliberate purr.

'Aw,' Bomi said. 'Can I pet her?'

And I followed Bomi. The lion's fur was lovely, deep and thick. When you scratched around her round, neat ears she leaned into your hand and the purr deepened.

Gry led her to the Waylord. Shetar sat down beside his chair and he put his hand out for her to sniff. She sniffed it thoroughly and then looked up at him, not with the long dog gaze: one keen cat glance. He put his hand on her head. She sat there with half-shut eyes, purring, and I saw the big talons of her forepaws working in and out gently against the slate floor.

◆ 5 ◆

When dinner was done, the Waylord invited our guests to come with him to his apartments, glancing at me to assure me I was welcome. We made our way at the slow pace of his lameness back through the corridors and past the deserted rooms and inner courts. We sat in the back gallery. The evening light was fading in the windows.

'I think we have a good deal to talk about,' the Waylord said to his guests. He looked at them both, and the flash of opal fire was in his eyes. 'Gry Barre says that you came to Ansul in part to find me. And Memer told me that her meeting with you was blessed by Lero. I am sure of that blessing. But may I ask why you sought me?'

'May I tell you all the story?' Caspro asked.

The Waylord laughed and said, '"Shall I allow the sun to shine, or permit the river to run?" That is what Raniu said when the great harper Moro asked him if he might play his harp in the temple.

Caspro began hesitantly. 'Because of what books were to me when I was a boy – because what was written was a light – a light in darkness to me—' He paused. 'Then, when I came down to the cities and began to learn how much there was to be learned, I was half in despair—'

'You were a calf in clover,' Gry said.

'Well, yes, that too.' We all laughed, and he went on more easily. 'At any rate, as I see it, making poetry is the least of what I do. Finding what other makers made, speaking it, printing it, recovering it from neglect or oblivion, relighting the light of the word – this is the chief work of my life. So when I'm not earning my living in the marketplace, I'm in the library or the bookdealer's stall or the scholar's den, asking about books and writings, learning about forgotten makers, those known only in their city or country. And everywhere I've been in Bendraman, Urdile, the City States, Vadalva, in every university or library or marketplace, the wisest, most learned people speak of the learning of Ansul and the Library of Ansul.'

'In the past tense,' said the Waylord.

'Waylord, I work with what's lost, buried, hidden. Lost by time and ill chance, maybe, or hidden from destruction, from the prejudice of a ruler or a priest. In the foundations of the old council halls of Mesun in Urdile we found the earliest of all the testaments of the *Life of Raniu*, written on calfskin and sealed in an unmarked vault five hundred years ago, in the reign of the tyrant Terensa. He drove out teachers and destroyed temples and writings throughout the city. He ruled for forty years. The Alds have ruled Ansul only seventeen years.'

'Memer's lifetime,' the Waylord said. 'A lot can be lost in seventeen years. A generation learns that knowledge is punished and safety lies in ignorance. The next generation doesn't know they're ignorant, because they don't know what knowledge was. Those who came after Terensa in Mesum didn't dig up the buried writings. They didn't know of them.'

'A rumor survived,' Caspro said.

'There are always rumors.'

'I follow them.'

'Was it some particular rumor that brought you here? The name of a lost maker, a lost poem?'

'Mostly the reputation of Ansul as the center of learning and of writing in all the Western Shore. What most drew me was the tale – the rumor – of a great library that was here even before the founding of the University of Ansul. In it were said to be writings from the days when we still spoke Aritan, and had some memory of the lands beyond the desert, from which we came. Perhaps there were even books brought from the Sunrise, across the desert, in the beginning of our history. I have longed for years to come here, to ask, to seek any knowledge of that library!'

The Waylord said nothing, made no response.

'I know that my quest puts me in some danger. It puts in worse danger every man I speak to about it – even if he doesn't answer.'

The Waylord nodded slightly. His face was expressionless.

'I know the Alds,' Caspro said. 'We lived among them some while.'

'That took courage.'

'Less than I ask of you.'

I could hardly bear it, the suppressed passion in both of them, the fire and fear and challenge. I wanted to say to them, shout at them, 'Trust each other! Can't you trust each other?' and knew it was foolish, childish, and wanted to cry.

Gry Barre nudged Shetar. The lion got up and lounged over to me and sat on her haunches in her peaceable, sleepy fashion right in front of my legs, so that I could scratch her ears. I did that, and the touch soothed me. Gry looked at us. She didn't quite wink, but I thought I read in her look something like, 'They're men; this is the only way they know how to do it.'

The Waylord had risen to fetch a candle. I should have done that, but he was already bringing the heavy iron candlestick to the table, awkwardly, having little grip in his hands. Gry lit the candle with the strike-box. The light bloomed, making the rest of the room dark and our faces vivid against the darkness and the faint glimmer of the windows.

Shetar gave a grunt and sank down at my feet in picture-book lion pose, front paws outstretched, eyes gazing at the light.

'I revised my opinion of courage,' the Waylord said, 'while I was in the Gand's prison. I thought it was something a man owed himself, like pride or self-respect. I learned that we owe it only to the gods.' His gaze too was on the steady yellow flame of the candle.

Caspro did not speak.

'I was taken there,' he went on, 'because they, like you, had heard tales and rumors. Tales and rumors that brought them here. To Ansul. Do you know why the Alds invaded my country and laid siege to my city?'

'I thought greed, envy of your green lands.'

'Why this green land? Vadalva is closer, and as unwarlike as we are. You say you lived a while in Asudar. Tell me, then, if I go astray: The Alds have a king, a Gand of Gands, who is also the high priest of Atth. His power is great. All slaves are his to claim. He commands the armies.'

Caspro nodded.

'The name of this priest-king who took the throne

of Asudar thirty years ago is Dorid. He believes that
Atth wishes him to combat evil on earth. Atth is
what the Alds call the only god they acknowledge; it
means Lord. The true name of Atth is not spoken.
All good belongs to Atth. But there is a great power
of evil, and it is called Obatth, the Other Lord.'

Again Caspro nodded.

The Waylord asked, 'Do you know the story of
the Thousand True Men?'

'The Alds say that if a thousand true soldiers
could be gathered together, Obatth could be van-
quished forever. Or, some say, a hundred.'

'And some say ten,' said Gry.

The Waylord smiled, though not with much
cheer. 'I like that version,' he said. 'Did they say
where these true men were to meet?'

'No.' Caspro looked at Gry, who also shook her
head.

'Well, the story was told me in a manner that
made it hard to forget. It was the son of our Gand
here, Iddor son of Ioratth, who told it to me. Many
times.' He paused for a while and then said, very
low, 'I don't like to speak it here in this house.
Forgive me. This is what I was told: All light and

righteousness belong to Atth, the Burning God, whose power is visible in the sun. There is nothing sacred outside the Fire of Atth. All fire is holy for his sake. The moon they despise, calling it the slave, the witch. The earth is a place of exile. A foul place, unholy, infested by demons, utterly cold and dark but for the light and warmth reflected on it by the sun of Atth. And on earth Obatth, the enemy of Atth, is manifest – in the evil fortunes of men, and the evil men do, and the evil spirits they worship. And most of all, in one certain place.

'In that place, all the foulness of earth gathers together, darkness drawing inward into earth, the reverse of light shining out from the sun. It is an anti-sun that eats light. It is black, wet, cold, vile. As the sun is being, it is unbeing. A void, a great hole in the earth, deep beyond depth. It is called the Night Mouth.

'And it is there that the Thousand True Men are to gather to bear the Fire of Atth into the kingdom of Obatth. They will enter the darkness, make war on the Other Lord and destroy him. Then they will come forth with their banners of flame, and all earth will burn as bright as the sun both night and day. All

demons and shadows will be driven into outer
darkness beyond the stars. And the sons of Asudar
will rule over all men in righteousness, worshipping
the Burning God.'

The Waylord's voice was monotonous and rough,
scarcely audible, and I saw that his hands were
clenched one in the other.

'Old traditions of Asudar said that the Night
Mouth was in the west, on the coast. Dorid the
priest-king in his city Medron ordered the lesser
priests of Atth to find this center of darkness. Some
thought the mountain Sul itself contained the Night
Mouth, but the others said no: Sul, they said, is a
volcano, it contains fire and so is sacred to Atth.
Opposite it – across the water from it – would be
the dark place, the bottomless well of evil. The
Night Mouth would be found here, in the city of
Ansul.

'It is supposed to be guarded by a wizard of
terrible powers, who can summon armies of evil
spirits, the foul emanations of the earth. And the
gods of the heathen will gather to defend it, the
thousand false gods.

'So the armies of Asudar were sent to take the

country and city of Ansul by force and find the Night Mouth. When it is found, King Dorid will send the Thousand True Men into it with banners of fire, a burning army. Light will banish darkness, and good will vanquish evil.'

He drew a harsh breath. He bit his lips and looked away from the candle, hiding his face in shadow.

'I never heard that tale,' Caspro said. His own voice was shaken. He spoke, I think, to give the Waylord time to recover himself. 'Tales of how earth is the battlefield of Atth and Obatth, yes. An unending war. And people in the desert knew there was a mountain called Sul far in the west, an uncanny place, but only because it's surrounded by the sea. Salt water they call the curse of Obatth . . . This tale of the Night Mouth must be a secret knowledge. Priestly lore.'

'Useful to justify an invasion,' said Gry.

'If so, it would be more widely known, wouldn't it? Do the common soldiers know the story, Waylord?'

'I don't know. I know they were told to search for certain things. Certain houses. Caves, wizards, idols, books . . . There are many caves in the hills above the city. And idols and books – there was no end of them in Ansul. The soldiers were diligent.'

We were all silent for a while.

'How are you governed?' Gry asked.

There was something in her voice; it wasn't as beautiful as her husband's voice, but there was something in it that relieved me, quieted me, the way touching the lion's fur did. When the Waylord answered her he sounded a little less strained.

'We're enslaved, not governed. The Gand Ioratth and his officers are all the law. For the most part, we of Ansul hold the city together by doing things as we used to do them, as best we can, while the Alds exact tribute, and punish blasphemy, and hold aloof. They've lived here as soldiers in a garrison ever since they took the city. They sent no colonists. They brought no women. They don't want to live here. They hate it, land and city and sea. The earth itself is a place of exile to them, and this is the worst of it.'

In the silence that followed, Shetar raised her head from her paws, said, 'Rrrawow!' in a deep, throaty voice, and yawned mightily.

'You're right,' Gry said to her. She and Caspro

rose to say good night, thanking the Waylord for his hospitality, and thanking me too.

I gave her an oil lamp with a mica shade to light their way to their room. I saw that both she and her husband touched the god-niche by the door as they left the room. I watched them go down the corridor side by side, his hand on her shoulder, the lion pacing softly after them and the glimmer of the lamp running along the bare stone walls.

I turned back to see the Waylord gazing at the candle, his face very weary. I thought how alone he was. His friends came and went again, and here he must stay. I had thought of his solitude as his choice, his nature, maybe because it came so natural to me. But he had no choice.

He looked up at me. 'What have you brought to Galvamand?' he said.

I was frightened by his tone. I said at last, 'Friends, I think.'

'Oh yes. Powerful friends, Memer.'

'Waylord—'

'Well?'

'This Night Mouth, this Obatth. Did they come here to the house, to Galvamand – the redhats, the soldiers – did they take you to prison, because they thought—?'

He didn't answer for a while. He sat stiffly, his shoulders hunched, as he did when in pain. 'Yes,' he said.

'But is it – is there anything here—?'

I didn't know what I was asking, but he did. He looked up at me, a fierce look. 'What they seek is theirs. It's in their hearts, not ours. This house hides no evil. They bring their darkness with them. They will never know what is in the heart of this house. They will not look, they will not see. That door will never open to them. You needn't fear, Memer. You can't betray it. I tried. I tried to betray it. Over and over. But the gods of my house and the shadows of my dead forgave me before I could do it. They wouldn't let me do it. All the hands of all the givers of dreams were on my mouth.'

I was very frightened now. He had never spoken of the torture. He was clenched and hunched and trembling. I wanted to go to him but did not dare.

He made a slight gesture and whispered, 'Go on. Go to bed, child.'

I went forward and put my hand on his.

'I'm all right,' he said. 'Listen. You did right to bring them here. You brought blessing. Always, Memer. Now go on.'

I had to leave him sitting there, shaking, alone.

I was tired, it had been a long day, an immense day, but I could not go to bed. I went to the wall under the hill and opened the door in it with the words written in air and went into the secret room.

As I went into it, all at once I was afraid. My heart went cold, my hair stirred on my neck.

That horrible image of a black sun that sucked out warmth and light from the world – it was like a hole in my mind, now, sucking out, leaving nothing but cold and emptiness.

I had always been afraid of the far end of this long, strange room stretching off into darkness. I had kept away from the shadow end, turned my back on it, not thought about it, told myself, 'That's something I'll understand later.' Now it was later. Now I had to understand what my house was built on.

But all I had to make understanding out of was that tale of a Night Mouth, that hateful image of the people I hated.

And Orrec Caspro's tale. A library, he had said. A great library. The greatest in the world. A place of learning, of the light of the mind.

I could not even look at the shadow end of the room. I wasn't ready yet for that, I had to gather my strength. I went to the table, the one I used to build houses under and pretend to be a bear cub in its den. I set down the lamp and laid my hands palm down on the table, pressing them hard on the smooth wood, to feel its smoothness, its solidity. It was there.

There was a book on it.

The two of us always returned books to the shelves before we left the room, an old habit of order the Waylord had from his mother, who had been his teacher as he was mine. I didn't recognise this book. It didn't look old. It must be one of those that people had brought him secretly to be hidden away, to be saved from the destruction of Atth. Occupied with learning all I could of the great makers of the past and the knowledge they had gathered, I had scarcely looked yet at the shelves that held those random, rescued, newer books. The Waylord must have set this one out for me while I went back to the market with Gry.

I opened it and saw it was printed, with the metal letters they use now in Bendraman and Urdile, which make it easy to make a thousand copies of a book. I read the title: *Chaos and Spirit: The Cosmogonies,* and under that the name Orrec Caspro, and under that the name of the printers, Berre and Holaven of Derris Water in Bendraman. On the next page were only the words, 'Made in honor and dear remembrance of Melle Aulitta of Caspromant.'

I sat down, facing the dark end of the room, for if I couldn't look at it neither could I turn my back on it. I drew the lamp closer to the book and began to read.

I woke there in the grey of early morning, the lamp dead, my head on the open book. I was chilled to the bone. My hands were so stiff I could barely write the letters on the air to leave the room.

I ran to the kitchen and all but crawled into the fireplace trying to get warm. Ista scolded and Sosta chattered but I didn't listen. The great words of the poem were running in my head like waves, like

flights of pelicans over the waves. I couldn't hear or
see or feel anything but them.

Ista was really worried about me. She gave me a
cup of hot milk and said, 'Drink this, you fool girl,
what are you taking sick for now? With guests in the
house? Drink it up!' I drank it and thanked her and
went to my room, where I fell on the bed and slept
like a stone till late in the morning.

I found Gry and her husband in the stableyard,
with the lion and the horses and Gudit and Sosta.
Sosta was neglecting her sewing to swoon around
Caspro, Gudit was saddling the tall red horse, and
Gry and Caspro were arguing. They weren't angry
with each other, but they weren't in agreement. Lero
was not in their hearts, as we say. 'You can't possibly
go there by yourself,' Gry was saying, and he was
saying, 'You can't possibly go there with me,' and it
was not the first time either had said it.

He turned to me. For a moment I felt almost as
swoony as Sosta, thinking that this was the man who
had made the poem that I had read all night and
that had remade my soul. That confusion went away
at once. This was Orrec Caspro all right, only not
the poet Caspro but the man Orrec, a worried man

arguing with his wife, a man who took everything terribly seriously, our guest, whom I liked. 'You can tell us, Memer,' he said. 'People saw Gry in the marketplace yesterday, saw her with Shetar – hundreds of people – isn't that true?'

'Of course it is,' Gry said before I could speak. 'But nobody saw inside the wagon! Did they, Memer?'

'Yes,' I said to him, and 'I don't think so,' to her.

'So,' she said, 'your wife hid in the wagon in the marketplace, and now stays indoors in the house, like a virtuous woman. And your servant the lion trainer emerges from the wagon and comes with you to the palace.'

He was obstinately shaking his head.

'Orrec, I travelled as a man with you for two months all over Asudar! What on earth makes it impossible now?'

'You'll be recognised. They saw you, Gry. They saw you as a woman.'

'All unbelievers look alike. And the Alds don't see women, anyhow.'

'They see women with lions who frighten their horses!'

'Orrec, I am coming with you.'

He was so distressed that she went to him and held him, pleading and reassuring. 'You know nobody in Asudar ever saw I was a woman except that old witch at the oasis, and she laughed about it. Remember? They won't know, they won't see, they can't see. I will not let you go alone. I can't. You can't. You need Shetar. And Shetar needs me. Let me go dress now – there's plenty of time. I won't ride, you ride, and we'll walk with you, there'll be plenty of time. Won't there, Memer? How far is it to the palace?'

'Four street crossings and three bridges.'

'See? I'll be back in no time. Don't let him go without me!' she said to me and Gudit and Sosta and perhaps to the horse, and she ran off to the back of the house, Shetar loping along with her.

Orrec walked to the gateway of the court and stood there straight and stiff, his back turned to us all. I felt sorry for him.

'Stands to reason,' Gudit said. 'Murderous snakes they are in that palace what they call it. Our Council House it was. Get over there, you!' The tall red horse looked at him with mild reproach and moved politely to the left.

'What a beauty you are,' I said to the horse, for he was. I patted his neck. 'Brandy?'

'Branty,' Orrec said, coming back to us with an air of dignified defeat that you could see went right to Sosta's heart.

'Ohhh,' she said to Orrec, and then trying to cover it up, 'Oh, can I, can I get you a . . .' but she couldn't think of anything to get him.

'He's a good old fellow,' Orrec said, taking up Branty's reins. He made as if to mount, but Gudit said, 'Hold on, wait a minute, have to look to the cinch here,' getting between him and the horse and throwing the stirrup up over the saddle.

Orrec gave up, and stood as patiently as the horse.

'Have you had him a long time?' I asked, trying to make conversation and feeling as foolish as Sosta.

'He's well over twenty. Time he had a rest from traveling. And Star as well.' He smiled a little sadly. 'We left the Uplands together – Branty and me, Star and Gry. And Coaly. Our dog. A good dog. Gry trained her.'

That got Gudit started off on the followhounds

that used to live at Galvamand and he was still talking about them when Gry reappeared. She wore breeches and a rough tunic. Men in Ansul wear their hair long, tied back, so she had merely combed out her braid and put on a worn black velvet cap. She had somehow darkened or roughened her chin. She had become a fellow of twenty-five or so, quick-eyed, shy, and sullen. 'So, are we ready?' she said, and her soft, burry voice had changed, becoming hoarse.

Sosta was staring at her, rapt. 'Who are you?' she asked.

Gry rolled her eyes and said, 'Chy the lion tamer. So, Orrec?'

He gazed at her, shrugged, laughed a little, and swung up onto the horse. 'Come on, then!' he said and set right off, not looking back. She and the lion followed behind him. She looked back at me as they passed through the gate, and winked.

'But where did he come from?' Sosta asked.

'Merciful Ennu go with them, that nest of murderous rats and snakes they're going to,' Gudit said hollowly, shuffling into the stable.

I went in to look after the gods and the ancestors and find out what Ista needed from the market.

◆ 6 ◆

Gudit told me that a messenger had come that
morning from the Council House, which the
Alds called the Palace of the Gand, to say Orrec
Caspro was to wait upon the Gand before midday.
Not saying please or why or anything, of course. So
they went, and so we waited. It was late enough
when they came back that I'd had plenty of time to
worry. I was out sitting on the edge of the dry basin
of the Oracle Fountain in front of the house when I
saw them coming along our street from the south,
Orrec afoot leading the horse, Chy the lion tamer
beside him, and the lion padding along behind with a

bored expression. I ran to meet them. 'It went well, it went well,' Orrec said, and Chy said, 'Well enough.'

Gudit was at the stableyard gate to take Branty – having horses in the stable was such joy to him he wouldn't let anybody else look after them for a moment – and Chy said to me, 'Come up with us.' In the Master's room, though she hadn't yet changed her clothes or washed her face, she became Gry again. I asked if they were hungry, but they said no, the Gand had given them food and drink. 'Did they let you under the roof?' I asked. 'Did they let Shetar in?' I didn't want to be curious about anything the Alds did, but I was. Nobody I knew had ever been inside the Council House or the barracks or seen how the Gand and the Alds lived there, for all of Council Hill was always guarded and swarming with soldiers.

'Tell Memer about it while I get out of these clothes,' Gry said, and Orrec told me, making a tale of it; he couldn't help it.

The Alds had set up tents as well as barracks, tents of the fashion they use travelling in their deserts. The tent in Council Square was high and very large, as large as a big house, all of red cloth with golden trimming and banners. It appeared, said Orrec, that the Gand actually governed from this tent rather than from the Council House, at least now that the rains had ceased. The tent would be sumptuously furnished, and would have movable, carved screens making rooms of a kind within it – Orrec had been made welcome in such great tents in his travels in Asudar. But here he was not brought under even that cloth roof. He was invited to sit on a light folding stool on a carpet not far from the open doorway of the tent.

Branty had been taken to the stables by a groom who handled him as if he were made of glass. The lion tamer and the lion stood some yards behind Orrec, with Ald officers guarding them. They, like Orrec, were offered paper parasols to protect them from the sun. 'I got one on account of Shetar,' Gry called to us from the dressing room. 'They respect lions. But they'll throw away the parasols, because we used them and we're unclean.'

They were offered refreshments at once, and a bowl of water was brought for Shetar. After they had waited about half an hour, the Gand emerged from the tent with a retinue of courtiers and officers.

He greeted Orrec most graciously, calling him prince of poets and welcoming him to Asudar.

'Asudar!' I burst out. 'This is Ansul!' Then I apologised for interrupting.

'Where the Ald is is the desert,' Orrec said mildly; I don't know whether they were his own words or an Ald saying.

The Gand Ioratth, he said, was a man of sixty or more, splendidly dressed in robes of linen inwoven with gold thread in the fashion of Asudar, with the wide, peaked hat that only Ald noblemen can wear. His manners were affable and his talk was shrewd and lively. He sat with Orrec and conversed about poetry: at first they spoke of the great epics of Asudar, but he also wanted to know about what he called the western makers. His interest was real, his questions intelligent. He invited Orrec to come regularly to the palace to recite from his own work and that of other makers. It would, he said, give him and his court much pleasure and instruction. He spoke as one prince to another, inviting, not ordering.

Some of the courtiers and officers joined in the conversation after a while, and like the Gand showed a thorough knowledge of their own epics and a curiosity, even a hunger, to hear poetry and story. They complimented Orrec, saying he was a fountain in the desert to them.

Others were less friendly. The Gand's son, Iddor, kept noticeably apart, paying no attention to the talk about poetry, standing inside the open tent with a group of priests and officers and chatting with them, until they grew so noisy that the Gand silenced them with a reproof. After that Iddor scowled and said nothing.

The Gand asked that the lion be brought to him, so Chy obliged, and Shetar did her useful trick, as Orrec called it: facing the Gand, she stretched out her front paws and bowed her head down between them, as cats do when they stretch – 'doing obeisance'. This pleased everybody very much, and Shetar had to do it several times, which was fine with her, since she got a small treat each time, even though it was her fasting day. Iddor came forward and wanted to play with her, dangling his feathered cap, which she ignored, and asking how strong she was, did she kill live prey, had she bitten people, had she killed a man, and so on. Chy the lion tamer answered all his questions respectfully, and had Shetar do obeisance to him. But Shetar yawned at him after doing a rather perfunctory bow.

'An unbeliever should not be permitted to keep a lion of Asudar,' Iddor said to his father, who replied, 'But who will take the lion from the master of the lion?' – evidently a proverb, neatly applied. At that, Iddor started to tease Shetar, provoking her by shouting and starting at her as if in attack. Shetar ignored him absolutely. The Gand, when he realised what his son was doing, stood up in a rage, told him he was shaming the hospitality of his house and offending the majesty of the lion, and ordered him to leave.

'The majesty of the lion,' Gry repeated, sitting down with us at last, her face clean, and dressed now in her silk shirt and trousers – 'I like that.'

'But I don't like what went on between the Gand and his son,' Orrec said. 'A snake's nest, as Gudit said. It will take careful treading. The Gand, though, he's a very interesting man.'

He's the tyrant that ruined and enslaved us, I thought, but didn't say.

'The Waylord is right,' Orrec went on, 'the Alds

are camped in Ansul like soldiers on the march. They seem amazingly ignorant of how people live here, who they are, what they do. And the Gand is bored with ignorance. I think he's seen that he'll probably finish out his life here and might as well make the best of it. But on the other hand, the people of the city don't know anything about the Alds.'

'Why should we?' I said. I couldn't stop myself.

'We say in the Uplands, it takes a mouse to really know the cat,' said Gry.

'I don't want to know people who spit on my gods and call us unclean. I call them filth. Look – look at my lord! Look what they did to him! Do you think he was born with his hands broken?'

'Ah, Memer,' Gry said, and she reached out to me, but I pulled away. I said, 'You can go to what they call their Palace and eat their food if you like and tell them your poetry, but I'd kill every Ald in Ansul if I could.'

Then I turned away and broke into tears, because I had ruined everything and didn't deserve their confidence.

I tried to leave the room, but Orrec stopped me.

'Memer, listen,' he said, 'listen. Forgive our ignorance. We are your guests. We ask your pardon.'

That brought me out of my stupid crying. I wiped my eyes and said, 'I'm sorry.'

'Sorry, sorry,' Gry whispered, and I let her take my hand and sit down with me on the window seat. 'We know so little. Of you, of your lord, of Ansul. But I know as you do that we were brought together here by more than chance.'

'By Lero,' I said.

'By a horse, and a lion, and Lero,' she said. 'I will trust you, Memer.'

'I will trust you,' I said to them both.

'Tell us who you are, then. We need to know one another! Tell us who the Waylord is – or what he was, before the Alds came. Was he the lord of the city?'

'We didn't have any lords.'

I tried to pull myself together to answer properly, as I did when the Waylord asked me, 'A little further, please, Memer?' I said, 'We elected a council to govern the city. All the cities on the Ansul Coast did. The citizens voted for the councillors. And the councils named the waylords. Waylords travelled among the cities and arranged trade so that the towns and the cities got what they needed from each other. And they kept merchants from cheating and usury, if they could.'

'It's not a hereditary title, then?'

I shook my head. 'You were a waylord for ten years. And ten more if your council named you again. Then somebody else took over. Anybody could be a waylord. But you had to have money of your own or from your city. You had to entertain the merchants and the factors and the other waylords, and travel all the time – even down into Sundraman, to talk with the silk merchants and the government there. It cost a lot. But Galvamand was a rich house, then. And people of the city helped. It was an honor, a great honor, being a waylord. So we still call him that. In honor. Although it means nothing now.'

I almost broke out in tears again. My weakness, my lack of control, scared me and made me angry, and the anger helped steady me.

'All that was before I was born. I only know it because people have told me and I've read the histories.'

Then my breath went out of me as if I had been hit in the stomach, and I sat paralysed. The habit of my lifetime had hold of me: I should not speak of reading, I should never say to anyone outside my household that I had read something in a book.

But Orrec and Gry, of course, didn't even notice. To them it was perfectly natural. They nodded. They asked me to go on.

I wasn't sure what I should and should not tell them, now. 'People like me are called siege brats,' I said. I pulled at my pale, fine, crinkly hair. I wanted them to know what I was but I didn't want to speak of my mother being raped. 'You can see . . . When the Alds took the city. That was when . . . But we drove them out again, and kept them out almost a year. We can fight. We don't make wars, but we can fight. But then the new army came from Asudar, twice as many men, and broke into the city. And they took the Waylord to prison and wrecked Galvamand. They tore down the university and threw the books into the canals and the sea. They drowned people in the canals and stoned them to death and buried them alive. The Waylord's mother, Eleyo Galva—'

She had lived in this room. She had been here when the soldiers broke into the house. I could not go on.

We were all silent.

Shetar paced by, lashing her tail. I reached out to her, to get away from what I'd been talking about, but she ignored me. He mouth was half open and she looked somehow more lionish than usual.

'She'll be in a bad mood all night,' Gry said. 'She got those rewards, at the palace, and it reminded her that she hasn't had a meal.'

'What does she eat?'

'Hapless goat, mostly,' Orrec said.

'Can she ever hunt?'

'She doesn't really know how,' Gry said. 'Her mother would have taught her. Halflions hunt in a clan, like wolves. That's why she tolerates us. We're her family.'

Shetar made a long, groaning, growling, singsong remark and paced down the long room again.

'Memer, if it isn't too hard for you to talk about it?' Orrec began, and when I shook my head, 'You said they destroyed the library of the university? Entirely?' I could tell he hoped I would deny it.

'The soldiers tried to tear down the library building, but it was stone and well built, so they broke the windows and wrecked the rooms, and brought the books out. They didn't want to touch them, they made citizens carry them and load them on carts and haul them to the canal and dump them in. There were so many books they piled up on the bottom of the canal and began to choke it, so they made people cart them down to the harbor. And unload the books and dump them off the piers. If they didn't sink right away they pushed people into the water after them. Once I saw a—' but this time I managed to stop myself, before I said that I had seen a book that had been salvaged from the sea.

It was in the secret room now, one of the northern scrollbooks, written on coated linen and rolled around wooden rods. The person who had found it cast up on the beach dried it out and brought it here. Though it had been weeks in the water, the beautiful writing could still be read. The Waylord showed it to me when he was working on it to restore the damaged text.

But I could not talk about the books, the old

books or the rescued books, in the secret room. Not even to Gry and Orrec.

It was safe, I hoped, to talk about ancient times, and I said, 'The university used to be here, long ago, in Galvamand.'

Orrec asked, and I told him what I knew, mostly as I had heard it from the Waylord, of the four great households of the city of Ansul: Cam, Gelb, Galva, Actamo. From earliest times they were the wealthiest families, with the most power in the Council. They built the finest houses and temples, paid for public rites and festivals, and gathered artists and makers, scholars and philosophers, architects and musicians, to live and work in their houses. That was when people began to call the city Ansul the Wise and Beautiful.

The Galvas had always lived here on the first rise of the hill above the river and the harbor, in the Oracle House.

'There was an oracle here?' Orrec asked.

I hesitated. I had given little thought to what the word meant until yesterday, the morning of the day Gry and Orrec came, as I stood by the dry basin of the fountain – the Oracle Fountain.

'I don't know,' I said. I started to say more, and did not. It was strange. Why had I never wondered why Galvamand was called the Oracle House? I did not even know what the oracle was, yet knew I must not speak of it – the way I knew, had always known, that I must not speak of the secret room. It was as if a hand was laid across my lips.

I thought then of what the Waylord had said last night, 'The hands of all the givers of dreams were on my mouth.' That frightened me.

They saw that I was confused and tongue-tied. Orrec changed the subject, asking about the house, and soon got me to telling its story again.

In those old days, the Galvas prospered, and both the house and the household grew, drawing to it people of art and learning and craft, and especially scholars and makers of poetry and tales. People came from all Ansul and even from other lands to hear them, learn from them, work with them. So over the years the university grew up here at Galvamand. All this back part of the house, both the upper and lower floors, had been apartments and classrooms and workrooms and libraries; there had been other buildings off the outer courts; and houses farther back on the hilltop had been hostels and domiciles for students and masters, workshops for artists and builders.

The poet Denios came here from Urdile when he was a young man. Maybe he had studied in the gallery where we had sat last night, for that had been part of the Library of Galvamand.

In the course of time, Luck, the god we call the Deaf One, turned away from the households of Cam, Gelb, and Actamo. As their wealth and well-being declined, their rivalry with Galva became rancorous. Partly in spite and envy, though they called it public spirit, they persuaded the Council to claim the university and its library for the city, taking it away from Galvamand. The Galvas accepted the ruling of the Council, though they warned that the old site was a sacred one and the new site might not be so blessed. The city built new buildings for the university down nearer the harbor. Almost all the great library that had been gathered here over the centuries was moved there. And I told Gry and Orrec what the Waylord had told me: 'When they began to take the books out of Galvamand, the Oracle Fountain in the forecourt began to fail. Little by little, as the books were taken out of the house, the water ceased to run. When they were done, it dried up entirely. It hasn't run for two hundred years . . .'

They opened the new university with ceremonies and festivals, and students and scholars came; but it was never so famous, so much visited, as the old Library of Galvamand. And then after two centuries the desert people came and tore down the stones, dumped the books into the canals and the sea, buried them in the mud.

Orrec listened to my story with his head in his hands.

'Nothing was left here at Galvamand?' Gry asked.

'Some books,' I said uncomfortably. 'But when the siege was broken the Ald soldiers came here right away, even before they went to the university. Looking for that . . . that place they believe in. They tore out the wooden parts of the house, and took the books, the furnishings— Whatever they found they took.' I was telling the truth, but I had a strong sense that Gry was aware that it wasn't the whole truth.

'This is terrible – terrible,' Orrec said, standing up. 'I know the Alds think writing is an evil thing –

but to destroy – to waste—' He was grieved and upset beyond words. He strode off down the room and stood at the western windows, where over the roofs of Galvamand and the lower city white Sul floated on the mist above the straits.

Gry went to Shetar and clipped the leash to her collar. 'Come on,' she said softly to me. 'She needs a walk.'

'I'm sorry,' I said, following her, despairing again at having so distressed Orrec. Everything I said was wrong. It was a day without Ennu, without any blessing.

'Was it you that destroyed the books?'

'No. But I wish—'

'If wishes were horses!' said Gry. 'Tell me, is there anywhere I could let Shetar off the leash to run? She won't attack if I'm anywhere near her, but it's less worrisome to let her go where there aren't people around.'

'The old park,' I said, and we went there. It is just above and east of the house, a broad gully in the hillside over the river where the Embankments divide it into the four canals. Trees grow thick on the slopes of the old park. The Alds never go there; they don't like trees. Nobody much goes there except children hunting rabbits or quail to get a bit of meat for their family.

I showed Gry what they call Denios' Fountain, near the entrance, and Shetar had a long drink from the basin.

There was not a soul about, and Gry let the lion off the leash. She bounded off, but not far, and kept coming back to us. Evidently she didn't much like the trees either, and didn't want to go far into the thick, neglected undergrowth. She spent a long time sharpening her claws on one tree, then another, and sniffed exhaustively on the tracks of some creature all round a great thicket of brambles. The farthest she got from us was in pursuit of a butterfly, which led her leaping and batting at it down a steep dark path. After she'd been out of sight around a bend for a while, Gry gave a little purring call. In a moment the lion reappeared, loping up at us through the shadows. Gry touched Shetar's head, and she followed us as we started wandering slowly back up through the woods.

'What a wonderful gift,' I said, 'to be able to call animals to you.'

'Depends on what you use it for,' Gry said. 'It certainly came in handy when we came down out of the Uplands and had to make a living. I trained horses while Orrec got his learning. I like that work . . . I admire the way the Alds train their horses. For them, beating your horse is worse than beating your wife.' She gave a little snort.

'How could you stand living in Asudar so long? Weren't you – didn't you get angry at them?'

'I didn't have the cause for anger you have,' she said. 'It was a little like living with wild animals – predators. They're dangerous, and not reasonable, by our standards. They make life hard. I felt sorry for the Ald men.'

I said nothing.

'They're like stallions or buck rabbits,' she went on, reflectively. 'Never a moment they're not anxious about a rival male, or a female getting loose. They're never free. They fill their world with enemies . . . But they're brave, and keep their word, and honor the guest. Like my people of the Uplands. I liked them well enough. I couldn't get to know any women, though, because I was pretending to be a man and had to keep away from them. That was tiresome.'

'I hate everything about them,' I said. 'I can't help it.'

'Of course you can't help it. What you've told us – how could you see them except as hateful?'

'I don't want to see them any other way,' I said.

I don't believe Gry ever didn't hear what people said, but sometimes she ignored it. She walked on a little and then turned to me on the path with a sudden grin. 'Listen, Memer! Why don't you come with us to the palace? Second groom. You make a fine boy. Fooled me completely. Would you like to? It's interesting. The Gand's a kind of king, how many chances do you get to meet a king? And you can hear Orrec – he's going to tell them the *Cosmogonies*. That could be risky, they're so stuck on Atth being the one and only god. But the Gand was asking him for it yesterday.'

I only shook my head. I longed to hear Orrec speak that poem, but not among a lot of Alds. I wouldn't say any more about how I hated them, but I certainly wasn't going to go be polite and meek and slavish to them.

After dinner the next day, though, Gry brought up the idea again. Evidently she had talked Orrec into it, for he made no objection; and to my dismay, the Waylord didn't either. He asked how dangerous they thought it might be. When they both said they trusted the Alds' law of hospitality, he said only, 'The hospitality they showed me wasn't of a kind I want Memer to know. But that our people and theirs know so little of one another, after so many years – that is shameful. For us as well as for them.' He looked at me thoughtfully. 'And Memer is a very quick learner.'

I wanted to protest, to say I refused to go anywhere near the Alds, I didn't want to learn anything from them or about them. But that would be wilful ignorance, a thing the Waylord despised. And also it would sound like cowardice. If Orrec and Gry were willing to risk going to the palace, how could I refuse?

The idea was more frightening the more I thought about it. Yet I was curious about the palace, the Alds, as Orrec and Gry talked about them. Everything had been the same in my life for so long that I'd wondered if it would always be the same –

the housework, the market; the empty rooms of Galvamand, the secret room and its treasures of reading and learning, and the dark strange part of it where I dared not go; no one to teach me anything new but my dear lord, no one but him to be with, to give my love to. Now by the coming of two people the house had come alive. The ancestors were awake, were listening – the souls, the shadows, and the guardians of sill and hearth. The One who Looks Both Ways had opened the door. I knew that. I knew that our guests had come on the path of Ennu and with Lero's blessing, and that to refuse what they offered me was to refuse the gift, the chance, the turning of the way.

'Do you want to go, Memer?' the Waylord asked me. I knew if I protested he wouldn't insist. I shrugged, not even speaking, as if it were a matter of no importance to me if I went or not.

He looked at me searchingly. Why did he agree to send me among our enemies? And I saw why: because I could go where he could not. Even if I was a coward, I could carry his courage. He was asking me to play my part as the heir of our house.

'Yes, I'll go,' I said.

That night for the first time in my life I dreamed of the man who was my father. He wore the blue cloak the soldiers wear. His hair was like mine, a dun, dull, crinkly mass too fine to comb, sheep hair. I could not see his face. He was climbing, clambering hastily over ruins, broken walls and stones, such as our city was full of. I stood in the street watching him. As he passed he looked straight at me. I could not see his face clearly, but I thought it was not a man's face but a lion's. He looked away again and climbed over a ruined wall, hurrying, as if pursued.

◆ 7 ◆

When Orrec Caspro set off the next time to entertain the Gand of the Alds of Ansul, his retinue was Chy the lion tamer, Shetar the lion, and Mem the groom.

Mem was anxious and uneasy. What if the Alds asked me to unsaddle Branty, or tried to talk groom-talk with me? They'd know in a moment that I didn't know a hock from a pastern. No fear, said Gry, they were just like Gudit, they wouldn't allow a strange boy in their stables with their prized horses. Anyhow, she'd keep me right beside her when we were at the Palace. All I had to do as Mem was walk through the streets at Branty's head, groom fashion, as if Orrec needed help managing his horse.

So I did that, feeling foolish and quite frightened. Branty was a comfort to me. He walked along, his shod hoofs ringing loud and regular on our stone-paved streets, his big head nodding up and down beside me, ears flicking forward and back; now and then he blew air out his nostrils. His big, dark eye had a kind look in it. He was old – older than I was – and had travelled over all the Western Shore. Where Orrec asked him to go he went with a noble patience. I wished I were like him.

We followed Galva Street up the low hill from Goldsmiths' Bridge to the square before the Council House. I looked at that building with a swell of pride. It is broad and tall, built of silvery-grey stone, with rows of high, delicate windows. Its dome of copper rises lightly above all the roofs of the city as Sul floats above the lower mountains. Steps go up from the great square to the terrace in front of the doors, where people used to make speeches and debate, when we governed ourselves. The Waylord had told me the terrace was so constructed that if you stood in front of the central doors and spoke only a little louder than usual your voice could be heard all over the square. But I'd never been up those steps; I'd never even walked on the square before. It belonged to the Alds, not the citizens.

In the middle of it stood the huge tent with its red peaks and long red banners flying from the poles, almost hiding the Council House.

An officer came to meet us as we approached the entrance to the square and ordered the blue-cloaked guards to let us pass.

Men came to meet us from the stables, off to the left of the square. I held Branty while Orrec dismounted, and an elderly Ald took the reins from me and with a little *tck-tck* to Branty led him away. Chy the lion tamer came up next to me, with Shetar short-leashed, and we followed Orrec across the pavement. There was a carpet in front of the tent and a folding chair and a parasol for Orrec; no seats for us, but a little boy, a siege brat, a slave, handed Chy a parasol of red paper. We stood behind Orrec. Chy at once gave me the parasol to hold over the three of us, and stood with arms folded in a lofty posture. I saw that this would make sense to the Alds, who would see me as Chy's or Orrec's slave.

The Alds' slaves here at their court all wore a robe or tunic of coarse striped cloth, grey and white or dun and white. Some were Alds and some my countrymen. They were all men or boys. The women would be kept elsewhere, indoors, hidden. And none of them would be Alds.

Various courtiers in various kinds of finery came out of the tent, and several officers came up from the barracks which the Alds built above the East Canal behind the Council House, where our voting booths used to be. When at last the Gand came out of the big tent, everybody stood up. Two Ald slaves followed him; one held a huge red parasol over his head, while the other held a fan in case the Gand needed to be cooled off. It was a mild spring day, the sun mostly veiled by light clouds, a soft sea wind blowing. Seeing the slaves stand there with their silly equipment I thought how stupid the Alds were – couldn't they look around and see they didn't need parasols, or fans, or the wide-brimmed hats the courtiers wore? Couldn't they see this wasn't the desert?

Imitating the behavior of the Ald slaves, I didn't look directly at the Gand Ioratth, but stole glances.

He had a heavy, seamed face, sallow like most Alds, with a short hawk nose and narrow eyes. The Alds' pale eyes always make me queasy, and I've thanked my ancestors many times for letting me have the dark eyes of my people. The Gand's sheep hair was short and grey, frizzing out under his hat; his eyebrows frizzed out too, and a short rim of close-cut grey beard followed his jawline. He looked tough and tired. He greeted Orrec with a smile that lightened his face and a gesture I had never seen any Ald make, opening out his hands from his heart in welcome with a bow of his head. It seemed a greeting to an equal. And he called Orrec 'Gand of the Makers'.

But he won't let him under his roof, I thought.

'Heathen,' they called us. A word we learned from them. If it meant anything, it meant people who don't know what's sacred. Are there any such people? 'Heathen' is merely a word for somebody who knows a different sacredness than you know. The Alds had been here seventeen years and still hadn't learned that the sea, the earth, the stones of Ansul are sacred, are alive with divinity. If anybody was heathen it was them, not us, I thought. So I stood stewing in my resentment and not listening to what the men said, Ioratth and Orrec, the two princes, the tyrant and the poet.

Orrec began to recite, and the viol of his voice woke me to hearing; but it was some Ald poem the Gand had asked for, one of their endless epics about wars in the desert, and I wouldn't listen.

I looked among the courtiers for the Gand's son Iddor, the one who had teased Shetar. He was easy enough to pick out. He wore a lot of finery, with feathers and cloth-of-gold ribbons on his fancy hat. He looked a good deal like his father, but was taller and handsomer, although very light-skinned. He was restless, always talking to a companion, fidgeting, gesturing, moving his body. The old Gand sat unmoving, intent on the story, his linen robe falling as if carved of stone, his short, hard hands spread on his thighs. And most of his officers listened as intently as he did, drinking in the words. Orrec's voice sang with passion, and I began hearing the story in spite of myself.

When he stopped, after a tragic scene of betrayal and reconciliation, the hearers all applauded by hitting their palms together. The Gand had a slave bring Orrec water in a glass. ('They'll break it, afterwards,' Chy murmured to me.) Plates of sweets were offered about, not to Chy or me. Ioratth leaned forward holding out a morsel of something to Shetar. Chy led her forward. She sat down, sniffed the candy politely, and looked away. The Gand laughed. He had a pleasant laugh that creased his whole face. 'Not food for a lion, eh, Lady Shetar?' he said. 'Shall I send for some meat?'

Chy, not Orrec, answered him, gruff and brief: 'Better not, sir.'

The Gand was not offended. 'You keep her to a diet, eh? Yes, yes. Will she do her bow again?'

I could not see that Chy moved or did anything, but the lion stood up and did a deep cat stretch in front of the Gand. While he laughed, she looked round for the little ball of bone marrow that was her reward, and Chy slipped it into her mouth.

Iddor had come forward and said now to Orrec, 'What did you pay for her?'

'I got her for a song, Gand Iddor,' Orrec said. He spoke still seated; he was tuning his lyre, an excuse for not rising. Iddor scowled. Orrec looked up from the instrument and said, 'For a tale, more truly. The nomads who had the cub and her mother wanted to hear the whole tale of *Daredar* told, so they'd know more of it to tell at their shows. I told it for the three nights it takes to tell, and for that my reward was the lion cub. We were all well satisfied.'

'How do you know that tale? How did you learn our songs?'

'I hear a tale or a song, and it's mine,' Orrec said. 'That's my gift.'

'That and the making of songs,' said Ioratth.

Orrec bowed his head.

'But where did you hear them?' the Gand's son insisted. 'Where did you hear *Daredar* told?'

'I travelled in northern Asudar, Gand Iddor. Everywhere the people gave me their songs and stories, telling and singing, sharing their wealth with me. They didn't ask for payment, not a lion cub, not even a copper penny – only a new song or an old tale retold. The poorest people of the desert are most generous in word and heart.'

'True, true,' the elder Gand said.

'Did you read our songs? Have you put them in books?' Iddor spat out the words 'read' and 'books' as if they were turds in his mouth.

'Prince, among the people of Atth I live by the law of Atth.' Orrec spoke not only with dignity but fiercely, a man whose honor has been challenged answering the challenge.

Iddor turned away, daunted either by Orrec's direct response or by his father's glare. He said, however, to one of his companions, 'Is it a man, then, playing that fiddle? I thought it was a woman.'

Among the Alds, only women play the plucked and bowed instruments of music, and only men the flutes and horns – so Gry told me later. All I understood then was that Iddor wanted to insult Orrec, or wanted to flout his father, and insulting Orrec was a way to do that.

'When you are refreshed, Maker, we should like to hear you speak verse of your own making,' Ioratth said, 'if you will forgive and enlighten our ignorance of the poetry of the west.'

It surprised me that the Gand spoke so formally and elaborately. He was an old soldier, no doubt about that, and yet everything he said was measured, even flowery, with archaic words and turns of phrase, pleasant to hear. It was the way you might expect a people to speak who shunned writing and made all their art of words aloud. Until now I had hardly heard an Ald say anything, only shout orders.

Orrec was quite able to give as good as he got in polite exchange as well as verbal duelling. Earlier, reciting from the *Daredar* epic, he had laid aside his northern accent and spoke like an Ald, blurring the harsher consonants and stretching out the vowels. Answering the Gand now he kept that softness. 'I am the last and least of that line of makers, Gand,' he said, 'and it is not in my heart to put myself before far greater men. Will you and your court permit me to say, rather than my own verses, a poem of the beloved Maker of Urdile, Denios?'

The Gand nodded. Orrec finished tuning his lyre, explaining as he did so that the poem was not sung, but that the voice of the instrument served to set the poetry apart from all words said before and after it, and also to say, sometimes, what no words could. Then he bowed his head to the lyre and struck the strings. The notes were plangent, clear, impassioned. The last chord died away, and he spoke the first words of the first canto of *The Transformations*.

Nobody moved till he was done. And they were silent for a long moment afterwards, just as the crowd in the marketplace had been. Then they were about to clap their hands in praise, but the Gand held up his hand in a sudden gesture – 'No,' he said. 'Again, Maker! If you will, speak us this marvel once again!'

Orrec looked a little taken aback, but he smiled and bowed his head to the lyre.

Before he touched the strings a man spoke loudly. It was not Iddor but one who stood near him among his troop: he wore a red-and-black robe and a red headdress that came down straight, boxlike, from a high red hat to his shoulders, hiding his head and leaving only his face visible. His beard had been singed off, leaving a burnt frizz along his chin. He carried a long, heavy, black stick as well as a short sword. 'Son of the Sun,' he said, 'is not once enough and more than enough to hear this blasphemy?'

'Priest,' Chy whispered to me. I knew he was a priest, though we didn't see them often. Redhats, we called them, and hoped never to see them, for when a citizen was to be stoned to death or buried alive down in the mudflats, it was the redhats who did it.

Ioratth turned to look at the priest. It was like the turn of a hawk's head, a quick, how-dare-you frown.

But he spoke mildly: 'Most Blessed of Atth,' he said, 'my ears are dull. I heard no blasphemy. I beg you to open my understanding.'

The man in the red headdress spoke with great assurance. 'These are godless words, Gand Ioratth. There is in them no knowledge of Atth, no belief in the revelations of his sacred interpreters. It is all blind worship of demons and false gods, talk of base earthly doings, and praise of women.'

'Ah, ah,' Ioratth said, nodding, not contradicting but not seeming shaken by this denunciation. 'It is true that the heathen poets are ignorant of Atth and his Burnt Ones. They perceive darkly and in error, yet let us not call them blind. The fire of revelation may yet come to them. Meanwhile, we who were forced to leave our wives long years ago, do you begrudge even our hearing a word about women? You the Blessed, the Fire-Burnt, are above pollution, but we are only soldiers. To hear is not to have, but it gives some comfort none the less.' He was perfectly solemn saying this, but some of the men about him grinned.

The man in the headdress began to reply, but the Gand abruptly stood up. 'In respect for the sacred purity of the Fire-Burnt,' he said, 'I will not ask the Blessed Rudde or his brothers to stay and listen longer to words that offend their ears. And any other man who does not wish to hear the heathen poet's songs may go. Since only he is cursed who hears the curse, as they say, those who have dull ears, like me, may stay and listen safely. Maker, forgive our disputes and our discourtesy.'

He sat down again. Iddor and the redhats – there were four of them – and the rest of Iddor's group all went back into the great tent, talking loudly, discontented. One man who stood near Ioratth also slunk away as unnoticeably as he could, looking anxious and unhappy. The rest stayed. And Orrec struck the lyre, and spoke the opening of *The Transformations* again.

The Gand let his people applaud at the end, this time. He had another glass of water brought to Orrec ('Fortune in crystal,' Chy hissed to me), and then he dismissed his retinue, saying that he wished to speak with the poet 'beneath the fern-palm', which evidently meant in private.

A couple of guards remained standing at the tent entrance, but the officers and courtiers went back into the big tent or to the barracks, and Chy and I were dismissed by the officious slave with the fan. We went to the stable side of the courtyard, following several men who, I realised now, had come from the stables or elsewhere to hear the poetry and had been standing all along unobtrusively on the fringe of the group. Some were soldiers, others hostlers, a couple of them were boys. Most of them were interested in Shetar. They wanted to get closer to her than Chy would let them get. They tried to strike up conversation, asking all the usual questions – what's her name, where did you get her, what does she eat, has she killed anybody. Chy's answers were curt and haughty, as befitted a lion tamer.

'Is he your slave?' a young man asked. I didn't realise he was talking about me until Chy answered, 'Prentice groom.'

The young man fell into step with me, and when I reached the shady wall and sat down on the cobbles, he sat down too. He looked at me several times and finally said, 'You're an Ald.'

I shook my head.

'Your dad was,' he said, looking very shrewd.

What was the use denying it, with my hair, my face? I shrugged.

'You live here? In the city?'

I nodded.

'Do you know any girls?'

My heart went up into my throat. All I could think was that he'd seen I was a girl, that he'd start shouting about pollution, defilement, blasphemy—

'I came here from Dur with my dad last year,' he said in a depressed tone, and then said nothing for a while.

Sneaking a longer glance at him I saw that he was a boy rather than a man, fifteen, sixteen at most. He didn't wear the blue cloak, but a tunic with a blue knot at the shoulder. He was bare-legged, big-boned, pale-skinned, with a soft face and pimples around his mouth. His frizz of sheep hair was yellowish. He sighed. 'The Ansul girls all hate us,' he said. 'I thought maybe you had a sister.'

I shook my head.

'What's your name?'

'Mem.'

'Well, look, Mem, if you knew some girls who,

you know, just wanted to be with some men for a while, I have some money. For you, I mean.'

He was graceless, detestable, and pitiful. He didn't even sound hopeful. I didn't make any answer at all. For all my fear and contempt of him, he made me want to laugh – I don't know why – he was so shameless. Like a dog. I couldn't actually hate him.

He went on about girls, just talking about his daydreams I suppose, and began to say some things that made me feel myself getting red in the face and restless. I said in a flat voice, 'I don't know any girls.' That shut him up for a while. He sighed and scratched his groin and finally said, 'I hate it here. I want to go home.'

Then go! I wanted to shout at him. I just said, 'Hunh.'

He looked at me again, so closely that it scared me all over again. 'Do you ever go with boys?' he asked.

I shook my head.

'I never have either,' he said in his sad, monotonous voice, which was no deeper than mine. 'Some of the fellows do.' The idea seemed to depress him so much that he said nothing more, until he said, 'Father would kill me.'

I nodded.

We sat in silence. Shetar was pacing up and down the courtyard with Chy in attendance. I wanted to be with them, but thought it would look odd if an apprentice groom walked up and down with the lion and the lion tamer.

'What do fellows do here?' the boy asked.

I shrugged. What did boys do? Scrounged for food and firewood, mostly, like everybody else in my city except the Alds. 'Play stickball,' I said finally.

He looked more depressed. Evidently he was not the game-playing type.

'What's so strange here,' he said, 'there's women everywhere. Out in the open. Women all over the place, but you can't . . . They don't . . .'

'Aren't there any women in Asudar?' I asked, playing stupid.

'Of course there's women. Only they aren't outside, all over the place,' he said in an aggrieved, accusing tone. 'They aren't always around where you see them all the time. Our women don't go flaunting around in the street. They stay home where they belong.'

I thought then of my mother, in the street, trying to get home.

A great, hot rage rose up through my body and if I had spoken then it would have been a curse, or I would have spat in his face; but I didn't speak, and the rage slowly died away to a cold, hollow sickness. I swallowed my saliva and willed myself to be calm.

'Mekke says there's temple whores,' the boy said. 'Anybody could go there. Only the temples were shut down, of course. So they do it in secret somewhere. But they still have them. They do it with anybody. You know anything about that?'

I shook my head.

He sighed.

Very carefully, I stood up. I needed to move, but move slowly.

'My name's Simme,' he said, looking up at me with a squinting smile, like a child.

I nodded. I moved slowly away – towards Shetar and Chy, for I did not know anywhere else to go. The blood was singing in my ears.

Chy looked me over and said, 'The Gand's about

done talking, I think. Go to the stables and ask them to bring the Maker's horse out. Say you want to walk him. All right?'

I nodded and went round into the great stable courtyard. For some reason I was no longer afraid of the men there. I asked after the Maker's horse, and they took me to Branty's stall. Branty was playing with a taste of oats. 'Have him saddled and brought out,' I said, as if they were slaves and I a master. The old man who had taken him from me at first went to obey my orders. I stood with my hands behind my back, looking over the beautiful horses in the long line of stalls. When the old man brought Branty out, I took his bridle without hesitation.

'He'd be about nineteen or twenty?'

'Older,' I said, with the same assurance.

'Good blood,' the old man said. He reached up to part Branty's forelock with thick, dirty, gentle fingers. 'I like big horses,' he said.

I gave a brief nod of approval, and walked away with Branty. Chy and Shetar were just at the entrance to the stable court, and Orrec was coming towards us. I gave him a knee up to mount, and we set off sedately for home. As we went out through

the gateway of the Council Square, past the Ald
guards in blue cloaks, I was overcome suddenly by
tears, they burst hot from my eyes, my mouth
quivered and jerked. I went walking on, seeing my
city, my beautiful city and the far mountain over the
straits and the cloud-swept sky through tears, until
they ceased.

◆ 8 ◆

Ista made one of her special dishes that night, what we call uffu, pastries stuffed with a bit of ground lamb or kid, potatoes, greens, and herbs, and fried in oil. They were crisp, greasy, delicious. Ista was grateful to Orrec and Gry not only because they had provided meat for the kitchen – we were sharing Shetar's dinner is the fact of it – but because they were our guests, restoring honor and dignity to the house by their presence, and giving her somebody new to cook for. They complimented the uffu, while she shrugged and growled and criticised her pastry for being tough. Can't get decent oil, she said, like we had in the good days.

After dinner the Waylord took our guests and me to the back gallery, and again we sat and talked. Three of us were very curious to know what the Gand Ioratth had said to Orrec beneath the fern palm. And Orrec was ready to tell us. He had news indeed.

Dorid, Gand of Gands, high priest and king of Asudar and commander of the Ald armies for nearly thirty years, was dead. He had died of a seizure over a month ago in his palace in the desert city Medron. His successor was a man named Acray, his nephew, or so called. Since the kings of Asudar were high priests, and priests of Atth were officially celibate, a king couldn't officially have a son, only nephews. Other nephews or claimants to the throne contested Acray's succession and had been killed in uprisings or behind the scenes. Medron had been in turmoil for some time, but by now Acray had seized firm hold of power as the Gand of Gands of all Asudar.

And this was evidently much to the Gand Ioratth's liking. From what he said, Orrec gathered that the new priest-king was less the priest and more

the king than Dorid had been. The palace factions
that had tried to keep Acray from the throne were,
like Dorid, followers of the cult of the Thousand
True Men – those who had declared a war of Good
against Evil, urging the invasion of heathen Ansul to
find and destroy the Night Mouth.

Acray's followers, it seemed, didn't put much
stock in the existence of the Night Mouth, especially
since the invading army had never been able to find
it. They considered the occupation of Ansul, though
it had brought some profit and luxury goods to
Medron, as a drain on the resources of the Ald army
and also a spiritually questionable enterprise. For the
Alds were a race apart, dwelling in their desert,
singularly favored by their single god. They had
always kept clear of the pollution of the unbelievers.
To continue to live among the heathen was to risk
their souls.

What should the Alds in Ansul do, then?

Ioratth, considering these matters aloud to Orrec,
had spoken remarkably plainly. The question, as he
saw it, was which would be more pleasing to Atth:
should the new Gand of Gands recall his soldiers
home to Asudar with all the loot they could bring,

or should he send settlers to colonise Ansul permanently?

'He put it just about like that,' Orrec said. 'Evidently the new ruler has asked Ioratth for his opinion, as a man who's lived all these years here among the heathen. And Ioratth sees me as disinterested, an impartial observer. But why does he see me so? And why does he trust me with his damned indecisions? I'm a heathen myself!'

'Because you're a maker,' the Waylord said. 'Therefore, to the Alds, a truth-speaker and a seer.'

'Maybe he has nobody else he can talk to,' Gry said. 'And whether or not you're a seer, you certainly are a good listener.'

'A silent one,' Orrec said, with some bitterness. 'What can I say to all this?'

'I don't know what you can say to Ioratth,' the Waylord said. 'But it may help you to know what little I know about him. In the first place, he took a woman of Ansul as a slave, a concubine, but it's said he treats her honorably. Her name is Tirio Actamo. She's the daughter of a great family. I knew her before the invasion. She was a beautiful, clever, spirited girl. All I know of her now is servants' gossip brought to me by others, but the gossip is that Ioratth honors her as a wife, and that she has great influence on him.'

'I wish I could talk with her!' Gry said.

'So do I,' the Waylord said, and his voice was wry and melancholy. After a pause he went on. 'Iddor is the Gand's son by a wife back in Asudar. They say Iddor hates Tirio Actamo. They also say he hates his father.'

'He taunts and defies him,' Orrec said, 'but seems to obey him.'

The Waylord sat silent for a while, then got up, went over to the god-niche, and stood before it. 'Blessed spirits of this house,' he murmured, 'help me speak truly.' He bowed his head and touched the worn sill of the niche, stood a moment longer, and came back to us. He spoke standing.

'It was Iddor and the priests who led the soldiers here to find their Night Mouth. They tortured the people of the house to make them reveal the entrance to the cave or sewer or whatever the Night Mouth might be. Some died in torture. The Alds kept me alive. They had—' he halted a moment and then went on, 'they had the most hope of me, since they perceived me as a witch. A priest, in their terms, but a priest of their anti-god. But I wasn't able to tell them what they wanted to know. Ennu laid her hand on my mouth and would not let me lie. Sampa stopped my tongue and would not let me speak the truth. All the souls of Galvamand came round me. The priests knew it. They were afraid of me, even while they . . . Not afraid of me but of the sacredness that came into me, the gathering of souls around me, the blessing of the gods and spirits of my house, my city, my land.

'After a while the priests didn't want to have anything to do with me, so Iddor himself was my only questioner. He feared me too, I think, but also he prided himself on his daring, since he believed me a great sorcerer and yet he could do what he liked with me. I proved his power, by being a toy for his cruelty. I had to listen to him. He talked and talked, always explaining to me, telling me over and over how the demon that filled me would come forth at last and tell him where to find the Night Mouth. When the demon came forth and spoke I would be allowed to die. All evil would die. Righteousness would rule the earth, and he, Iddor, would sit by the throne of the King of Kings, burning in glory. He talked and talked. I tried to lie to him, and I tried to tell him the truth. But they would not let me.'

He had not sat down as he spoke, and now he went back to the god-niche, put his hands on the sill of it, and stood there in silence a while. I heard him whisper blessing on Ennu and the house-gods. Then he turned to us again.

'All that time, all the time Iddor held me prisoner, I never saw his father. Ioratth kept away from the prison cells and had no part in the witch hunts. Iddor constantly complained to me about his father, railed at him, saying he was impious, contemptuous of priests and prophecies, and flouted the order of the Gand of Gands to find the Night Mouth. 'I obey my god and my king, he does not,' he said. But in the end, whether at Ioratth's order or not, I was let go. The hunts for caves and demons died down. Now and then Iddor or the priests would raise up a scare, finding a book to destroy or a scholar to torture. Ioratth let them do it, I suppose to satisfy the Gand of Gands that the quest was still going on. He had to walk carefully, since his son was of the king's party and he was not.

'But now, it looks as if Ioratth has a king of his own kind, and the power Iddor and the priests had will be suddenly reduced. This could be a dangerous moment.'

He sat down with us again. 'Though he had spoken painfully, he did not seem troubled now, only grave and weary; and as he looked around at us, a gentleness came into his face, as if, returned from a journey, he saw people he loved.

'Dangerous because . . .' Gry said, and Orrec finished her half question: 'Because Iddor, seeing his faction losing power, might try to seize power?'

The Waylord nodded. 'I wonder where the Ald soldiers stand on this,' he said. 'No doubt they'd like to go home to Asudar. But they respect their priests. If Iddor defied his father, and the priests were with Iddor, which of them would the soldiers obey?'

'We can do some listening at the palace,' Gry said. She glanced at me, I didn't know why.

'There's another element of danger, or hope, or both,' the Waylord said, 'which I tell you of, asking you for your silence. There's a group of people who hope to rouse Ansul against the Alds. A group that for a long time now has been laying plans for rebellion. I know of it only through friends. I don't take part in making its plans, I don't even know with any certainty how strong it is. But it exists. Seeing a power struggle in the palace, such a group might try to act.'

Now at last I knew what Desac came to talk about, and why I was always sent away when he met with the Waylord. That sent a rush of anger through me. Why hadn't I been allowed to listen to talk of rebellion, of rising against the Alds, fighting them, driving them out? Did Desac think I'd be afraid? Or go blabbing about it like a child? Did he think, because I had sheep hair, that I'd betray my people?

Gry wanted to know more about this group, but the Waylord was unable or unwilling to say much about it. Orrec was silent, brooding, till he asked at last, 'How many Alds are here in Ansul – in the city? A thousand, two thousand?'

'Over two thousand,' the Waylord said.

'They're greatly outnumbered.'

'But armed and disciplined,' Gry said.

'Trained soldiers,' Orrec said. 'It gives them an edge . . . But still. All these years—'

I burst out, 'We fought! We fought them in every street, we held out for a year – till they sent an army twice as large – and then they killed and killed – Ista told me that in the days after the city fell, the canals were so choked with the dead that the water couldn't run—'

'Memer, I know your people were overrun and overmatched,' Orrec said. 'I didn't mean to question their courage.'

'But we're not warriors,' said the Waylord.

'Adira and Marra!' I protested.

His gaze rested on me a moment. 'I didn't say we couldn't have heroes,' he said. 'But for centuries we settled our affairs by talking, arguing, bargaining, voting. Our quarrels were fought with words not swords. We were out of the habit of brutality . . . And the Ald armies seemed endless. How much more would they destroy? We lost heart. We have been a crippled people.'

He held up his broken hands. His face was strange, wry; his eyes looked very dark.

'As you say, Orrec, they have the edge,' he said. 'Having one king, one god, one belief, they can act single-mindedly. They're strong. Yet the single can be divided. Our strength embraces multitude. This is our sacred earth. We live here with its gods and spirits, among them, they among us. We endure with them. We've been hurt, weakened, enslaved. But only if they destroy our knowledge are we destroyed.'

◆　◆　◆

TWO DAYS after that, when we went to the Council Square again, I found out why Gry had given me that glance when she said, 'We can do some listening.' She wanted Mem the apprentice groom to talk to the Ald stableboys and cadet soldiers who hung around to hear Orrec recite. 'Keep an ear out,' she said. 'Ask about the new Gand in Medron. About the Night Mouth. You were talking for a long time with one of those boys the other day.'

'The pimply one,' I said.

'He took a shine to you.'

'He wanted to know if I'd sell him my sister for sex,' I said.

Gry whistled, a soft little down-note, *tiu*.

'Endure,' she said softly.

The Waylord had used that word. I took it as my

guide word, my orders. I would obey. I would endure.

This time, when the Gand came out of the great tent to hear Orrec, Iddor and the priests didn't follow him. Partway through the recitation a noise began inside the tent, a lot of loud chanting and drum banging – evidently the priests performing a ceremony. Some of the courtiers around the Gand looked disturbed, others shrugged and whispered. Ioratth sat imperturbable. Orrec finished the stanza and fell silent.

The Gand gestured to him to go on.

'I would not show disrespect to those who worship,' Orrec said.

'It is not worship,' Ioratth said. 'It is disrespect. Proceed, if you will, Maker.'

Orrec bowed and went on with the piece, another Ald hero tale. When it was done, Ioratth had him brought a glass of water and began to talk with him, several of the courtiers joining in. And I, obeying my orders, slipped back towards the group of boys and men in the shade of the stable wall.

Simme was there. He came right over to me. He was bigger than I was, a tall, strong boy. There were fair, fuzzy hairs among the pimples around his mouth – the Alds are hairier than my people, and many have beards. Yet when I saw the way he greeted me, almost cringing, hoping that I liked him, I thought: he's a little boy.

All I knew was my city and my house and books, while he had travelled with an army and was a soldier in training, but I knew I knew more than he did, and was tougher. He knew it, too.

It made it hard to hate him. There's some virtue in hating people who are stronger than you, but to hate somebody weaker is contemptible and uncomfortable.

He didn't know what to talk about, and at first I thought we wouldn't be able to talk at all, but then I thought to ask him something I really wanted to know. 'Where did you hear what you were talking about the other day,' I said, 'all that stuff about temples and prostitutes?'

'Some of the men,' he said. 'They said you heathens had these temples, where they had these orgies with these priestesses of this goddess, this demoness, that made men, you know, have sex with the priestesses. The demoness possessed them. And they'd have sex with any man. Anybody who came along. All night.'

He'd brightened up considerably at the thought.

'We don't have any priestesses,' I said flatly. 'Or priests. We do our own worship.'

'Well, maybe it was just women who went to this temple, and the demoness made them have sex with anybody. All night.'

'How could people get inside a temple?'

In Ansul, the word temple usually means a little shrine on the street or in front of a building or at a crossways – altars, places to worship at. Many of them are just god-niches like the ones inside houses. You touch the sill of the temple to say the blessing, or lay a flower as an offering. Many street temples were wonderful little buildings of marble, two or three feet high, carved and decorated, with gilt roofs. The Alds had knocked those all down. Some temples were hung up in trees, and the Alds left them, thinking they were birdhouses. In fact if a bird nested in a temple it was a joyful thing, a blessing, and a lot of the old tree temples had swallows and sparrows and thrushes in them year after year. The best luck of all was an owl. The owl is the bird of the Deaf One.

I knew that to the Alds a temple meant a full-sized building. I didn't care.

My question did get his mind off the notion of all-night sex, anyway. He frowned and said, 'What do you mean? Everybody goes into temples.'

'What for?'

'To pray!'

'What do you mean, 'pray'?'

'Worship Atth!' Simme said, staring.

'How do you worship Atth?'

'You go to the ceremony?' he said, in a questioning tone, incredulous that I didn't know what he was talking about. 'And the priests sing and drum and dance, and they speak the words of Atth? You know! You're down on your hands and knees? And you knock your head on the ground four times and say the words after the priests.'

'What for?'

'Well, if you want something, you pray to Atth, you knock your head on the ground and pray for it.'

'Pray *for* it? How do you pray *for* something?'

He was beginning to look at me as if I was feebleminded.

I returned the look. 'You don't make sense,' I said. I was in fact rather curious to understand his idea of praying, but I didn't want him to start feeling superior to me. 'You can't *pray* for things.'

'Of course you can! You pray to Atth for life and health, and, and, and everything else!'

I did understand him. Everybody cries out to Ennu when they're frightened. Everybody prays to Luck for things they want; that's why he's called the Deaf One. But I said, contemptuously, 'That's begging, not praying. We pray for blessing, not for things.'

He was both shocked and stymied. He looked sullen. He said, 'You can't be blessed. You don't believe in Atth.'

Now I was shocked. To say to someone that they couldn't be blessed, that was horrible. Simme didn't seem like a person who could even think such a cruel thing. I finally said, much more cautiously, 'What do you mean, 'believe in'?'

He stared at me. 'Well, to believe in Atth is – is to believe Atth is god.'

'Of course he is. All the gods are god. Why shouldn't Atth be?'

'What you call gods are demons.'

I thought about it for a while. 'I don't know if I believe there are demons, but I do know the gods. I don't understand why you have to 'believe' in only one god and none of the others.'

'Because if you don't believe in Atth you're damned and when you die you'll turn into a demon!'

'Who says so?'

'The priests!'

'And you believe *that?*'

'Yes! The priests know about stuff like that!' He was getting more and more unhappy, and spoke angrily.

'I don't think they know much about Ansul,' I said, realising, a little late, that antagonising him was not the best way to get information out of him. 'Maybe they know all about Asudar. But things are different here.'

'Because you're heathens!'

'Right,' I said, nodding, agreeing. 'We're heathens. So we have a lot of gods. But we don't have any demons. Or priests. Or temple prostitutes. Unless they're about six inches high.'

He was silent, scowling.

'I heard the army came looking for a specially bad place here,' I said after a while, trying to speak in a more friendly way and feeling both devious and exposed. 'Some sort of hole in the ground where all the demons are supposed to come from.'

'I guess so.'

'What for?'

'I don't know,' he said. He looked very glum, screwing up his pale eyes and frowning.

We were sitting on the pavement in the shade of the wall. I began scratching criss-cross patterns in the dust on the paving stone.

'Somebody said your king in Medron died,' I said, as easily as I could. I used our old word, king, not their word, gand.

He merely nodded. Our discussion had discouraged him. After a long time he said, 'Mekke said maybe the new High Gand would order the army back home to Asudar. I guess you'd like that.' He glanced at me sullenly.

I shrugged. 'Would you?'

He shrugged.

I wanted to make him go on talking, but didn't know how.

'That's fit-fat,' he said.

Now I looked at him as if he was crazy, till I saw he was looking down at the pattern I'd made on the dusty stone. He reached over and drew a horizontal line in one square of the criss-cross.

'We call it fool's game,' I said, and drew a vertical line in another square. We played to a draw, as you always do in fool's game unless you really are a fool. Then he showed me a game called finding the ambush, where you each have a hidden criss-cross with a square marked off, the ambush, and you guess in turn where the other person's ambush is, and the one who finds the other's ambush first is the winner. Simme won two out of three, which cheered him up and made him talkative.

'I hope the army gets moved back to Asudar,' he said. 'I want to get married. I can't get married here.'

'Gand Ioratth did,' I said, and then was afraid I'd gone too far, but Simme just grinned and made a lewd chuckling noise.

"Queen' Tirio?' he said. 'Mekke says she was one

of those temple prostitutes to start with, and she put a spell on the Gand.'

I'd had enough of him and his temple prostitutes. 'There were never any temples,' I said. 'We had festivals. All over the city. Processions and dances. But you Alds stopped them. You killed anybody who danced. You were so afraid of your stupid demons.' I got up, rubbed out the criss-cross with my foot, and stalked off to the stable.

Once I got to the stables I didn't know what to do. I was ashamed of myself. I had not endured. I had run away. I looked in at Branty, who acknowledged me with a half nicker. He was lipping up a little treat of oats delicately, making them last. The old hostler was perched up on a sawhorse nearby, watching him with what looked to me like adoration. He nodded to me. Branty went on twiddling his oats. I leaned up against a post and folded my arms and hoped I looked aloof and unapproachable.

And here came Simme across the stableyard, slouching and cringing and grinning like a dog that's been yelled at.

'Hey, Mem,' he said, as if we'd parted days ago instead of two minutes ago.

I nodded at him.

He looked at me the way the old hostler looked at Branty.

'My father's horse is over there,' he said. 'Come see her. She's from the royal stables in Medron.'

I let him lead me across the yard to the facing stalls to show me a fine, nervous, bright-eyed sorrel mare with a light mane, like the horse that had run at me in the market. Maybe it was that horse. She eyed me sideways over the door of the stall and shook her head.

'She's named Victory,' Simme said, trying to pat the mare on the neck; she tossed her head and moved back in the stall. When he tried again, she turned at him, showing her long yellow teeth. Simme drew his hand back quickly. 'She's a real warhorse,' he said.

I gazed at the horse as if judging it from a deep knowledge and experience of horses, nodded again rather patronisingly, and sauntered back across the yard. To my relief, Chy and Shetar were just looking in the gateway. Several horses, seeing or smelling the lion, neighed and kicked in their stalls. I hurried over to Chy, while behind me Simme called, 'See you tomorrow, Mem?'

On our way back to Galvamand I told them of my efforts to cross-examine Simme, which I thought completely foolish and fruitless; but they, and later the Waylord, listened intently. They remarked on Simme's apparent lack of knowledge or interest when I spoke indirectly of the Night Mouth, and on his saying he had heard that the new Gand of Gands might recall the army to Asudar.

'Did he say anything about Iddor?' Gry asked.

'I didn't know how to ask.'

'Is he a bright fellow?' the Waylord asked.

I said, 'No. He's stupid.' But I was ashamed, saying it. Even if it was true.

The day had been very warm, and the evening was mild. Instead of sitting in the gallery after dinner, we went out to the small outer courtyard that opens from it. It is sheltered by the house walls on two sides and marked off on the other two by slender columned arcades. The hill to the east rises immediately behind the house, and the scent of flowering shrubs was in the air. We sat looking north to the open evening sky faintly tinged with green.

'The house is built into the hillside, isn't it?' Orrec said, looking up at the north windows of the Master's room, above this court, and the walls behind walls and roofs behind roofs of the ancient building.

'Yes,' the Waylord said, and I don't know what was in his tone, but the hairs on my neck stirred.

He went on after a little while, 'Ansul is the oldest city of the Western Shore, and this is the oldest house in Ansul.'

'Is it true that the Aritans came from the desert a thousand years ago, and found all these lands we know empty of humankind?'

'Longer than a thousand years, and from farther than the desert,' the Waylord said. 'From the Sunrise, they said. They were people of a great empire far in the east. They sent explorers into the desert that bordered their lands to the west, and at last a group found a way across the desert – hundreds of miles wide, they say – to the green valleys of the Western Shore. Taramon led that group. Others followed. The books are very old, fragmentary, hard to understand. Many of them are lost, now. But it seemed they said that the people who came here were driven out of the Sunrise lands.' He said a line of verse in Aritan, and then in our tongue: "The riverless waste that guards the exile's spring . . .' We are the children of those exiles.'

'And no one has ever come from the east since then?'

'Nor gone back to the east.'

'Except the Alds,' said Gry.

'They went back into the desert, yes, or stayed there, but only the western border of it, where there are springs and rivers. East of Asudar, they say, for a thousand miles the sun is the Gand of Gands and the sand is his people.'

'We live on the far edge of a world we know nothing of,' Orrec said, gazing at the pale, deep sky.

'Some scholars think Taramon and the others were driven out because they were sorcerers, people who had uncanny powers. They think gifts such as you in the Uplands have were common among the people who came from the Sunrise, but have died out among us over the centuries.'

'What do you think?' Gry asked.

'We have no such gifts as those here now,' the Waylord said rather carefully. 'But the earliest records of Ansul tell of people coming to be healed by women of the house of Actamo, who could restore sight to the blind and hearing to the deaf.'

'Like the Cordemants!' Orrec said to Gry, and Gry said, 'Backwards – as I thought!' They were about to explain this to us, when Desac came suddenly from the door of the gallery out into the court where we sat.

Like all the Waylord's regular visitors, he let himself into and through the old part of the house, which was never locked. Ista sometimes fretted about the risk, but the Waylord said, 'There are no locks on the doors of Galvamand,' and that was that. So Desac appeared now, startling Shetar. The halflion stood up with her head down and her ears flattened in a nasty, snaky way, and glared at him. He stopped short in the doorway.

Gry hissed a reproof at Shetar, who grunted and sat down, still glaring.

'Welcome, my friend, come sit with us,' the Waylord said, while I hurried to find a chair. Desac meanwhile took my chair next to the Waylord. That was like him. He did not have bad or coarse manners, but people who did not interest him did not exist for him. To him I was a furniture bringer, about as important as the furniture. He was single-minded, like the Alds. Perhaps soldiers have to be single-minded.

By the time I'd found a manageable chair and brought it out, he had been introduced to Orrec and Gry, and the Waylord must have told them that this was the leader of the resistance, or Desac had told them so himself, for that's what they were talking about. I sat down to listen.

Desac took notice of me then. Furniture should not have ears. He looked from me to the Waylord with the plain intent of having me sent away as usual.

'Memer knows a soldier's son, who told her that some of the Alds talk of the army being recalled to Asudar,' the Waylord said to Desac. 'And the boy called Tirio Actamo Queen Tirio, as a common joke. Have you heard that title?'

'No,' Desac said stiffly. He shot another glance at me. He looked a little like Shetar glaring with her ears flat (though she by now had decided to ignore him, and was industriously washing a hind paw).

'What we say here must go no farther than this courtyard,' he announced.

'Of course,' said the Waylord. He spoke as kindly and easily as ever, but the effect was rather like Gry's hiss at the lion. Desac looked away from me, cleared his throat, rubbed his chin, and spoke to Orrec.

'Blessed Ennu sent you here, Orrec Caspro,' he said, 'or the Deaf One called you to us, in the very hour of our need.'

'Need for me?' said Orrec.

'Who can better call the people to arms than a great maker?'

Orrec's face went still and his bearing stiff. After a moment of silence he said, 'I'll do what's in my power to do. But I'm a foreigner.'

'Against the invader we are all one people.'

'I've been more at the Palace than in the marketplace. At the Gand's beck and call. Why should your people trust me?'

'They do trust you. They speak of your coming as a sign, a portent that the great days of Ansul are about to return.'

'I'm not a portent, I'm a poet,' Orrec said. His face

was hard as rock now. 'A city rising against tyranny will find its own speakers.'

'You'll speak for us when we call you,' Desac said, with equal certainty. 'We've sung your poem "Liberty" for ten years now here in Ansul, in hiding, behind doors. How did that song get here, who brought it? From voice to voice, from soul to soul, from land to land. When we sing it aloud at last, in the face of the enemy, do you think you'll be silent?'

Orrec said nothing.

'I'm a soldier,' Desac said, 'I know what makes people fight to win. I know what a voice like yours can do. And I know that's why you came here when you did.'

'I came because the Gand asked me to come.'

'He asked you because the gods of Ansul moved his mind. Because our hour is coming. The balance changes!'

'My friend,' said the Waylord, 'the balance may be changing, but are the scales in your hands?'

Desac held out his empty hands with a dry smile.

'There's no sign of unrest among the Ald soldiers which we might take advantage of,' the Waylord said. 'We're not certain if there's any change yet in

Ald policy. And we don't know what's going on between Ioratth and Iddor.'

'Ah, but that we do know,' Desac said. 'Ioratth intends to send Iddor back to Medron with a retinue of priests and soldiers. Seemingly to seek guidance from the new Gand Acray, actually to get Iddor and his priests out of Ansul. Tirio Actamo's servant Ialba passed that word this morning to the slaves we're in touch with at the palace. She's been a faithful informer.'

'Then you intend to wait till Iddor is gone before you move?'

'Why wait? Why let the rat escape the trap?'

'You plan to attack? The barracks?'

'An attack is planned. Not where or when they might expect it.'

'I know you have some arms, but have you the men?'

'Arms we have, and men enough. The people will join with us. We are twenty to one, Sulter! All these years of tyranny, enslavement, insult, defilement, the rage of all these years will burst out like fire in straw, everywhere in the city. All we need is to see how many we are, how few they are! All we need is a voice, a voice to summon us!'

His passion shook me, and I could see it had shaken Orrec, at whom he was looking now. An uprising, a revolt – to turn on those arrogant men in blue cloaks, drag them off their horses, use them as they had used us, cow them as they had cowed us, drive them out, out, out of our city, out of our lives – Oh! I had wanted that so long! I would follow Desac. I saw him truly now: a leader, a warrior. I would follow him as the people followed the heroes of old, through fire and water, through death.

But Orrec sat there with his face set, silent.

And Gry, watchful as her lion, silent.

In that tense silence the Waylord said, 'Desac: if I ask concerning this – if I am answered – would you hear the answer?' He said the word *ask* with a strange emphasis.

Desac looked at him, at first evidently not understanding, then with a frown. He began a question, but the Waylord's expression checked him. Desac's hard, sad, weathered face changed slowly, becoming open, uncertain. 'Yes,' he said, hesitant, then again more strongly, 'Yes!'

'Then I will,' the Waylord said.

'Tonight?'

'The time is so near?'

'Yes.'

'Very well.'

'I'll come tomorrow morning,' Desac said, standing up, alive with energy. 'Sulter, my friend, I thank you from my heart. We will see – you will see – your spirits will speak for us.' He turned to Orrec – 'And your voice will call us, you'll be with us, I know. And we'll meet here again, free men, in a free city! The blessing of Lero and all the gods of Ansul on you all, and on the souls and shadows of Galvamand who hear us now!' He strode out, soldierly, exultant.

Orrec, Gry, and I looked at one another. Something important had been said, some promise had been made, which we three did not understand. The Waylord sat not looking at anyone, his face somber. Finally he glanced around at us. His gaze rested on me.

'Before there was a city here,' he said, 'before there was a house built here, the oracle was here.' Then he spoke in Aritan: '"They came here across the deserts, the weary people, the exiles. They came over the hills above the Western Sea and saw white Sul across the water. In the hillside was a cave, and from the cave ran a spring. On the darkness of the air in the cave they saw words written: *Here stay.* So they drank the water of that spring, and built their city there.'"

◆ 9 ◆

We parted for the night soon after that, and the Waylord said to me, 'Come to the room, Memer.'

So a little later I went back through the house and drew the letters in the air and entered the hidden room that goes back under the hill in darkness.

He came in some while later. I had lighted the oil lamp on the reading table. He set down the small lantern he carried but did not blow it out. He saw I had Orrec's book open on the table, and smiled a little.

'You like his poetry?'

'Above any other. Above Denios!'

He smiled again more broadly, teasingly. 'Ah, they're all very well, these moderns, but none of them is a match for Regali.'

Regali lived a thousand years ago, here in Ansul, writing in Aritan; the language is difficult and the poetry is difficult and I had not got very far with Regali, though I knew how well the Waylord loved her.

'In time,' he said, seeing my expression. 'In time . . . Now, I have a good deal to tell and to ask, my Memer. Let me talk to you a while.' We sat at the table facing each other in the soft sphere of light the lamp made. Around it the high, long room darkened away; here and there shone the glimmer of a gold-stamped word on the spine of a book, and the books themselves were a silent gathering, a dark multiplicity.

He had said my name with such tenderness that it almost frightened me. But his face was grim as it was when he was in pain. When he spoke it was with difficulty. He said, 'I have not done well by you, Memer.'

I began to protest, wanting to say he had given me

all the treasures of my life, – love, loyalty, learning, – but he stopped me, gently, though still with that grim look. 'You were my comfort,' he said, 'my dear comfort. And I looked only for comfort. I let hope go. I did not pay my debt to those who gave me life. I taught you to read, but I never let you know that there was more to read than tales and poetry . . . Here. I gave you what was easy to give. I told myself, she's only a child, why should I burden her . . .'

I was aware of the darkness of the room behind my back; I felt it as a presence.

He went on, doggedly. 'We were talking of gifts that run in the blood, in a lineage, like Gry's family, the Barres, who can speak with animals, or the Actamos, who could heal. We Galvas, whose ancestors inhabit this house as souls and shadows, we have – not a gift maybe, but a responsibility. A bond. We are the people who live in this place. *Here stay.* We stay here. Here, this house. This room. We guard what is here. We open the door and close it. And we read the words of the oracle.'

As he said the word, I knew he was going to say it. It was the word he had to say and I had to hear. But my heart went cold and heavy in me.

'In my cowardice,' he said, 'I told myself it was unnecessary to speak of it to you. The time of oracles was past. It was an old story that was no longer true . . . Truth can go out of stories, you know. What was true becomes meaningless, even a lie, because the truth has gone into another story. The water of the spring rises in another place. The Fountain of the Oracle has been dry for two hundred years . . . But the spring that fed it still runs. Here. Within.'

He sat facing me and that end of the room where it stretches into shadow, becoming darker and lower; he was no longer looking at me, but into that darkness. When he was silent I listened for the faint voice of the running water.

'I saw my duty and clung to it: to keep and guard what little was left – the books here, the books people brought me to preserve, the last of our treasure, the last of the glory of Ansul. And when you came here, into this room, that day, and we spoke of letters, of reading – you remember?'

'I remember,' I said, and the memory warmed me a little. I looked at the shelves of books I had read and knew and loved, my friends.

'I told myself you were born to do the same, to take my place, to keep the one lamp burning. And I clung to that comfort, denying that I had any other duty to carry out, anything else to teach you.

'When your body is broken the way mine was, the mind too becomes misshapen, weak—' He held out his hands. 'I can't trust myself. I am too full of fear. But I should have trusted you.'

I wanted to say, to plead with him, 'No, don't, you can't trust me, I'm weak, I'm afraid too!' but the words wouldn't come out.

He had spoken harshly. After a while he went on, and the tenderness was back in his voice. 'So,' he said, 'a little more history. All the history you've patiently learned, you so young – all this weight of years on you, obligations undertaken by people dead for centuries! You've borne it all, you'll bear this too.

'Your house is the House of the Oracle, and we are the readers of the oracle. It is here, in this room. You learned to write the words that let you enter before you knew what writing was. And so you'll know how to read the words that are written.

'The first were those I spoke just now: *Here stay.*

'In the early times, all the people of the Four

Houses could read the oracle. That was their power, their sacredness. As the exiles of Aritan settled the coast and began to make towns elsewhere, still they came back to Ansul, to the Oracle House. They'd bring their questions: Is it right to do this? If we do that, what will happen? They'd come to the fountain and drink of it, and ask the blessing, and ask their question there. Then the readers of the oracle would go into the house, into the cave, into the dark. And if the question was accepted, they would read the answer written on the air.

'Sometimes, also, when they went into the darkness they would see words shining, though no question had been asked.

'All these words of the oracle were written down. The books they were written in were called the Galvan Books. Over the years the Galvas, who built their house at the oracle cave, became the sole keepers of the books, interpreters of the words, the voice of the oracle – the Readers.

'That led to jealousy and rivalry, in the end. It might have been better if we'd shared our power. But I think we weren't able to. The gift gives itself.

'The Galvan Books themselves weren't only

records of the oracles. Sometimes the writing in them altered though no hand had touched it, or a Reader would open a book and find in it words no one had written there. More and more often the oracle spoke on the pages of the books, not on the darkness of the cave.

'But often the words themselves were dark. Interpretation was needed. And there were the answers to questions that had not been asked . . . So the great Reader Dano Galva said, "We do not seek true answers. The strayed sheep we seek is the true question. The answer follows it as the tail follows the sheep."'

He had been watching his thoughts in the air behind me; now he looked back at me, and was silent.

'Have you – have you read the oracle?' I asked at last. I felt as if I hadn't spoken for a month; my throat was dry and my voice thready.

He answered slowly. 'I began to read the Galvan Books when I was twenty, with my mother as my guide. The most ancient of them first. The words in those are fixed, they no longer change. But the oldest are the most obscure, because they didn't write the question with the answer, and so you have to guess the sheep from the tail . . . Then there are many books from later centuries, both questions and answers. Often both are obscure, but they repay study. And then, after they moved the library out of Galvamand, there were fewer questions. And the answers may change, or vanish, or appear with no question asked. Those are the books you cannot read twice, any more than you could drink the same water twice from the Oracle Spring.'

'Have you asked it a question?'

'Once.' He gave a brief laugh and rubbed his upper lip with the knuckles of his left hand. 'I thought it was a good question, direct and plain, such as the oracle seems to respond to. It was when Ansul was first besieged. I asked: *Will the Alds take the city?* I got no answer. Or if I did, I was looking in the wrong book.'

'How did you – How do you ask?'

'You'll see, Memer. I told Desac, tonight, I'd ask the oracle about the rebellion he plans. He knows of it only as an old story, but he knows that if it spoke it might help his cause.'

He studied me a moment. 'I want you with me. Can you do that? Is it too soon?'

'I don't know,' I said.

I was stiff with fear, cold, mindless fear. The hair on my neck and arms had been standing up ever since he began to speak of the books, the oracle books. I didn't want to see them. I didn't want to go where they were. I knew where they were, which books they were. At the thought of touching them my breath stuck in my throat. I almost said, 'No, I can't.' But the words stuck too.

What I finally said took me by surprise. I said, '*Are* there demons?'

When he did not answer, I went on, the words bursting out of me hoarse and unclear, 'You say I'm a Galva, but I'm not – not only – I'm both – neither. How can I inherit this? I never even knew about it. How can I do something like this? How can I take this power, when I'm afraid – afraid of demons – the Alds' demons – because I'm an Ald too!'

He made a little sound to halt me and soothe me. I fell silent.

He asked, 'Who are your gods, Memer?'

He asked it the way he might ask me, when he

was teaching me, 'What does Eront say in his *History of the Lands Beyond the Trond?*' And I gathered my mind together and answered him as I would answer then, trying to say truly what I knew.

'My gods are Lero. Ennu who makes the way easy. Deori who dreams the world. The One Who Looks Both Ways. The keepers of the hearthfire and the guardians of the doorway. Iene the gardener. Luck, who cannot hear. Caran, Lord of the Springs and Waters. Sampa the Destroyer and Sampa the Shaper, who are one. Teru at the cradle, and Anada who dances on the grave. The gods of the forest and the hills. The Sea Horses. The soul of my mother Decalo, and your mother Eleyo, and the souls and shadows of all who lived in this house, the former dwellers, the forerunners, who give us our dreams. The room-spirits, my room-spirit. The street-gods and the crossway-gods, the gods of the market and the council place, the gods of the city, and of stones, and the sea, and Sul.'

Saying their names I knew they were not demons, that there were no demons in Ansul.

'May they bless me and be blessed,' I whispered, and he whispered the words with me.

I stood up then and walked towards the doorway and back to the table, only because I had to move. The books, the books I knew, my dear companions, stood solid on the shelves. 'What do we have to do?' I asked.

He stood up. He picked up the small lantern he had brought. 'First the darkness,' he said. I followed him.

We went all the way down the long room, past the shelves where the books I feared were. The lantern gave small light, and I could not see them clearly. Beyond those last shelves the ceiling grew lower, and the light seemed less. I heard the sound of running water clearly now.

The floor had become uneven. Pavement gave way to dirt and rocks. His lame gait grew slower and more cautious.

I saw in the lantern's flickering light a small stream of water that ran from the darkness and dropped down into a deep basin, vanishing underground. We passed the basin and followed beside the water, upstream, on a rocky path. Shadows dodged away from the lantern, quick, huge, and shapeless, running black across raw rock walls. We walked deep into a high tunnel, a long cave. The walls drew closer as we kept walking farther.

The light glittered in the water of a welling spring and trembled reflected on the rock roof above. The Waylord stopped. He raised the lantern, and shadows leapt wildly. He blew it out, and we stood in darkness.

'Bless us and be blessed, spirits of the sacred place,' his voice said, low and steady. 'We are Sulter Galva of your people and Memer Galva of your people. We come in trust, honoring the sacred, following truth as we are shown it. We come in ignorance, honoring knowledge, asking to know. We come into darkness for light and into silence for words and into fear for blessing. Spirits of this place who made my people welcome, I ask an answer to my question. Will a rebellion, now, against the Alds who hold our city, fail or prevail?'

His voice made no echo off the rock walls. Silence snuffed it out utterly. There was no sound but the trickle of the spring, and my breathing, and his. It was absolutely dark. My eyes fooled me again and again, making faint lights flash, and colors blur and vanish in the black in front of me, that sometimes seemed to be right up against my eyes like a blindfold, and then deep and far as a starless sky, so that I feared to fall as if standing on a cliff's edge. Once I thought I saw a glimmer taking form, the shape of a letter, but it went out suddenly, utterly, as a spark goes out. We stood a long time, long enough that I began to feel the rock pressing through my thin shoe soles and the ache in my back from not moving. I was dizzy because there was nothing in the world, no thing at all, only blackness and the sound of water and the pressure of the rock under my feet. No air moved. It was cold. It was still.

I felt warmth, his warmth, a light touch on my arm. We murmured the blessing and turned round. Turning, I became dizzier, disoriented. I didn't know which way I was facing in this utter dark – had I turned halfway or clear round? I reached out and found him there, the warmth, the touch of the cloth of his sleeve; I took hold of it and followed him. I wondered why he did not light the lantern, but dared not speak. It seemed a long way we went, far longer than the way in. I thought we were going the wrong way, deeper and deeper into the dark. I wouldn't believe it when I first began to see a change, a dimness growing out of darkness ahead of us, not visibility yet, but the promise of it. I let go his arm then. But he, lame, took my arm, and held it till we could see our way.

When we were in the room again the space around us was airy and welcoming, and everything was distinct, full of a warm light, even down here at the cave end, the shadow end.

He looked at me searchingly. Then he turned and went to the shelves that had been built where the rock of the cave mouth gave place to plastered wall. Through the plaster here and there a rough cornice of rock stuck out. The shelves were set into the wall, not built out from it. On them were books, some small, some large and coarsely bound, some standing, others lying, maybe fifty or so in all. Some shelves were empty or held only a volume or two. The Waylord looked at the shelves as one does when seeking a book but not certain which or where it is, scanning. He looked again at me.

I looked at once for the white book, the book that had bled. I saw it instantly.

He saw where I was looking. He saw that I could

not take my eyes from it. He went forward and took the white book from the shelf.

I stepped back when he did so, I couldn't help it. I said, 'Is it bleeding?'

He looked at me, and at the book; he let it fall open gently in his hands.

'No,' he said. He held it out to me.

I took another step back from it.

'Can you read it, Memer?'

He turned it and held it out to me again, open. I saw the small, square, white pages. The right-hand page was blank. On the left-hand page there were a few words written small.

I took a hard step forward, and a second step, my hands clenched. I read the words aloud: *Broken mend broken.*

The sound of my voice was terrible to me: it was not my voice at all but a deep, hollow, echoing sound swelling out all round my head. I cried out, 'Put it back, put it away!' and turned and tried to walk back towards the lamp that shone in a sphere of gold far off at the other end of the room, but it was like walking in a dream, I could move my legs only slowly, heavily. He came and took my arm, and

together we made our way back. It grew easier for
me as we went. We reached the reading table. That
was like coming home, coming into firelight out of
the night, a haven.

I sat down in the chair with a great, shuddering
sigh. He stood a little while stroking my shoulders
gently, then went round the table and sat down
facing me, as we had been before.

My teeth chattered. I wasn't cold any longer, but
my teeth chattered. It was a while before I could
make my mouth obey me at all.

'Was that the answer?'

'I don't know,' he murmured.

'Was it – was it the oracle?'

'Yes.'

I took a while longer to bite my lips, which felt
stiff as cardboard, and tried to make my breath come
evenly.

'Had you read in that book before?' I asked him.
He shook his head.

'I saw no words,' he said.

'You didn't see – on the page—?' I gestured, to
show that the words had been on the left-hand page,

and I saw my fingers begin to write the letters on the air. I made them stop.

He shook his head.

That made it even worse.

'Was – what I said, was it the answer to the question you asked?'

'I don't know,' he said.

'Why didn't it answer *you?*'

He said nothing for quite a while. At last he said, 'Memer, if you had asked the question, what would it have been?'

'*How can we be free of the Alds?*' I said at once, and saying it I felt that again I was speaking with another voice, a loud deep voice not mine. I closed my mouth, I snapped my teeth shut on the thing that spoke through me, used me.

And yet that was the question I would have asked.

'The true question,' he said, with a half smile.

'The book bled,' I said. I was determined now to speak for myself, not to be spoken through – to say what I would say, to take control. 'Years and years ago, when I was little. I went down to the shadow end. I told you that, I told you part of it. I told you I thought one of the books made a noise. But I didn't tell you I saw that one. That white book. And I took it from the shelf, and there was blood on the pages. Wet blood. Not words, but blood. And I never went back. Not until tonight. I— If – If there are no demons, all right, there are no demons. But I am afraid of what is in that cave.'

'So am I,' he said.

◆   ◆   ◆

WE WERE both tired, but there was no question of sleep yet. He relit the small lantern, I put out the lamp, he drew the words on the air, and we went out of the room, through the corridors, back to the north courtyard where we had sat earlier that evening. A great ceiling of stars stood over it. I blew out the lantern. We sat there in starlight, silent for a long time.

I asked, 'What will you tell Desac?'

'My question, and that I received no answer.'

'And – what the book said?'

'That is yours to tell him or not, as you choose.'

'I don't know what it means. I don't know what

question it was answering. I don't understand it. Does it make sense at all?'

I felt that I'd been tricked, that I'd been made use of without being told what for, as if I were a mere thing, a tool. I had been frightened. Now I was humiliated and angry.

'It makes the sense we can make of it,' he said.

'That's like telling fortunes with sand.' There are women in Ansul who, for a few pennies, will take a handful of damp sea sand and drop it on a plate, and from the lumps and peaks and scatters of the sand they foretell good fortune and bad, journeys, money ventures, love affairs, and so on. 'It means whatever you want it to mean.'

'Maybe,' he said. After a while he went on, 'Dano Galva said that to read the oracle is to bring rational thought to an impenetrable mystery . . . There are answers in the old books that seemed senseless to those who heard them. *How should we defend ourselves from Sundraman?* they asked the oracle, when Sundraman first threatened to invade Ansul. The answer was, *To keep bees from apple blossoms.* The Councillors were irate, saying the meaning was so plain it was foolish. They ordered an army to be raised to

build a wall along the Ostis and defend it from
Sundraman. The southerners crossed the river,
knocked down the wall, defeated our army, marched
here to Ansul City, killed those who resisted them,
and declared all Ansul a protectorate of Sundraman.
Ever since then they've been excellent neighbors,
interfering with us very little, but greatly enriching us
with trade. It was not a recommendation but a
warning: To keep bees from apple blossoms is to
have trees that bear no fruit. Ansul was the blossom
and Sundraman the bee. That's clear now. It was
clear to the Reader, Dano Galva; as soon as she read
it she said it meant we should offer no resistance to
Sundraman. For that she was called a traitor. From
that time on the Gelb and Cam and Actamo clans
said the Council should not consult the oracle, and
pressed for the university and the library to be
moved from Galvamand.'

'Much good the oracle did the Reader and her
house,' I said.

'"The nail's hit once, the hammer a thousand
times."'

I thought that over. 'What if one doesn't choose
to be a tool?'

'You always have that choice.'

I sat and looked up at the great depths of stars. I thought that the stars were like all the souls who lived in former times in this city, this house, all the thousands of spirits, the forerunners, lives like distant flames, lights far and farther away in the great darkness of time. Lives past, lives to come. How could you tell one from the other?

I had wanted to ask why the oracle couldn't speak plainly, why it couldn't just say *Don't resist*, or *Strike now*, instead of cryptic images and obscure words. After looking at the stars, that seemed a foolish question. The oracle was not giving orders but just the opposite: inviting thought. Asking us to bring thought to mystery. The result might not be very satisfactory but it was probably the best we could do.

I gave an enormous yawn, and the Waylord laughed.

'Go to bed, child,' he said, and I did.

Making my way to my room through the dark halls and corridors I expected to lie awake, haunted by the strangeness of the cave and by the words I had read and the voice that had spoken through me saying them: *Broken mend broken.* I touched the god-niche by the door, fell into my bed, and slept like a stone.

✦ 10 ✦

When Desac came the next day, I wasn't with the Waylord, I was helping Ista with the wash. She and Bomi and I had the boilers going soon after dawn, set up the cranked wringer, strung the wash lines, and by noon had filled the kitchen courtyard with clean sheets and table linens blinding white and snapping in the windy, hot sunlight.

In the afternoon, walking in the old park with Shetar, Gry told me what had occurred in the morning.

The Waylord had come to the Master's room to say that Desac wished to speak with Orrec. Orrec asked Gry to come with him. 'I left Shetar behind,'

Gry said, 'since she seems to dislike Desac.' They went down to the gallery, and there Desac again tried to make Orrec promise to go out and speak to the people of the city, rousing them to drive out the Alds, when the moment came.

Desac was eloquent and urgent, and Orrec was distressed, divided in mind, feeling that this was not his battle, and yet that any battle for freedom must be his. If Ansul rose up against tyranny, how could he stand aside? But he was given no choice in time or place, and also no real knowledge of how this rebellion was to be made. Desac was clearly wise to say so little about it, since its success depended on it being a surprise; yet, as Orrec told her, he didn't like being used, he'd rather be included.

I asked what the Waylord had said, and Gry said, 'Almost nothing. Last night, you know, when Sulter said he'd "ask", and Desac jumped at it? – Well, nothing at all was said about that. They'd said it before we came down, no doubt.'

I hated not to be able to tell her anything about the oracle; I didn't want to keep anything from Gry. But I knew it was not mine to speak of, or not yet.

She went on, 'I think Sulter is worried about

numbers. More than two thousand Ald soldiers, he said. Most of them near the palace and the barracks. At least a third armed and on duty, and the others close to their weapons. How can Desac move a large enough force against them without alerting the guards? Even at night? The night guards are mounted. Asudar horses are like dogs, you know, they're trained to give a signal if they sense anything amiss. I hope that old soldier knows what he's doing! Because I think he's going to do it pretty soon.'

My mind moved swiftly, thinking of fighting in the streets. *How can we be free of the Alds?* With sword, knife, club, stone. With fist, with force, with our rage unleashed at last. We would break them, break their power, their heads, their backs, their bodies . . . *Broken mend broken.*

I was standing on a path among great bushes. The sun was hot on my head. My hands were dry, swollen, and sore from hot water and handling linens all the morning. Gry stood near me, watching me with alert concern. She said gently, 'Memer? Where were you?'

I shook my head.

Shetar came bounding along the path to us. She

halted, holding up her head with a proud and conscious air. She opened her fierce, fanged mouth, and a small blue butterfly came fluttering out and flew off, quite unconcerned.

We both laughed uncontrollably. The lion looked a little embarrassed or confused.

'She's the girl that spoke blossoms and bells and butterflies!' said Gry. 'You know about her – when Cumbelo was King?'

'And her sister spoke lice and lugworms and lumps of mud.'

'Oh, cat, cat,' Gry said, tugging at the fur behind Shetar's ears till the lion rolled her head with pleasure, purring.

I could not put it all together. Fighting in the streets, darkness in the cave, terror, laughter, sunlight on my head, starlight in my eyes, a lion who said a butterfly.

'Oh, Gry, I wish I understood *something*,' I said. 'How do you ever make sense out of what happens?'

'I don't know, Memer. You keep trying, and sometimes it does.'

'Rational thought and impenetrable mystery,' I said.

'You're as bad as Orrec,' she said. 'Come on. Come home.'

That night Orrec and the Waylord talked about the Gand Ioratth, and I found I could listen without closing my mind. Maybe it was because I had seen the Gand twice now, and despite the hateful pomp, and the cringing slaves, and my knowledge that if the whim took him he could have us all buried alive, what I had seen was a man, not a demon. A hard, tough, wily old man who loved poetry with all his heart.

Orrec spoke almost to my thought: 'This fear of demons, devilry – it's unworthy of him. I wonder how much of all that he believes, in fact.'

'He may not fear demons much,' the Waylord said. 'But so long as he can't read, he'll fear the written word.'

'If I could just take a book there and open it and read from it – the same words I speak without the book—!'

'Abomination.' The Waylord shook his head. 'Sacrilege. He'd have no choice but to hand you over to the priests of Atth.'

'But if the Alds decide to stay here, to rule Ansul,

to deal with its neighbors, with other lands and nations, they can't go on abominating what trade is based on – records and contracts. And diplomacy – let alone history, poetry! Did you know that in the City States, "ald" means idiot? 'No use to talk to him, he's an ald.' Surely Ioratth has begun to see the disadvantage they're at.'

'Let's hope that he has. And that the new king in Medron sees it.'

But I began to be impatient with this talk. The Alds weren't going to decide to stay here, rule us, deal with our neighbors. It wasn't up to them. I found myself saying, 'Does it matter?'

They all looked at me, and I said, 'They can go be illiterate all they please in Asudar.'

'Yes,' the Waylord said, 'if they'll go.'

'We'll drive them out.'

'Into the countryside?'

'Yes! Out of the city!'

'Are our farmers able to fight them? And if we chased them clear home to Asudar – won't the High Gand see it as an insult and threat to his new power, and send more thousands of soldiers against us? He has an army. We do not.'

I didn't know what to say.

The Waylord went on, 'These are considerations which Desac dismisses. He may well be right to do so. 'Forethought, bane of action.' But do you see, Memer, now that things are changing among the Alds themselves, I have my first hope of regaining our liberty by persuading them that we're more profitable to them as allies than as slaves. That would take time. It would end in a compromise not a victory. But if we seek victory now and fail, hope will be hard to find.'

I could say nothing. He was right, and Desac was right. The time to act was upon us, but how to act?

'I could speak for you to Ioratth better than I could speak for Desac to the crowd,' Orrec said. 'Tell me, are there people in the city who would talk in these terms to Ioratth, if he agreed to some negotiation?'

'Yes, and outside the city, too. We've kept in touch over the years with all the towns of the Ansul Coast, scholars and merchants, people who were waylords and mayors and officers of the festivals and ceremonies. Boys run messages from town to town, wagoneers carry them along with the cabbages. The soldiers seldom search for written messages, they'd rather have nothing to do with sacrilege and wizardry.'

'"O Lord Destroyer, give me an ignorant enemy!"' Orrec quoted.

'In the city, some of the men I've talked about this with over the years are with Desac now. They seek any way to get the Ald yoke off our neck. They're ready to fight. But they might be willing to talk. If the Alds will listen.'

◆　◆　◆

ORREC WAS not summoned to the palace the next day. Late in the morning he went down to the Harbor Market, on foot, with Gry. He didn't give any advance notice, no tent was set up, but as soon as he walked into the market square people recognised and followed him. They didn't press very close to him, partly because of Shetar, but they made a moving circle round him, greeted him, called out his name, and shouted, 'Recite, recite!' One man shouted, 'Read!'

I didn't walk with them. I was in boy's clothes, as usual when I went in the streets, and didn't want to be seen as Mem the groom with Gry, who wasn't in disguise. I ran round to the raised marble pavement in front of the Admirals' Tower and climbed up on the base of the horse statue there, from which I had a good view of the whole market. The statue is the work of Redam the sculptor, carved from one great block of stone; the horse stands foursquare, strong and heavy, his head raised and turned to the west, looking out to sea. The Alds had destroyed most statues in the city but left this one untouched, perhaps because it was a horse; certainly they didn't know that the sea gods, the Seunes, are imagined and worshipped in the form of horses. I touched the Seune's big stone left front hoof and murmured the blessing. The Seune returned the blessing to me in the form of shade. It was a hot day already, and going to get hotter.

Orrec took his position where the tent had been on the first day he spoke here, and the people crowded round him. The pedestal I was on soon filled up with boys and men, but I hung on to my place right between the horse's front legs, shoving back hard when people shoved me. Many of the stall keepers in the market tossed a cloth over their goods and joined the crowd to listen to the maker, or stood on a stool by their booth to see over the heads of the throng. I saw five or six blue cloaks in the crowd, and soon a troop of mounted Ald soldiers came down the Council Way to the corner of the square, but they stopped without trying to push into the crowd. There was a great hum of noise, talking and laughing and shouting, and it was a shock when all that human commotion ceased at once, dropped into utter silence, at the first note of Orrec's lyre.

He said a poem first, Tetemer's love poem 'The Hills of Dom', an old favorite all up and down the Ansul Coast. When he had spoken it he sang the refrain with the lyre, and the people sang with him, smiling and swaying.

Then he said, 'Ansul is a small land, but her songs are sung and her tales are told through all the Western Shore. I first learned them far to the north, in Bendraman. The makers of Ansul are famous from the farthest south to the River Trond. And there have been heroes here in peaceful Ansul and Manva, brave warriors, and the makers have told of them. Hear the tale of Adira and Marra on the Mountain Sul!'

A great, strange sound went up from the crowd, a kind of moaning roar both of joy and of grief. It was frightening. If Orrec was daunted, if the response he got was more than he'd expected, he didn't show it. He lifted his head proudly and sent his voice out strong and clear: 'In the days of the Old Lord of Sul, an army came from the land of Hish . . .' The crowd stood completely motionless. I was fighting tears the whole time. The story, the words, were so dear to me, and I had only known them in silence, in secret, in the hidden room, alone. Now I heard them spoken aloud among a great crowd of my people, in the heart of my city, under the open sky. Across the straits the mountain stood blue in the blue haze, its peak sharp white. I held on to the stone hoof of the Seune and fought my tears.

The tale ended, and in the silence one of the Ald horses gave a loud, ringing whinny, a regular warhorse cry. It broke the spell. The crowd laughed, moved, and began crying out, 'Eho! Eho! Praise to the Maker! Eho!' Some were shouting, 'Praise to the heroes! Praise to Adira!' The mounted troop up at the east edge of the square shifted as if they were forming to ride into the crowd, but the people paid no attention and did not move away from them. Orrec stood quietly, his head bowed, for a long time. The tumult did not die away, and at last he spoke through it, not out-shouting the crowd, but as if speaking in an ordinary tone, though his voice carried amazingly: 'Come on, sing with me.' He raised his lyre, and as they began to quieten, he sang out the first line of his song 'Liberty': 'As in the dark of winter night . . .'

And we sang it with him, thousands of voices. Desac was right. The people of Ansul knew that song. Not from books, we had no more books. From the air – from voice to voice, from heart to heart, down through all the western lands.

When it was done and the moment of silence passed, the tumult rose again, cheers and calls for more, but also shouts as of anger, and somewhere in the crowd a deep-voiced man called out, 'Lero! Lero! Lero!', and other voices took it up as a chant, with a fast beat on a mounting tune. I had never heard it, but I knew it must be one of the old chants, the songs of festival, procession, worship that had been sung in the streets when we were free to praise our gods. I saw the mounted troop pushing their way into the crowd, which caused enough commotion that the chant lost force and died away. I saw Orrec and Gry making their way down the steps to the east, not across the square but behind the Ald troop. The crowd was still resisting the horsemen, though slowly giving way to them – it's very hard not to get out of the way of a horse coming straight at you, I can testify. I slid down from the pedestal and wriggled through the crowd till I got onto Council Way, ran up it and cut across behind the Customs House, and met my friends on the way up West Street.

A mob of people were following them, but not closely, and most of them didn't come farther than the bridge over North Canal. The maker, the singer, is sacred, not to be intruded on. While I was still up on the pedestal I saw people touching the place where Orrec had stood on the pavement above the Admiralty steps, touching it for the blessing; and no one would walk across it that spot for a while. In the same way, they followed him at a distance, calling out praise and jokes and singing his hymn to liberty. And again for a moment that chant rose up, 'Lero! Lero! Lero!'

We said nothing as we climbed the hill to
Galvamand. Orrec's brown face was almost grey with
fatigue, and he walked blindly; Gry held his arm. He
went straight to the Master's room. Gry said he
would rest there a while. I began to see the cost of
his gift.

◆　◆　◆

EARLY IN the evening I was down in the stable
court playing with a new batch of kittens. Bomi's
cats had been quite shy and retiring ever since Shetar
appeared, but kittens have no fear. This lot was just
old enough to be wildly funny, chasing one another
over and through a woodpile, falling over their tails,
stopping to stare with their little, round, intent eyes,
and flying off again. Gudit had been exercising Star
out on the horsepath. He stood watching the
kittens with a glum and disapproving air. One got
into trouble, scrabbling straight up a post and then
sticking there, crying, not knowing how to get back
down; Gudit gently picked it off the post, like a burr,
and gently put it back on the woodpile, saying,
'Vermin.'

We heard the clatter of hoofs, and a blue-cloaked officer rode in and halted his horse in the archway.

'Well?' said Gudit in a loud, belligerent tone, straightening up his hunched back as well as he could and glaring. Nobody rode into his stableyard uninvited.

'A message from the Palace of the Gand of Ansul to the Maker Orrec Caspro,' said the officer.

'Well?'

The officer looked curiously at the old man for a moment. 'The Gand will have the Maker attend him at the palace late tomorrow afternoon,' he said, politely enough.

Gudit gave a brief nod and turned his back. I also looked away, picking up a kitten as an excuse. I knew that elegant sorrel mare.

'Hey, Mem,' somebody said. I froze. I turned around reluctantly, and there was Simme standing inside the stableyard. The officer was backing his mare out of the archway. He spoke to Simme as he turned the horse, and Simme saluted him.

'That's my dad,' Simme said to me, with transparent pride. 'I asked him if I could come along with him. I wanted to see where you live.' His smile was fading as I stared at him, saying nothing. 'It's, it's really big,' he said. 'Bigger than the Palace. Maybe.' I said nothing. 'It's the biggest house I ever saw,' he said.

I nodded. I couldn't help it.

'What's that?'

He came closer and bent over to see the kitten, which was squirming in my hands and needling me fiercely.

'Kitten,' I said.

'Oh. Is it, is it from that lion?'

How could anybody be so stupid?

'No, just a housecat. Here!' I passed the kitten to him.

'Ow,' he said, and half dropped it. It scampered off with its tiny tail in the air.

'Claws,' he said, sucking his hand.

'Yes, it's really dangerous,' I said.

He looked confused. He always looked confused. It was unseemly to take advantage of anybody so confused. But it was almost irresistible.

'Can I see the house?' he asked.

I stood up and dusted my hands. 'No,' I said. 'You can look at it from outside. But you can't go in.

You shouldn't have come even this far. Strangers and foreigners stop in the forecourt until they're invited farther. People with manners dismount in the street and touch the Sill Stone before they come into the forecourt.'

'Well, I didn't know,' he said, backing away a little.

'I know you didn't. You Alds don't know anything about us. All you know is that we can't come under your roof. You don't even know that you can't come under ours. You are ignorant.' I was trying to hold back the flood of shaking, triumphant rage that swelled in me.

'Well, look. I was hoping we could be friends,' Simme said. He said it in his hangdog way. But it took some courage to say it at all.

I walked towards the arch, and he came with me.

'How can we be friends? I'm a slave, remember?'

'No you aren't. Slaves are . . . Slaves are eunuchs, you know, and women, and . . .' He ran out of definitions.

'Slaves are people who have to do what the master orders. If they don't, they're beaten or killed. You say you're the masters of Ansul. That makes us slaves.'

'You don't do anything I tell you to do,' he said. 'You aren't any kind of slave.'

He had a point there.

We had come out of the stableyard and were walking under the high north wall of the main house. It was built of massive squared stones for ten feet up from the ground; above that was a storey of finer stonework with tall double-arched windows, and high above that carved cornices supported the deep eaves of the slate roof. He glanced up at it several times, quickly, askance, the way a horse eyes something that spooks him.

We came round into the forecourt, which goes the whole width of the house. It's raised a step above the street and separated from it by a line of arcaded columns. The pavement is of polished stones, grey and black, fitted into a complex geometrical pattern, a maze. Ista told me how they used to dance the maze on the first day of the year, the spring equinox, in the old days, singing to Iene who blesses growing things. The pavement was dirty; dust and leaf litter had blown across it. It was a big job to sweep it. I tried sometimes, but I never could keep it clean. Simme started to walk across the maze.

'Get off that!' I said. He jumped, and followed me down the step between the columns into the street, staring with a startled, innocent look, almost like the kittens.

'Demons,' I said with a grin, a snarl, gesturing to the grey-and-black pattern of the stones. He didn't even see it.

'What's that?' he said. He was looking at the stump of the Oracle Fountain.

The fountain is to the right as you face the great doors. The basin is green serpentine – Lero's stone – ten feet or so across. The water had sprung from a central jet; the bronze spout stuck up, now, out of a marble lump so broken and disfigured you could hardly see that it had once been shaped as an urn and carved with watercress leaves and lilies. Dust and dead leaves lay in the basin.

'A fountain full of demon water,' I said. 'It ran dry centuries ago. But your soldiers smashed it all the same, to get the demons out.'

'You don't have to talk about demons all the time,' he said sullenly.

'Oh but look,' I said, 'see, around the base of the urn, those little carvings? Those are words. That's

writing. Writing's black magic. Written words are all
demons, aren't they? You want to go nearer and read
them? Want to see some demons close up?'

'Come on, Mem,' he said. 'Lay off.' He glared at
me, hurt and resentful. That was what I wanted,
wasn't it?

'All right,' I said after a while. 'But look, Simme.
There isn't any way we can be friends. Not till you
can read what the fountain says. Not till you can
touch that stone and ask blessing on my house.'

He looked at the long, ivory-colored Sill Stone set
into the center of the step, worn into a soft hollow
by the hands that had touched it over all the
centuries. I bent down now and touched it.

He said nothing. He turned at last and went away
down Galva Street. I watched him go. There was no
triumph in me. I felt defeated.

*   *   *

ORREC CAME to dinner that evening, recovered and
hungry. We talked first of his recitation, he and Gry
and I telling the Waylord what he had said and how
the crowd had responded to it.

Sosta had been down to the market to hear him

and now was swoonier than ever, gazing at him across the table with her face gone all soft and loose, till he had to take pity on her. He tried to joke, but that didn't work, so he tried to turn her mind from him to her real future, asking where she would live after she married. She managed to explain that her betrothed had chosen to join our household and be a Galva. Orrec and Gry, who had a great interest in the ways people do things, asked all about our customs of marriage-bargain and chosen kinship. Mostly Sosta gazed, mute with adoration, and the Waylord answered; but when Ista sat down with us at table she had a chance to boast about her son-in-law to be, which she loved to do.

'It seems hard that he and Sosta can't see each other all this time before the wedding,' Gry said. 'Three months!'

'Betrothed couples used to be able to meet at any public occasion,' the Waylord explained. 'But now we have no dances or festivals. So the poor things have to catch glances in passing . . .'

Sosta blushed and smirked. Her betrothed strolled by regularly with his friends every evening, just when Ista and Sosta and Bomi happened to be sitting out in the sidecourt facing Galva Street to take the air.

After dinner the rest of us went to the little north court. We found Desac already there waiting. He came forward and took Orrec's hands and called blessing on him. 'I knew you'd speak for us!' he said. 'The fuse is lit.'

'Let's see what the Gand thinks of my performance,' said Orrec. 'I might get a critical commentary.'

'Has he sent for you?' asked Desac. 'Tomorrow? What time?'

'Late afternoon – is that right, Memer?'

I nodded.

'Will you go?' the Waylord asked.

'Of course,' said Desac.

'I can scarcely refuse,' Orrec said. 'Though I could ask to postpone.' He looked at the Waylord, alert to catch the meaning of his question.

'You must go,' Desac said. 'The timing is perfect.' His tone was brusque and military.

I could see Orrec didn't like being told he must go. He kept his eyes on the Waylord.

'No profit in postponement, I suppose,' the

Waylord said. 'But there may be some danger in going.'

'Should I go alone?'

'Yes,' Desac said.

'No,' Gry said in a calm, flat voice.

Orrec looked at me. 'Everybody gives orders except us, Memer.'

'"The gods love poets, for they obey the laws the gods obey,"' the Waylord said.

'Sulter, my friend, there's danger in any undertaking,' Desac said with a kind of impatient compassion. 'You're walled up here, away from the life of the streets, the doings of the people. You live among shadows of ancient times and share their wisdom. But a time comes when wisdom is in action – when caution becomes destruction.'

'A time comes when the will to act defeats thought,' the Waylord said grimly.

'How long must I wait? There was no answer given!'

'Not to me.' The Waylord glanced very briefly at me.

Desac did not notice that. He was angry now. 'Your oracle is not mine. I was not born here. Let books and children tell you what to do. I'll use my head. If you distrust me as a foreigner you should have told me years ago. The people who are with me trust me. They know I never wanted anything but the freedom of Ansul and the restoration of the bond with Sundraman. Orrec Caspro knows that. He stands with me. I'll go now. I'll come back here to Galvamand when the city is free. Surely you'll trust me then!'

He turned and strode out of the courtyard, not through the house but down the broken steps at the open north end. He turned the corner of the house and was gone. The Waylord stood silent, watching him.

After a long time Orrec asked, 'Was I the fool who lit the fire?'

'No,' the Waylord said. 'A spark from the flint, maybe. No blame in that.'

'If I go tomorrow I will go alone,' Orrec said, but the Waylord smiled a little and looked at Gry.

'You go, I go,' she said. 'You know that.'

After a while Orrec said, 'Yes, I do. But,' to the Waylord, 'if I went too far today, the Gand may be forced to punish me, to show his power. Is that what you fear?'

The Waylord shook his head. 'He'd have sent soldiers here. It's Desac I fear. He will not wait for Lero.'

Lero is the ancient, sacred soul of the ground where our city stands. Lero is the moment of balance. Lero is a great round stone down in the Harbor Market, so poised that it might move at any time and yet has never moved.

The Waylord soon excused himself from us, saying he was tired. He gave me no sign to follow or come to him later. He went into the house, slow and lame, holding himself upright.

I woke again and again that night, seeing the words in the book, *Broken mend broken*, hearing the voice say them, my mind going over them, over and over them, trying to make them into meaning.

✦ 11 ✦

The next morning I did the house worship very early and then went down to both markets, not only to buy the food we needed but to see what was going on in the city. I thought everything would be changed, everybody would be ready for a great thing to happen, as I was. But nobody seemed ready for anything. Everything was just as always, people in the streets hurrying, not looking at one another, keeping out of trouble; Ald guards in blue cloaks swaggering at the corner of the marketplace; vendors in their stalls, children and old women bargaining and buying and creeping home on the byways. No tension, no excitement, nobody saying anything unusual. Only once I thought I heard somebody crossing the Customs Street bridge whistle a few notes of the tune of 'Liberty'.

When Orrec and Chy set off for the Council House late in the afternoon they went on foot. They took Shetar, but not me. There was no reason to have a groom without a horse, and they were concerned that there might be danger. I was relieved. I didn't want to face Simme, because every time I thought of him my heart sank with shame.

But as soon as they were gone I knew I couldn't stay at home. I couldn't bear to sit in the house waiting. I had to be closer to the Council Hill, where they were. I had to be near them.

I dressed in my women's clothes, with my hair done up in a knot instead of worn long like a child or a man, so that I was Memer the girl instead of Mem the groom or Nobody the boy. I wanted to wear my own clothes because I needed to be myself. Perhaps I had to put myself into a little danger, to feel that I was with them.

I walked along Galva Street quickly, not looking up, as women always walked, till I came to Goldsmiths' Bridge over the Central Canal. The gold

of Ansul had mostly gone to enrich Asudar; many of
the shops on the bridge had long been closed, but
some still sold cheap trinkets and worship-candles
and such. I could go into one of the shops, out of the
thoroughfare, and keep watch for my friends.

Even though nothing had been going on in the
markets, and there was no sign of any agitation here
at the bridge nearest the Council Hill, and the two
Ald foot soldiers on guard duty were lounging on
the bridge steps playing dice, I couldn't rid myself of
the feeling that something was happening or about
to happen – a sense that some great thing overhead
was bending and bending, about to break.

I stood in the shadow of a shop doorway. I'd
talked a little with the old man who kept the shop,
telling him I was waiting to meet a friend; he nodded
knowingly and disapprovingly, but let me stay. Now
he dozed behind his counter with its trays of wooden
beads, glass bangles, and incense sticks. Not many
people went by outside. There was a little god-niche
by the door frame and I touched the sill of it now
and then, whispering the blessing.

As if in a dream I saw a lion pace by, lashing its
tail.

I came out of the shop and fell into step with my friends, who looked only mildly surprised. 'I like your hair that way,' Gry said. She was dressed as Chy, but was no longer playing the role.

'Tell me what happened!'

'When we get home.'

'No, please, now!'

'All right,' Orrec said. We were on the steps at the north end of the bridge. He turned aside at the bottom, where a railed marble pavement projects out over the canal; from it a narrow flight of stairs leads down to a pier for boats and fishermen. We descended those steps to the canal bank, right under the bridge, out of sight of the street. The first thing we did was go down and touch the water, with a word of blessing for Sundis, the river that makes our four canals. Then we all squatted there, watching the brownish-green, half-transparent water run. It seemed to carry urgency away with it. But pretty soon I said, 'So?'

'Well,' Gry said, 'the Gand wanted to hear the story Orrec told in the market yesterday.'

'Adira and Marra?'

They both nodded.

'Did he like it?'

'Yes,' Orrec said. 'He said he didn't know we had warriors like that. But he particularly liked the Old Lord of Sul. He said, 'There is the courage of the sword and the courage of the word, and the courage of the word is rarer.' You know, I wish I knew some way to bring him and Sulter Galva together. They're men who would understand each other.'

That would have offended me a few days earlier. Now it seemed right.

'And nothing unusual happened? He didn't ask you to sing 'Liberty', did he?'

Orrec laughed. 'No. He didn't. But there was a little commotion.'

'The priests started a chanting worship in the tent again, just when Orrec started reciting,' Gry said. 'Loud. Drums. Lots of cymbals. Ioratth went black as a thundercloud. He asked Orrec to stop, and sent an officer into the tent. And the head priest came right out, all in red with mirrors, very gorgeous he was, but grim as death. He stood there and said the holy worship of the Burning God was not to be interrupted by vile heathen impieties. Ioratth said the ceremony of sacrifice was to be at sunset. The priest said the ceremony had begun. Ioratth said it was two hours yet till sunset. The priest said the ceremony had begun and would continue. So Ioratth said, 'An impious priest is a scorpion in the king's slipper!' And he sent for slaves and had a carpet set up on poles to make shade, by the arcade above the East Canal, and we all trooped over, and Orrec went on.'

'But Ioratth lost the round,' Orrec said. 'The priests carried on with their sacrifice. Ioratth finally had to hurry over to the big tent so he wouldn't miss the whole thing.'

'Priests are good at making people jump,' Gry said. 'There's a lot of priests in Bendraman. Bossing people about.'

'Well,' Orrec said, 'they're held in honor, and they perform important rites, so they get to meddling with morals and politics . . . Ioratth's going to need support from his High Gand against this lot.'

'I think he sees you as support,' Gry said. 'A way to begin making some kind of link with people here. I wonder if that's why he sent for you.'

Orrec looked thoughtful, and sat thinking it over. A horse galloped by on the street high above us, with a loud, hard clackety-clackety of shod hoofs on stone. The sleek surface of the water ruffled and roiled out in the middle of the canal. The sea wind that had blown all day had died away, and this was the first breath of the land wind of evening. Shetar, who had lain down on the dirt, sat up and made a low singsong snarling noise. The fur along her spine was raised a little, making her look fluffy.

The water rippled against the lowest marble step and the pilings of the pier. There was a smoky tint in the fading, red-gold light on the wooded hills above the city. Everything down here by the water was peaceful, and yet it was as if a breath were being held, as if everything held still, poised. The lion stood up, tense, listening.

Again a horse galloped past, up on the bridge above us – more than one horse, a racket of hoofs, and the sound of running feet on the bridge, and shouting, both up there and in the distance. We were all afoot now, staring up at the marble railing and the backs of the houses on the bridge. 'What's going on?' Orrec said.

I said aloud, not knowing what I said, 'It's breaking, it's breaking.'

The shouting and yelling were directly above us

now, horses neighed, there was trampling of feet, more shouting, scuffling. Orrec started up the stairs and stopped, seeing people at the marble railings, a crowd of people, fighting or struggling, yelling orders, screaming in panic. He ducked as something came hurtling over the railing, a huge dark thing that crashed onto the mud by the staircase with a heavy sodden thud. Heads appeared at the top of the stairs, men peering down, gesturing, shouting.

Orrec had leapt down off the stairs. He said, 'Under the bridge!' We all four ran to hide under the low last arch of the bridge where it joined the shore, where the men on the bridge could not see us.

I saw the thing that had fallen. It was not huge. It was only a man. It lay like a heap of dirty clothes near the foot of the steps. I could not see the head.

No one came down the steps. The racket up on the bridge died suddenly, completely, though somewhere in the distance, up towards the Council House, there was a great, dull noise. Gry went to the fallen man and knelt by him, glancing up once or twice at the railing above her from which she might be seen. She came back soon. Her hands were dark with mud or blood. 'His neck's broken,' she said.

'Is he an Ald?' I whispered.

She shook her head.

Orrec said, 'Stay here a while, or try to get back to Galvamand?'

'Not by the street,' Gry said.

They both looked at me, and I said, 'By the Embankments.' They didn't know what I meant. 'I don't want to stay here,' I said.

'Lead on,' said Orrec.

'Should we wait till dark?' Gry asked.

'It'll be all right under the trees.' I pointed up the canal to where great willows stooped out over the bank. I was desperate to get home. I feared for my lord, for Galvamand. I had to be there. I set out, keeping away from the water and close to the wall, and soon we were under the willows. A couple of times we stopped to look back, but there was nothing to be seen from down here but the backs of the houses on the bridge, and across the canal, the wall and treetops and rooftops. No sound came to us from the streets. The air was thick, and I thought I smelled smoke.

We came to the Embankments, the great stone walls like fortresses that hold and divide the River Sundis where it comes out of the hills. Like all the

children of Ansul I had played on the Embankments, climbing the steep steps cut into the walls,
leaping the gaps, running across the narrow bridges
of chained planks that connect the banks for the use
of workmen and dredgers. Our game then was to
dare one child to cross the plank bridge while the
others jumped on it so that it bounced up and down
wildly in the water. Our game now was to dare
Shetar to cross. She took one look at the flimsy set
of planks with water slipping and sliding over them,
and crouched with her shoulders up and her tail
down, saying very clearly, *No*.

Gry immediately sat down beside her and put a
hand on her head behind the ears. She and Shetar
seemed to be having a discussion. I saw that much,
but in my haste I'd already started across the bridge.
Once you start you can't stop, keeping going is the
whole trick of it. I went on across and then stood on
the far bank, feeling foolish and desperate, until I
saw Gry and Shetar both get up, and set out across
the canal – Gry stepping steadily from plank to
plank, and the lion swimming beside her, holding her
fierce head clear of the water. Orrec followed Gry.

Once on shore Shetar shook herself, but cats can't

shake water off like dogs. Her coat was black with wet in the twilight, and she looked shrunken, lean, and small. She showed her white teeth in a mighty snarl.

'There's another bridge and a boat,' I said.

'Lead on,' Orrec said.

I led them across the abutment to the East Canal; we crossed that as we had crossed the other; then up by the steep narrow side-cut stairs onto the great wedge-shaped abutment that separates the East Canal from the river itself, across it, and down again to the river. By then it was getting quite dark. We crossed the river on the line-ferry that is always there. The boat was on our side; we got in and pulled across. The current is strong, and it took both Orrec and me to haul us. Shetar did not want to get into the boat, did not want to be in the boat, and growled all the way across, sometimes making a short coughing roar. She was shivering with cold or fear or rage. Gry talked to her now and then, but mostly just kept a hand on her head behind the ears.

The lineferry landing is at the foot of the old park. Gry took the leash off and Shetar leapt up into the darkness of the woods and vanished. We followed her, finding our way through the trees, up to the paths where Gry and Shetar and I had walked, and so down again to Galvamand, coming at it from the northeast. The lion ran before us like a shadow in the shadows. The house stood huge, dark, and silent as a hill.

I thought in panic, 'It's dead, they're dead.'

I ran ahead of the others across the court, into the house, calling out. There was no answer. I ran through the Waylord's apartments, all in darkness, and on back to the secret room. My hand shook so that I could barely write the words to open the door. There was no light in the room but the faint glimmer of the skylights. No one was there. No one but the books that spoke, the presence in the cave.

I closed the door and raced back through the dark corridors and galleries to the part of the house where people lived. There was a gleam of warm light across the great court. They were all gathered in the pantry where we ate – the Waylord, Gudit, Ista, Sosta, and Bomi, and Gry and Orrec had joined them there. I stopped short in the doorway. The Waylord came to me and took me for a moment in his arms. 'Child, child,' he said. And I clung to him with all my strength.

We sat round the table; Ista insisted that we eat the bread and meat she had set out, and in fact I was ravenous. We told one another what we knew.

Gudit had been over at a beer house near the Central Canal where he and his old friends, all stablemen, hostlers, grooms, used to meet and sit and talk slowly about horses. 'All of a sudden,' he said, 'we heard a lot of noise, up on the Council Hill. Then there was smoke rising, a great black fume of smoke.' Trumpets were blown, and Ald soldiers, mounted and afoot, came rushing past, all heading up along Council Way. Gudit and his friends made their way as far as Galva Street, but a big crowd was already there at the entrance to the Council House square, both Alds and citizens, 'yelling and carrying on, and the Alds had their swords out,' he said. 'I don't like crowds. I decided to go home. It stood to reason.'

He tried to go along Galva Street, but the way was blocked by mobs of citizens, and there seemed to be fighting ahead. He had to go round by Gelb Street to West Street. Over on our side of town things seemed quieter, but he saw people heading towards the Council House; and as he came up to

Galvamand a troop of mounted Alds went by at the gallop, swinging their swords in the air and shouting, 'Out of the streets! Into your houses! Clear the streets!'

We confirmed that there had indeed been fighting on Galva Street, at Goldsmiths' Bridge, and a man thrown to his death from the bridge.

A friend of Bomi's had come running in soon after Gudit came home, reporting that 'everybody said' the Council House was on fire. But a neighbor running home said it was the Alds' big tent in the Council courtyard that had been set afire, and the Alds' king had burned up inside it with a lot of the red priests.

Beyond this there was no news, for nobody dared go out in the street, in the dark, with Ald soldiers all over the place.

Ista was very frightened. I think the terrors of the fall of the city seventeen years ago came back to her that night and overwhelmed her. She set out food for us and ordered us to eat, but she didn't eat a bite herself, and her hands trembled so that she hid them on her lap.

The Waylord ordered her and the girls to bed,

telling them that Orrec and Gry would be guarding the front of the house. 'With the lion,' he said. 'You needn't worry. Nobody is going to get past the lion.'

Ista nodded meekly.

'And Gudit is with the horses, as always. And Memer and I will keep watch in the old rooms. It may be a friend will come by in the night and bring us news. I hope so.' He spoke so mildly and cheerfully that Ista and the girls took heart, or at least pretended to. When we'd cleaned up the kitchen they went off together with brave goodnights. They had seen Gry posted at the top of the front steps, just inside the great door, where she and Shetar could see anything and anybody that came along the street or entered the front court. Orrec made himself the link among the rest of us, checking in with Gudit now and then, and with the Waylord, and patrolling the deserted south side of the house.

For we all dreaded the same thing, more or less obscurely: that Galvamand would again be the target of the Alds' fear or revenge.

The hours of the night passed quietly. I went up several times to the Master's rooms, where I could look out over the city. There was no sign of anything unusual. The slope of the hill hides the Council House from us; I peered that way to see smoke rising or the glow of fire, but there was nothing. I came down again to rejoin the Waylord in the long gallery. We talked a little, then we sat in silence. The night was warm, a soft night of early summer. I intended to go back up to the upstairs windows, but I was sound asleep in my chair when voices roused me.

I jumped up in terror. There was a man at the far end of the room, standing in the courtyard doorway. 'Can I stay, can you hide me?'

'Yes, yes,' the Waylord said 'Come in. Is there anyone with you? Come in. You'll be safe here. Did anyone follow you?' He spoke in a mild, peaceable tone, with no urgency to his questions. He drew the man into the room. I ran past them to see if anyone else was there. I saw someone standing out in the courtyard, a dark form in starlight, and almost cried out in warning – but it was Orrec.

'Fugitive,' he whispered.

'Did anybody follow him?'

'Not that I can see. I'll go back round. Keep watch here, Memer.'

He went quickly back through the arcade. I stood in the doorway, watching out, and listening to the Waylord and the fugitive.

'Dead,' the man was saying, in a hoarse whisper. He kept coughing as he spoke. 'They're all dead.'

'Desac?'

'Dead. All of them.'

'Did they attack the Council House?'

'The tent,' the man said, shaking his head. 'The fire—' He broke into violent coughing. The Waylord brought him water from the carafe on the table and made him sit down to drink it. He sat near the lamp, and I could see him. I didn't know him, he wasn't one of the people who came to the house. He was a man of thirty or so, his hair wild, his clothes and face smeared with dirt or ash or blood. They were, I realised, the striped clothes worn by slaves serving at the Palace. He sat crouched in the chair, struggling to get his breath.

'They set fire to the tent,' the Waylord said.

The man nodded.

'The Gand was in it? Ioratth?'

Again he nodded. 'Dead, they're all dead. It

burned like straw, it was like a bonfire, it burned . . .'

'But Desac wasn't in the tent, was he? – No, drink some more water, tell me later. How should I call you?'

'Cader Antro,' the man said.

'Of Gelbmand,' the Waylord said. 'I knew your father, Antro the blacksmith. The Gelbs used to lend me horses when I was Waylord. Your father was very particular about their shoes. Is he still alive, Cader?'

'He died last year,' the man said. He drank off the water and sat exhausted and dazed, staring in front of him.

'We set the fire and got out,' he said, 'but they were there, they came round us, they pushed us back, back into the fire. Everybody screaming and pushing. I got out. I crawled out.' He looked down at himself with bewilderment.

'Were you burned? Hurt?' The Waylord went closer to him to look him over, and touched his forearm. 'You're burned there, or cut. Let's have a look at it. But first, tell me how you got here, to Galvamand? Were you alone?'

'I crawled out,' Cader repeated. He was not in the quiet room with us, he was in the fire. 'I crawled . . . I got over above the East Canal, I jumped down. They were fighting back there, all over the square, killing people. I went . . . down . . . Clear to the seafront. There were guards riding down all the streets. I hid behind the houses. I didn't know where to go. I thought they might come here. To the Oracle House. I didn't know where to go.'

'You did quite right,' the Waylord said in the same soothing and matter-of-fact tone. 'Let me get a better light here and have a look at that arm. Memer? Would you bring me more water, and a cloth?'

I didn't want to leave my guard post, but it did seem that the man had come alone and unpursued. I fetched a basin and water, cloths and the herbal salve we kept for kitchen burns and cuts; and I cleaned and dressed the burn on Cader's arm, my hands being defter at such work than the Waylord's. After being looked after, and drinking a little cup of the old brandy the Waylord kept for the Feast of Ennu and for emergencies, Cader seemed less dazed. He thanked us and haltingly asked blessing on the house.

The Waylord asked him a few more questions, but he was unable to tell us much more. A small group of Desac's people – some of them slaves of the Alds and some like Cader posing as slaves – had infiltrated the great tent and set fire to it at several places while the ceremony was going on. But the plan went wrong. 'They didn't come,' Cader kept saying. Some of the conspirators, like Cader and Desac, were caught leaving the burning tent; others, who were to be waiting in the square to strike down the Alds as they fled from the fire, had themselves been struck down, or had not been able to get anywhere near the tent – Cader did not know which. He began to weep as he tried to talk about it, and to cough again. 'Come, come on, enough,' the Waylord told him, 'you need to sleep.' And he took him off to his own room and left him there.

When he came back I asked him, 'Do you think they're all dead? Desac, the Gand? What about the Gand's son? He was there, in the tent.'

The Waylord shook his head. 'We don't know.'

'If Ioratth is dead and Iddor is alive, he'll take over, he'll rule,' I said.

'Yes.'

'He'll come here.'

'Why here?'

'For the same reason Cader came here. Because this is the heart of everything in Ansul.'

The Waylord, standing in the doorway looking out at the starlit court, said nothing.

'You should go to the room,' I said. 'You should be there.'

'To the oracle?'

'To be safe.'

'Oh,' he said, with a little laugh, 'safe . . . Maybe I will yet. But let's wait out the darkness and see what daylight brings.'

It was still not daylight, though, when looking from the upper windows I saw a fire, southwest of us, down somewhere near the ruined university buildings. It glowed, died down, blazed up again. There were sounds of unrest, horses clattering down distant streets, a trumpet call, faint troubling sounds of voices, many voices. Whatever the disaster in Council Square had been, the city was not cowed or pacified.

Just as the darkness began to grey and the sky to lighten above the hills behind the city, Orrec came in. With him was Sulsem Cam of Cammand, a lifelong friend of the Waylord, a fellow scholar, who had brought many rescued books to Galvamand. Now he brought news.

'Hearsay is all we have, Sulter,' he said. He was a man of sixty or so, courteous, cautious, very mindful of his own and others' dignity – 'a Cam through and through', the Waylord called him. Even now he spoke quite precisely. 'But we have it from more than one source. The Gand Ioratth is dead. His son Iddor rules. A great many of our people are dead. Desac the southerner and my kinsman Armo died in the fire in the great tent. The Alds still have the city in their grip. Riots and fires and street fighting have broken out all night here and there. People are stoning the soldiers from roofs and windows as they pass. But the attacks on the Alds have no leader that we know of. They're random, scattered. The Alds have an army, we have not.'

I remembered someone saying that, days ago it seemed, months ago; who had said it?

'Let Iddor be certain of his army, then,' the Waylord said. 'We have a city, they do not.'

'Bravely said. But Sulter, I am afraid for you. For your household.'

'I know it, my friend. I know that's why you came here, at risk to yourself. I am grateful. May all the gods and spirits of my house and yours go with you: and go home now, before it's daylight!'

They clasped each other's hands, and Sulsem Cam went back as he had come.

The Waylord went to check on the fugitive, who was fast asleep, then out to the little basin fountain in the back atrium to wash, as he did every morning, and then he began the rounds of the daily worship, as he did every morning. At first I thought I couldn't possibly do the worship, but it seemed to draw me. I went out and picked Iene's leaves and put them at her altar, and started round to all the god-niches to dust them and say the blessings.

Ista was up and bustling in the kitchen. She said the girls were still asleep, having been awake half the night. Going towards the front of the house I heard voices in the great inner courtyard.

Gry stood on the far side, talking with a woman. The first sunlight was just striking the roofs above the open courtyard, and the air was sweet and summer-cool; the two women stood by the wall in shadow, one in white, one in grey, under a flowering vine, like figures in a painting. Everything was charged, intense, vivid.

I crossed over to them. 'This is Ialba Actamo,' Gry said to me, and to the woman, 'This is Memer Galva.'

Ialba was small, slight, a delicate woman in her thirties, with keen eyes. She wore the pale striped dress of the palace slaves. We greeted each other cautiously.

'Ialba brings us news from the palace,' Gry said.

'Tirio Actamo sends me,' the woman said. 'I bring word of the Gand Ioratth.'

'He's dead?'

She shook her head. 'He is not. He was hurt in the attack and the fire. His son had him carried into the Palace and told the soldiers he was dying. We think he'll announce his death. But he's not dead! The priests took him to the prison there. With my lady. She's with him there. If Iddor kills him, she'll die with him. If the officers knew he was alive they might rescue them. But there's no one I can speak to there – I hid all night, I came here by the hill paths

– My lady said to go to the Waylord, tell the Waylord he is not dead.' Her voice was level, light, and even, but I realised that she was shaking, her whole body shivering, quivering, as she spoke.

'You're cold,' I said. 'You've been out all night. Come to the kitchen.'

And she came meekly with me.

When I said her name to Ista, Ista looked her over and said, 'You're Benem's daughter. I was at your mother's wedding. We were friends, your mother and I. You were always Lady Tirio's favorite, when you were just a child, I remember that. Sit down, sit down, I'll have something hot here in just a moment. Why, your clothes are all wet! Memer! Take the girl to my room and find her some dry clothes!'

While I did that, Gry ran back to give Ialba's news to the Waylord and Orrec; and I rejoined them soon, leaving Ialba in good hands. I brought with me a basket of bread and cheese, for I was hungry and thought the others might be too. We sat and ate and talked – what did the news Ialba carried mean, what could we do? 'We need to know what is going on!'

the Waylord said in frustration, and Orrec said, 'I'll go and find out.'

'Don't you show your nose in the streets,' Gry said fiercely. 'Everybody knows you! I'll go.'

'They know you, too,' he said.

'Nobody knows me,' I said. I swallowed a last mouthful of bread and cheese and stood up.

'Everybody in this city knows everybody else,' Orrec said, which was more or less true. But my being recognised as the half-blood boy or girl who did the shopping for Galvamand was no great danger, and to the Ald soldiers I was completely insignificant.

'Memer, you should be here,' the Waylord said.

If he had commanded me to stay I would have obeyed, but it was a protest rather than a command, or so I took it. 'I will be careful, and I'll be back in an hour,' I said. I had already changed into boy's clothing, and now I let my hair down and tied it back and started out, leaving by the north courtyard. Gry followed me and gave me a hug. 'Be careful, lion,' she murmured.

◆ 12 ◆

I looked in at the stables. Gudit was walking
Branty round the court, scowling; he nodded to
me. He had set out pitchforks and other tools ready
to use as weapons. He would die defending the
stable, the horses, Galvamand. As I crossed the
forecourt, still shadowed by the house and the rise of
the hills, my breath stuck in my throat, because I
saw the old man with his bald head and his hunched
back and his pitchfork facing a cavalry troop with
lances and bare swords, and I saw him cut down, I
saw him die. Like the heroes of old. Like the
warriors of Sul.

Galva Street lay empty before and behind me as I

crossed the North Canal Bridge. The city seemed very silent. Again my breath caught: was it a deathly silence, despite the sweet morning sunlight and the scent of flowering trees? Where were my people?

I cut through the back ways past Gelbmand and over by Old Street, heading for the Harbor Market. I didn't dare go towards Council Hill. I was nearly at the marketplace, and still spooked by the silence of the city, when I heard shouting, some way off, towards Council Way, and then the repeated summons of a shrill Ald trumpet. I ran back up West Street, out in the open, since there was no one about, until I got back to Gelb Street. Down it came a couple of Ald horsemen, just as Bomi had described them, riding at a canter, waving bared swords, shouting, 'Clear the streets! Into your houses!'

I ducked behind a broken shrine of Ennu, and they didn't see me. They rode on, and soon I heard the hoofbeats and the distant shouts on the Downway, passing the Foothill Market. I touched the sill of the shrine and said the blessing and went on the byways between houses back up to Galvamand. I had hoped to join a crowd and be invisible and learn what was going on, but there were no crowds. Only soldiers. That was all I had learned, and it was heavy news.

Gry and Shetar were waiting for me at the front door of Galvamand. Four men had come to the back of the house, she said, all of them known to the Waylord, all of them members of Desac's conspiracy. They had been posted, yesterday, on the East Canal with a force that was to attack the Alds in the Council House courtyard when the great tent was set afire; but not all of them had got there when the fire started, earlier than planned. The Ald soldiers had been very quick to gather and defend themselves, and soon took the offensive. The rebel force was broken apart and men were cut down as they tried to escape. They had scattered out over the city. These four spent the night first hiding in the ruins of the university, then making guerrilla attacks on Ald troops. They made their way to Galvamand because the word was all over the city that whoever wanted to fight for Ansul should go there, to the Waylord's house, the House of the Oracle.

'For refuge? Or to make a stand?' I asked Gry.

'I don't know. They don't know,' she said. 'Look.'

A troop of seven or eight men came running round the corner from West Street towards us. They were citizens, not Alds. One of them had a bandaged arm and they all looked fairly desperate. I went out on the steps and faced them. 'Are you coming here?' I called.

'The Alds are coming here,' the one in the lead answered. He stopped at the Sill Stone and touched it. 'Blessing on the souls of the household, living and having lived. The soldiers at the Council House – they'll be here soon. So we're told. Tell the Waylord to lock his doors!'

'I doubt he will,' I said. 'Will you help us guard them?'

'That's what we're here for,' he said. The others were coming up and touching the Sill Stone. One of them said, 'There's the lion, look.'

'Will you come in?' I said.

'No, we'll stay here and wait for them, I think,' the leader said. He was a dark-faced fellow; he had lost his hair tie, and his mane of long black hair made him look wild, but he spoke quietly. 'There'll be others coming. If you had any water, though . . .'

He looked wistfully at the dry basin of the broken fountain.

'Go around to the side, there, to the stable,' I said. 'There's running water. Ask Gudit to let you in.'

'I know Gudit,' one of the men said. 'He's my dad's friend. Come on.' They trotted on round to the stable. Already another, larger group was coming along the street from the other direction, from the Downway, twenty men or more, some of them armed with edge-tools, one brandishing an Ald saber. We made them welcome, and they too were thirsty, after what one of them called a hot night's work, so we sent them around to get a drink at the stables.

At least Gudit wouldn't be standing there alone with his pitchfork, as I had imagined him.

I ran in to tell the Waylord I was back safe and report to him that the city seemed empty, but that the forecourt of Galvamand was now getting rather crowded, and the rumor was that Ald soldiers were coming here.

This was confirmed by all the people who came. They kept arriving, a few at a time, members of Desac's conspiracy, or men and boys who had joined them after the aborted coup at the Council Square. They all said Desac and the Gand had both died in the fire. Some said hundreds of soldiers had been killed in the square, others said the dead were almost all citizens and the Alds were as strong as ever.

As the morning went on, there were more and more women among the people who came to Galvamand, walking in groups, some with a distaff in hand, a few with a baby in a sling. One group of five old women came, all carrying stout sticks and looking about grimly. Four stooped to touch the Sill Stone; the fifth, who was crippled with arthritis and couldn't stoop, just swept her stick across it with a short and testy blessing that sounded more like a swearword.

I stood in the doorway of the house, at the top of the steps, thinking it was like a market fair, or a recitation, or a festival – a sacred ceremony of the old days, such as I had never seen – the people of the city gathering, talking, chatting, idling, waiting, excited yet patient . . . But they would have worn finer clothes to a festival. They would have brought flowering branches to a festival, not swords, knives, daggers, pruning hooks, sticks.

Two men with crossbows had posted themselves one on each side of the door.

There was a great noise, southward down Galva Street, in the direction of the Council House: trumpets and horns braying, drums beating, a roar of voices. The noise went on for some while, ceased, began again.

A little boy of seven or eight came running down the street, his feet flying, his hair flying. 'It's the new Gand!' he shouted. 'He's there with all the soldiers! And there's redhats making speeches!'

Everybody gathered round him. A man took him up on his shoulders and he piped out the message he had heard, which sounded very strange in his thin, sweet voice: 'The Gand Ioratth is dead, the Gand Iddor rules! All hail the Son of the Sun, the Sword of Atth, the Lord Iddor, who comes to subdue the enemies of Atth and destroy the demons of Ansul!'

Like an echo, far down the street, trumpets and horns blared out again, voices roared, drums thumped.

From the crowd round Galvamand there was a

groaning mutter of response. People shifted uneasily. I saw several groups climb over the low wall into the neglected gardens across the street, getting out of harm's way.

I turned and ran into the house again, back through court and corridor to the old rooms, where Orrec and the Waylord stood talking with Per Actamo and some other men of the Actamo household. They turned to me. I said, 'Orrec, maybe you could come speak to the people.'

They all stared at me.

'The new Gand and the army are on the way here,' I said. 'People don't know what to do.'

'You should go,' the Waylord said to Orrec – not meaning go out to the people, but meaning go up into the hills, escape. 'Now.'

'No, no,' Orrec said. He put his hand on the Waylord's arm.

They both held still, silent, for a moment. Then the Waylord turned away.

'It will all be gone,' he said aloud in utter despair and grief. 'The books lost, the makers dead.' He hid his face with his broken hands.

We all stood silent, shaken by that cry.

The Waylord looked up at last; he looked at me.

'Will you come with me, Memer? Can I save you, at least?'

I could not answer. But I could not follow him.

He saw that. He came and kissed my forehead and blessed me. Then he went off, walking very lame, to the back of the house, to the hidden room.

'Will he be safe?' Orrec asked me.

'Yes,' I said.

Even inside the walls of Galvamand we could hear the sound of the trumpets now.

With nothing further said, we all went forward through the great courtyard and the high gallery to the front doors of the house, where Gry and Shetar stood like a statue of a woman and a lion.

I went to Gry and put my arm around her, because I had to have somebody to hold. I had let my dear lord go, I had not held him, I had let him walk away alone to be safe, to live, not to be hurt again. But I had to have somebody to hold.

Gry put her arm around me. We stood there in the doorway of the house. Per Actamo and the others went outside, but Orrec kept back, behind us. He knew that if he came out on the steps and the crowd saw him, he must act, he must speak, and he was not ready to act or speak. The time had not come.

People came, still crowding into the street and the gardens across it, people of Ansul, more and more of them. I couldn't even see the grey-and-black maze of the forecourt; it was a moving pavement of people, alive as it hadn't been in all my lifetime. The crowd gathered and gathered. Galva Street itself was crowded now both north and south as far as I could see.

The trumpets sounded again, a noise that thrilled in the blood, and the drums beat nearer.

There was a wave in the crowd in the street south of us like a tidal bore driving up a canal, pushing everything before it; people shouted, screamed, clambered up onto curbs and walls, making way for the force that drove them, forced them out of the street, pushed them aside: mounted Ald guards, their curved swords slashing and sweeping the air, their horses rearing and striking out with their hoofs. They came straight through the crowd in the streets and stopped in front of Galvamand, a compact troop of fifty or more horsemen. With them, among them, defended by them, eight or ten red-clad, redhatted priests rode close round a man in the broad, pointed hat of the Ald nobility, cloaked in flowing gold.

Behind the mounted troop many people were still in panic, trying to get out of the way, while others struggled to go to the help of those who had been struck down or trampled. There was great confusion and great fear. But all the people I could see all the way down the street were men and women of Ansul. If there were more soldiers coming behind the cavalry, they had not made their way through the crowd.

A circle of emptiness had formed all round the cavalry troop in the forecourt, like the space that had been round Gry and Shetar that first morning at the market, but much larger. I could see the figures of the maze on the pavement inside the circle of snorting, fidgeting horses.

The group of redhat priests rode forward to the steps of the house, and the man in gold rode forward from among them. It was the Gand's son, Iddor, the big, handsome man. The cloak he wore shone like the sunlight itself. He stood in the stirrups and raised his sword high. He shouted out words which

I could not hear over the shouting of his soldiers and the strange noise of the crowd, the groaning roar.

Then all at once all sounds nearby died out, leaving only the noise of the crowds farther away, who could not see what was happening.

What I saw, what the soldiers and the nearby crowd and Iddor saw, was Gry, who came out of the door with Shetar, unleashed, beside her. Woman and lion paced forward and descended the wide steps slowly, walking straight at Iddor.

And he drew back.

Maybe he couldn't keep his horse from flinching, maybe he pulled the reins: the white horse and its gold-cloaked, dazzling rider drew back a step, and back a step again.

Gry stood still and the lion stood motionless beside her, snarling.

'You cannot come into this house,' Gry said.

Iddor was silent.

A little, soft, jeering whisper began to run through the crowd.

Down the street, far down, a trumpet sounded. It broke the paralysis. Iddor's horse backed again and then stood steady. Iddor stood in the stirrups and shouted out in a powerful voice: 'The Gand Ioratth is dead, murdered by rebels and traitors! I his heir, Iddor, Gand of Ansul, claim vengeance. I declare this house accursed. It will be destroyed, its stones will fall, and all its demons will perish with it. The Mouth of Evil will be stopped and silenced. The one God will reign in Ansul! God is with us! God is with us! God is with us!'

The soldiers shouted those last words with him. But then their shouts went ragged, as another sound began, a murmur that spread and spread through the crowd: 'Look! Look! Look at the fountain!'

I was still standing in the doorway, between the crossbowmen who guarded the door of Galvamand, their bows ready to fire, both aimed at Iddor. A man had come to stand beside me there. I thought it was Orrec, then I did not know who it was, a tall man, his hand held out, pointing straight at the Oracle Fountain. The basin with its broken jet was just within the empty circle of the guards.

I saw him then. I saw him, for once, as he had been, and as my heart had always known him: a tall, straight, beautiful man, smiling, with fire in his eyes. I followed his pointing hand and saw what the people below were seeing – a thin jet of water that leapt up into the light. It poised there and fell away to crash with a silvery racket in the dry basin. It sank, leapt up again, higher and stronger, and the voice of the falling water filled the air.

'The fountain,' people cried, 'the Oracle Fountain!' There was a movement forward, pressing in on the cavalrymen, as people tried to see better or to reach the fountain itself. An officer shouted an order, and the horsemen began to turn their horses outward to face the crowd. But their close ranks had been broken, and the officer's voice was lost in a new roar of sound.

The Waylord put his hand on my shoulder and said, 'Come with me, Memer.'

Gry and Shetar had drawn aside, on the steps above to the fountain. I went with the Waylord out onto the broad top step, where he halted and spoke.

'Iddor of Medron, son of Ioratth,' the Waylord said, and his voice was like Orrec's, it filled the air, it commanded the ear, it held the mind, and the great crowd was still. 'You lie. Your father lives. You imprisoned him and falsely claimed his power. You betray your father, you betray your soldiers who serve you faithfully, you betray your god. Atth is not with you. He abhors the traitor. And this house will not fall. This is the House of the Fountain, and the Lord of the Springs protects it, sending it the blessing of his waters. This is the House of the Oracle, and in the books of this house your fate and ours is written!'

He had in his left hand a book, a small one, and he held it up now as he strode down the steps. He was not lame, he was lithe and quick. I went beside him. I saw Shetar's laughing snarl as we passed her. We stopped a few steps above the pavement, so our faces were on a level with Iddor's as he sat on his nervous horse. The Waylord held the book up, open, right in Iddor's face. I could see the man in the shining cloak control himself, force himself not to flinch away from it.

'Can you read it, son of Ioratth? No? Then it will be read to you!'

And then there was a ringing in my ears. I cannot truly say what it was I heard, nor can anyone who was there that morning, but it seemed to me that a voice cried out, a loud, strange voice that rang out all around us, over the forecourt where the fountain leapt, and rang echoing off the walls of Galvamand. Some say it was the book itself that cried out, and I think it was. Some say that it was I, that it was my voice. I know I read no words in that book – I could not see its pages. I don't know whose voice it was that cried out. I don't know that it was not mine.

The words I heard were, *Let them set free!*

But others heard other words. And some heard only the crashing water of the fountain in the great silence of the crowd.

What Iddor heard I don't know.

He shuddered away from the book, crouching in the saddle and hunching his shoulders as if against something that struck at him. His hands must have tightened on the reins to urge his horse forward or pull it back, but awkwardly, so that the horse reared up and bucked, unseating him. The shining figure in cloth of gold jerked and slipped and slithered down and staggered on the ground, while the squealing horse backed away and away, half dragging him with it. We stood still on the steps; Gry and Shetar had come to stand with us, and Orrec had joined us.

The priests closed in around Iddor, some trying to assist him from horseback, others dismounting.

Across this knot of confusion the Waylord's voice rang clearly: 'Men of Asudar, soldiers of the Gand Ioratth, your lord is held prisoner in the palace. Will you go set him free?'

Then it was Orrec whose voice rang out. 'People of Ansul! Shall we see justice done? Shall we go free the prisoner and the slaves? Shall we take freedom into our own hands?'

A wild yell went up at that, and the crowd began to surge down the street towards the Council Housel. 'Lero! Lero! Lero!' – the deep chant ran through them. They flowed around the cavalrymen like the sea flowing around rocks. The officer shouted out orders, the trumpet blew a brief command, and the horsemen, some moving in a body and some straggling out behind, all began to go with the crowd, amid them, borne with them, down Galva Street towards the Council House.

The red hatted priests had got Iddor back up on his horse. Shouting to one another, they followed the mass of the crowd. None of the soldiers that had escorted them had waited for them.

Orrec spoke briefly with Gry and now rejoined Per Actamo and the small group of men who had come to stand with the Waylord and me on the steps. 'Go, follow them!' the Waylord said urgently, and Orrec and the others set off after Iddor and the priests.

Not all the crowd joined in the rush down Galva Street to the palace. People stayed in the street and on the forecourt, many of them women and older people. They all seemed both drawn to and awed by that high jet of water and the lame man who now hobbled down the steps to the basin and sat down awkwardly on its broad rim.

He was as I had always known him, not straight and tall but bent and lame, but he was my heart's lord then and always.

He looked up at the leap and spray of the jet catching the morning sunlight above the shadow of the house. His face shone with water or tears. He reached down and laid his hand on the water, still rising in the wide stone bowl. I had followed him and stood close by him. He was whispering the praise to Lero and the Lord of the Springs, over and over. People rather timidly gathered at the fountain's rim, and they too touched the water, and looked up at the sunlit jet, and spoke to the gods of Ansul.

Gry came to me, holding Shetar now on a close leash, often putting a hand on her head; the lion was still snarling and yawning, still excited and enraged by the noise, the crowds. I saw why Gry had not tried to follow Orrec, though I knew she must long to. I said, 'Gry, I can keep Shetar here.'

'You should go,' she said.

I shook my head. 'I stay here,' I said. Those words came from my own heart, in my own voice, and I smiled with joy as I said them.

I looked up at the column of water that leapt from the cylinder of bronze and towered high, breaking into a great bright-showering blossom at the top. The silvery crash and racket of its fall were wonderful. I sat down on the broad green lip of the basin and did as the Waylord did: I put my hands on the water and in it, and let the spray fall on my face, and gave thanks and praise to the gods and shadows and spirits of my house and city.

Gudit came around the corner of the courtyard. He carried a pitchfork. He halted and looked around at the scattered, quiet people.

'They gone, then?'

'To the palace – the Council House,' Gry called back.

'Stands to reason,' the old man said. He turned and started to trudge back to the stables; then he turned again and stared at the fountain.

'Merciful Ennu,' he said at last. 'She's running again!' He scratched his cheek, stared a while longer, and went back to his horses.

✦ 13 ✦

I can tell what happened at the Council House as Orrec and Per Actamo told us afterwards. The troop of priests surrounding Iddor forced their way forward through the crowd in Galva Street. Orrec and Per managed to keep directly behind them. When they came to the Council Square, the soldiers guarding it shouted, 'Let the Gand Iddor pass!' and began to open the way for the troop of priests. But Iddor and his redhats rode straight past, gaining speed as the crowd thinned out. Orrec thought they making for the Isma Bridge to escape from the city, but they were circling round the back of the Council House to get to the entrance door on the far side, above the Alds' barracks. Soldiers guarded the four-foot-high stone wall that marked off the back court. At Iddor's shouted command, they opened the gate, and the troop of priests galloped in.

But with them came a mob of citizens, who had joined Orrec and Per following the priests past the entrance to the square. Soldiers attacked the citizens as they came pushing in the open gate and swarming over the wall, and citizens mobbed the soldiers. Iddor and his redhats broke through the confusion, leapt off their horses, and made straight for the back door of the Council House. Orrec and Per kept right behind them through the mêlée – the tail of the comet, Orrec said.

Before they knew what was happening they were inside the Council House, still on the heels of Iddor and the priests, who were so intent on getting where they were going that they paid no attention to their pursuers. They all raced through a high hallway and down a flight of stairs. At the foot of the stairs was a basement corridor dimly lit by small windows high in the wall at ground level. Where this corridor opened into a large, low guardroom, the priests and Iddor halted, shouting orders – at guards posted there, or at an opposing force coming from the square? Orrec said it was all shouting and confusion for a while, Alds yelling at Alds. He and Per had held back; now they went forward cautiously to the doorway.

The red-hatted priests and a troop of soldiers stood facing each other, the officers demanding to see the Gand Ioratth, the priests saying, 'The Gand is dead! You cannot defile the rites of mourning!' The priests had their backs against a door and stood firm. Iddor was barely visible among them. He had cast off his golden hat and cloak somewhere. A priest advanced on the officers, formidable in his tall red hat and robes, his arms raised, shouting that if they did not disperse he would curse them in the name of Atth. The soldiers drew back from him, cowed.

Then all at once Orrec strode straight at the priest, shouting, 'Ioratth is alive! He is alive in that room! The oracle has spoken! Open the door of the prison, priests!' – or so Per reported his words. Orrec himself recalled only shouting out that Ioratth was not dead, and then the officers shouting, 'Open the door! Open the door!' And then, he told us, 'I ducked back out of it,' for swords and daggers flashed out on both sides, the soldiers attacking the priests who defended the door, driving them away and down the farther corridor. An officer sprang forward and unbolted and flung open the door.

The room beyond was black, unlighted. In the glimmer of lantern light in the doorway a wraith appeared, a white figure out of the darkness.

She wore the striped gown of an Ald slave, torn and streaked with filth and blood. Her face was bruised, one eye swollen shut, and her scalp was covered with blackened, clotted blood where her hair had been torn out by handfuls. She gripped a broken stake in her hand. She stood there, Orrec said, like a candle flame, luminous, trembling.

Then she saw the man who stood beside Orrec, Per Actamo, and her face slowly changed. 'Cousin,' she said.

'Lady Tirio,' Per said. 'We're here to set the Gand Ioratth free.'

'Come in, then,' she said. Orrec said she spoke as gently and civilly as if she were welcoming guests into her home.

The struggle in the corridor had intensified and then quieted. One of the soldiers brought in a lantern from the guardroom, and light and shadow leapt round the officers as they entered the prison chamber. Per and Orrec followed them. It was a large, low room, earth-floored, with a foul, damp, heavy smell. Ioratth lay on a long chest or table, his arms and legs chained. His hair and clothing were blackened and half burnt away, and his legs and feet were bloody and crusted with burns. He reared up his head and said in a voice like a wire brush on brass, 'Let me loose!'

While his officers were busy getting the chains off him, he saw Orrec and stared. 'Maker! How did you get here?'

'Following your son,' Orrec said.

At that Ioratth glared round and wheezed out in his smoke-ruined voice, 'Where is he? Where is he?'

Orrec, Per, and the officers looked round, ran back to the guardroom. Four priests were being held there by soldiers. The rest were gone, Iddor with them.

'My lord Gand,' said one of the officers, 'we'll find him. But if now – if you'd show yourself to the troops, my lord – They believe you're dead—'

'Hurry up, then!' Ioratth growled.

As soon as they freed his arms he reached out and

caught the hand of the woman who stood silent beside him.

When they got his legs free he tried to stand up, but his burnt feet would not bear his weight; he cursed and sat back down abruptly, still gripping Tirio Actamo's hand. The officers grouped round him to carry him in a chair hold. 'With her,' he said, gesturing impatiently. 'With them!' gesturing at Orrec and Per.

So the whole group stayed together as they went up the stairs to the high gallery that encircles the Council Chamber and along it to the front of the great building, through its anteroom. They came out into blazing sunlight under the columns of the portico, on the speakers' terrace that looks out over the Council Square.

The whole vast expanse of the square was a mass of people, and more still were pushing into it from every entrance, a greater number of people than Orrec had ever seen, the citizens outnumbering the Ald forces by thousands.

When Iddor, the man they thought their new lord and general, had ridden on past the entrance from Council Way with no signal to them, the

bewildered soldiers began to heed the growing rumor
that the Gand Ioratth was alive. Confused, divided
in allegiance, some turning on others as traitors to
Ioratth or to Iddor, they had broken ranks. Citizens
had pushed into the square, armed with whatever
they had. Before real fighting began, realising how
outnumbered they were, the officers quickly rallied
the soldiers and pulled them together out of the
crowd. Most of the Alds now stood on the steps of
the Council House and the pavement in front of it.
In their blue cloaks, they formed a solid half circle
facing the Ansul crowd, their swords bared, not
threatening attack directly but not yielding.

The crowd, though tumultuous, kept back, leaving a ragged no-man's-land between their front ranks
and the soldiers.

'There was an awful stink of burning,' Orrec told
us. 'Vile – hard to breathe. The air was full of dust,
fine black dust, hanging there, the ash and cinders
the crowd had trodden and trampled and kicked into
the air. And I saw a strange thing sticking up out of
that roil and press of people. It looked like the prow
of a wrecked ship. I realised at last it was part of the
frame of the great tent, with burnt canvas clinging to

it. And there were whirlpools in the sea of people, places where men who'd been killed or wounded in the rush into the square were lying, while some people still pressed on past them and others stopped to protect them. And the noise, I didn't know human beings could make a noise like that, it was terrifying, it never ceased, a kind of huge howling . . .'

He thought he could not force himself to go forward and stand facing that mob. His head swam with panic. The officers he was with were also clearly frightened and uncertain, but they carried their Gand forward staunchly. And they shouted out, 'The Gand Ioratth! He lives!'

The soldiers below turned, stared up, saw him, and began to shout, 'He lives!'

Ioratth was saying irritably to the men carrying him, 'Put me down!' and they finally obeyed. He got a firm grip on the arm of one of them with one hand, and on Tirio's shoulder with the other. He managed to take a step forward, grimacing with pain, and to stand there facing the crowd. The roar of his soldiers' salute dominated the bellowing of the crowd for a while, but soon the terrible noise was growing again, drowning the shouts of 'He lives!' in shouts of 'Death to the tyrant! Death to the Alds!'

Ioratth raised his hand. The authority of that ragged, fire-scarred, shaky figure brought silence. And he spoke – 'Soldiers of Asudar, citizens of Ansul!'

But his smoke-hoarsened voice did not carry. They could not hear him. One of the officers stepped forward, but Ioratth ordered him back. 'Him, him!' he said, gesturing Orrec forward. 'They'll listen to him! Talk to them, Maker. Quiet them down.'

The crowd saw Orrec then, and a roar went up from them. They shouted, 'Lero! Lero!', and 'Liberty!'

Amid that tumult, Orrec said to Ioratth, 'If I speak to them, I speak for them.'

The Gand nodded impatiently.

So Orrec raised his hand for silence, and a rumbling, muttering silence spread out through the huge mob.

He told us that he'd had no idea what he would say from one word to the next, and couldn't remember what he said. Others remembered well, and wrote down his words later: 'People of Ansul, we have seen the water of the dead fountain run. We have heard the voice that was silent speak. The oracle bade us set free. And so we have done this day. We have set free the master, we have set free the slave. Let the men of Asudar know they have no slaves, let the people of Ansul know they have no masters. Let the Alds keep peace and Ansul will keep peace with them. Let them sue for alliance and we will grant them alliance. In living token of that peace and that alliance, hear Tirio Actamo, citizen of Ansul, wife of the Gand Ioratth!'

If the Gand was taken aback, it didn't show on his battered, sooty face; he stood there, not able to do much more than keep standing, holding on to Tirio while she spoke. Her voice was clear and valiant but very frail, and all the crowd in the square went silent to hear her, though there was still a hoarse continual tumult of noise from all the nearby streets.

'May the gods of Ansul be blessed again, who will bless us with peace,' she said. 'This is our city. Let us hold it as we always held it, lawfully. Let us be a free people once again. Luck and Lero and all our gods be with us!'

The deep chant of 'Lero! Lero!' rose up from the crowd following on her words. Then a man broke forward from the crowd, shouting out, 'Give us our city! Give us back our Council House!'

Those who were there said that was the most dangerous moment of all: if the crowd had simply pressed forward in its huge irresistible force to occupy the Council House and had met the army standing firm, they would have fought, and Ald soldiers fight to the death. It was Ioratth who prevented a slaughter, rasping out orders to his officers, who shouted them full voice and relayed them by trumpet calls, rallying the soldiers and shifting the whole mass of them rapidly over from the Council House steps to the area east of it, clearing the steps for the wild crowd who had began to flood up and surge into the building. It was the soldiers' discipline, Orrec said, that saved them and the thousands of citizens who would have died in such a battle. The Gand's order had been, 'Down arms,' and not one soldier raised his sword even when shoved, struck, or pushed aside by exultant, vengeful civilians.

To escape the onrush of the mob, Orrec and Per stayed with the knot of officers, who chair-lifted Ioratth again and ran with him to the east end of the terrace and down the side steps to join the ranks that were reforming there. Tirio, Per, and Orrec followed them. A litter was fetched for the Gand. When they got him settled, he promptly summoned Orrec.

'Well said, Maker,' he said, half audible, with a kind of grim salute. 'But I have no authority to make an alliance with Ansul.'

'Best obtain it, my lord,' said Tirio Actamo in her silvery voice.

The old Gand looked up at her. Evidently he saw her bruises, her puffed eye, her torn hair and blood-clotted scalp clearly for the first time. He sat up staring, glaring, shouting in a whisper, 'The damned – the damned traitor – Atth strike him dead! Where is he?'

The officers looked at one another.

'Find him!' wheezed the Gand, and began to cough.

Tirio Actamo knelt beside the litter and put her hand on his. 'Ioratth, you must be quiet a while,' she said.

He laughed through his coughing and gripped her hand. Looking up at Orrec, he said, 'Married us, did you?'

IT SEEMED a long time before Orrec came back to us at Galvamand, yet it was still early afternoon of that day that had already been as long as a year.

The Waylord had come in at my urging for some food and a brief rest, but then he returned to the reception hall that ran along the front of the house, called the high gallery. It had never been used in my lifetime and had no furnishings. Its doors, the wide front doors of Galvamand, stood open now. He asked for chairs and benches to be brought, and there were plenty of willing hands to bring them, not only from other rooms but from houses nearby. He sat down there and made himself available to all who came.

And they came, dozens of people, hundreds. They came to see the Oracle Fountain run, and to hear those who had been there tell how the oracle had spoken and what it had said; that was when I first learned that not all had heard the same words, or that as the words were repeated they were changed and changed again. People came to see the Waylord, Galva the Reader, to greet him, to take counsel with him. Many who came were working men and women, others were or had been merchants, magistrates, mayors of wards of the city and members of the Council. They were all poor because we were all poor, you couldn't tell shoemakers from shipmasters by their clothes. Some of the working people came in only to bless the gods of the house and greet the Reader of the Oracle with awed and joyful respect and be gone again, but others stayed along with the mayors and councillors, the merchants and members of great households, to sit and talk about what was happening and air their opinions on what could and should be done. So I first saw what it was to be a citizen, and what it was to be a Waylord, too.

I stayed with him to wait on his needs and because he asked me to be there. I found it difficult, because people looked at me with awe and fear. Some of them made the gesture of worship to me. I felt utterly false and foolish, and had no idea what to say to anybody. But they had the Waylord to talk to. And fortunately I had to go to the kitchen pretty often to give a hand to Ista, who was almost crazy with excitement and anxiety. The house was full again at last – 'It's like the old days!' she said over and over – but she had no food to offer the guests of the house. 'I can't even offer them water!' she said, tears of rage springing into her eyes. 'I haven't got enough drinking cups!'

'Borrow them,' said Bomi.

'No, no,' Ista said, offended at the thought, but I said, 'Why not?' – and Bomi darted off to extort drinking cups from neighbors. I went back to the reception hall and spoke to Ennulo Cam, the wife of Sulsem Cam who had come last night – a year ago! – and had returned now with his wife and son to sit and talk with the Waylord and the others. I explained our need to her, and very soon a couple of boys from Cammand brought us a half-hundred heavy glass goblets, telling Ista, as they had been bidden, 'A gift from our house to the blessed House of the Fountain.' It was hard for Ista to take offense at that, though she scowled. From then on she kept Bomi and Sosta frantic, fetching water for every guest and taking back and washing out the goblets. She still wanted to offer food, of course, to everyone, but I did not see my way to begging on that scale. I said to her that the people came to talk, not eat. She scowled again, bit her lip, and turned away. I realised then that I had given her an order, and she had taken it.

I went to her and put my arms round her. She hadn't cuffed me for years, but she never had been one for hugs. 'Bymother,' I said, 'don't fret! Be happy with the spirits and shadows of our house. Our guests want nothing more than the water of the Oracle Fountain.'

'Ah, Memer! I don't know what to think!' she said, getting loose from me, with a hasty pat on my shoulder.

None of us knew what to think, that day.

When Orrec came back at last, he was the comet, not the tail: a stream of people followed him from the Council Square. He was the hero of the city. He stopped at the Oracle Fountain and looked up at the ceaseless silver jet of water with the same laughing amazement I had seen on so many faces. Gry came to meet him there. Shetar was shut away in the Master's rooms (where, Gry had told me, she was sulking and tearing strips out of the poor mangy old carpet). Orrec and Gry held each other for a long time before they went up the steps and into the reception hall.

Everybody crowded after them. Once he had greeted the Waylord, Orrec had to tell the whole story that I've just written of the morning's events at the Council House. Some of it we already knew from people who had been back and forth from Galvamand and the square, but the pursuit of Iddor and the priests to the prison chamber and the finding of Ioratth and Tirio was news to us – as was the disappearance of Iddor.

If Orrec couldn't tell us what he had said to the crowd, there were plenty of people who could: 'He said, "Let them beg for alliance and we'll grant them alliance!"' one old man shouted out. 'By the Harrow of Sampa, let 'em beg! Let 'em crawl! And we'll give or not give in our own good time!'

That was the mood of the city, that day: fiercely joyous, belligerent, barely restrained from vengeance.

Ioratth had ordered his soldiers to keep off the streets and stay within the barracks area south and east of the Council House, which they surrounded with a cordon of guards. Wanting access to the Council stables where their horses and some of their men were, the soldiers tried to cordon off a passage between the barracks and the stables, but the crowd in the square got ugly; stones were thrown; and the Gand ordered his men to stay where they were, whether in the barracks or the stableyards.

The Alds were taking care to offer no provocation and show no fear. Their position could too easily become, perhaps already was, a state of siege. Once the habit of fear was broken, the citizens would realise that the conquerors who had mastered them for so long were dependent on them for supplies – and were, however formidable and well armed, vastly outnumbered. If the restraint Ioratth imposed on his men was mistaken for weakness, for unwillingness to fight, there could yet be a massacre.

They talked about that in the reception hall. And they talked about Desac and his group, what their plan had been and how it had gone wrong. The man who had taken refuge with us, Cader Antro, was there, and his story was confirmed and enlarged by others. The arsonists were Ansul slaves, used as servants and sweepers by Ald courtiers; the idea of burning the great tent had come from one of them to begin with. They had secretly admitted to the tent other conspirators dressed as slaves, but armed, and with them had prepared so that fires would start up in several places at once, engulfing the tent in flame, while Desac's men, rushing into the square from two directions, would attack the soldiers on guard. All that was to take place at the sunset ceremony, so that Iddor and Ioratth and many officers and courtiers would be in the tent when the fire broke out.

But, because Iddor wanted to disturb Orrec's recitation, the priests began the ceremony earlier than planned, and so the time of the assault had to be changed, and word of the change didn't get to all the conspirators. The ceremony was already ending when the fires were set. Ioratth came late and was still there praying, but Iddor and the chief priests had just left the tent. The fire spread with terrible quickness, and all of Desac's people who were there attacked, but the soldiers were quick to rally and seemed fearless of the fire, the promised embrace of their Burning God. In the fighting and the smoke and confusion, evidently only Iddor and the priests saw Ioratth stagger free of the flames. They seized and carried him to the Council House, while the soldiers drove the conspirators, those who tried to

flee and those who tried to attack, into the furnace of
the fire to be burned alive. Desac was one of them.

I could only think of that black foul dust of ash
and cinder Orrec had told us of, kicked up by the
feet of the crowds.

The people hearing the story were silent for a
while before they began to talk again.

'So Iddor saw his chance,' one man said, 'with the
old Gand as good as dead.'

'Why did he put him in prison? Why not finish
him off?'

'It's his father, after all.'

'What's that to an Ald?'

I thought of Simme, how proud he was of his
father, even of his father's horse.

'He was going to get his own back on the old
man. Seventeen years he's been waiting!'

'And the old man's Ansul mistress.'

'Torture them for the pleasure of it.'

That brought a silence. People glanced uneasily at
the Waylord.

'So where's he got to, that one, with his redhats?' a
woman asked. People hated the Ald priests worse
than they hated the soldiers. 'I say they'll find him

hiding. They'd never get through the streets alive, that lot.'

She was right. We heard about it later that day, as news was constantly brought down the street to us by dusty, excited, exhausted people coming from the square. The citizens swarming through the Council House, retaking it for the city, throwing out all the goods and furniture of the Ald courtiers and officers who had used it for their quarters, came on Iddor and three priests hiding in a tiny attic room in the base of the dome. They were taken down and locked in the basement room, the torture chamber, where Ioratth and Tirio had been locked for a night. Where Sulter Galva had been locked for a year.

That news relieved our hearts. We had suffered much from Iddor's belief that he had been divinely sent to drive out demons and destroy evil, and we all felt now that with him imprisoned, disgraced, the power of that belief was broken. We had to deal with an enemy still, but a human enemy, not a demented god.

And it was a relief also to know that the wild crowd going through the Council House hadn't torn the priests to pieces when they found them, but had locked them away to wait for some kind of justice – whether ours or the Alds'.

'We may treat Iddor better than his father would,' said Sulsem Cam.

'I doubt he'd be gentle with him,' Orrec said wryly.

'No gentler than your lady and her lion,' said Per Actamo, who had rejoined Orrec here and helped him retell their exploits and adventures to newcomers wanting to hear it all over again all afternoon. 'That was the beginning of the end of Iddor – when he flinched and drew back in front of all the crowd! Where is your lion, Lady Gry? She should be here to be praised.'

'She's in a very bad temper,' Gry said. 'It's her fasting day, and I've had to keep her indoors. I'm afraid she's eaten part of the carpet.'

'Give her a feast, not a fast!' said Per, and people laughed and called for the lion – 'the only Ald on our side!' So Gry went and fetched Shetar, who was indeed in a sullen mood. She had not appreciated the swimming and boating of the night before, or the crowd scenes of the morning; she sensed the continuing tension in the city, and like all cats she detested uproar, excitement, change. She paced into the reception hall with a singsong snarling *warrawarrawarra* and a yellow glare. Everyone made her plenty of room. Gry led her up to the Waylord and had her do her stretching bow; and people laughed again and praised her. They asked for her to do her obeisance again, for Orrec, for Per, for a little boy of three who was there with his parents; and so Shetar got a good many treats, and began to cheer up.

It was evening. The big room was growing shadowy. Ista, along with Ialba, Tirio's companion who had brought us such important word last night, came with lighted lamps. Ista had told me that that was always the signal for guests to leave, in the old days. And as if the ways and customs of our people had been given back to us today, all the visitors rose, one after another, and took their leave of the Waylord. They spoke to Orrec and Gry, and to me, and as they passed through the door they spoke to the souls and shadows of the house. As they passed the fountain leaping up into the evening air they blessed the Lord of the Springs and Waters, and as they crossed the Sill Stone they bent down to touch it.

⋄ 14 ⋄

Lying in bed that night, sleep seemed as far from me as the moon, and I relived all the long day. I saw again Gry and her lion stand facing the priests and soldiers and the gold-cloaked man. I saw the leap of the fountain into the sunlight. I saw the Waylord stride out and down the steps beside me, saw him hold up a book before Iddor and us all, and heard that strange piercing voice – *Let them set free* . . . The cry echoed in my mind with the other words I myself had cried out or that had been said through me, *Broken mend broken*, and for a moment I thought I understood.

Yet I was mystified again, remembering that when

I went to the front of the house with Orrec and the others, the Waylord had gone back to the secret room, seeming in despair, taking refuge. He could not have gone clear back into the cave of the oracle – there had been not time enough for that. He must have gone straight to the shadow end, taken that book from the shelves there, and come back all the way through the rooms and corridors and courts of the great house, to stride forward to face Iddor – not lame, not a broken man, but healed and whole. For that brief time. For the time needed.

Had he questioned the oracle? Had he known what the book said? What book was it?

I had seen it only as a small book in his hand. I had not seen its pages. I had not, could not have read from it. Surely it had been the book that spoke, not I. I was no longer certain now even of the words – had they been *Let them set free*, or *Be set free*, or only *Set free*? I could hear the voice in my mind but not the words. That troubled me. I struggled to hear them but they slipped away from me as if through clear water. I saw the fountain, the morning sunlight over the roofs of Galvamand brightening the high blossom of the water . . .

And then it was morning indeed, early daylight dim on the walls of my little room.

And it was the holiday of Ennu, who makes the way easy for the traveller, speeds the work, mends quarrels, and guides us into death. People say she goes before the dying spirit as a black cat, stopping and looking back if the shadow hesitates, sitting patiently, waiting for it to follow her. Few of our gods are given any figure or image, only Lero in stones, and Iene in the oak and willow; but Ennu is often carved as a little cat, smiling, with opal eyes. I had such a figure that had been my mother's; it sat in the niche beside my bed, and I kissed it every morning and night. Ennu's house-shrine in Galvamand is in the old inner courtyard, an incurved shell of stone on a pedestal, with the tracks of a cat carved across the floor of it, very faint, nearly worn away by the fingers that have touched them in blessing over the centuries. I got up and dressed, and took a bowl out to the Oracle Fountain for water, and a handful of meal from the kitchen bin, and went to that shrine to make her offering. The Waylord met me there, and we spoke the praise of Ennu together.

Ista had breakfast ready for us, and then it was as

the day before: the Waylord took his place in the front gallery of the house, and people came to talk to him and to one another all day long. The community of Ansul was knitting itself together, remaking itself, here.

The Waylord wanted me there with him. He said to me that the people wanted me there. And it was true, though few of them spoke to me except in greeting, a deeply respectful greeting that made me feel as if I were pretending to be somebody important. Sometimes a child was sent forward to give me flowers, dropping them on my lap or at my feet and then running away. After a while I was so flower-bedecked I felt like a roadside shrine.

I tried to understand what I was to them. They saw in me the mystery of what had happened yesterday – the fountain, the voice of the oracle. I was that mystery. The Waylord was their familiar friend and leader, a link to the old days. I was a new thing among them. He was Galva. I was the daughter of Galva, and through me the gods had spoken.

But they were quite content for me not to speak. I

was to smile and say nothing. Enough mystery is enough.

They wanted to talk with the Waylord and with one another, to argue, to debate, to break out of seventeen years' silence, full of words and passion and argument. And they did that.

Some who came said they ought to be at the Council House, holding their meeting there, and as the idea excited them they were all ready to go off to the House that moment and reclaim it as the seat of our government. Selsem Cam and Per Actamo talked easily and quietly of the need to gather strength before they moved, of the need to plan and act upon plan: how could the Council meet if they had not held elections? Ansul had always been wary, they said, of men who claimed power as their right.

'In Ansul we don't take power, we lend it,' said Selsem Cam.

'And charge interest on the loan,' the Waylord added dryly.

What the older people said carried weight with younger people, who had little or no memory of how Ansul had ruled itself and were uncertain how to begin to restore a government they could not remember. They listened to Per because he was Orrec's companion, Adira's Marra, the second hero of the city. Also I saw that when any man of the Four Houses spoke, people listened with respect, a respect based on nothing but habit, tradition, the known name; but useful now, because it gave some structure and measure to what might otherwise have been a competition in opinion-shouting. Sulter Galva, the most respected of all, in fact said very little, letting the others talk out their passions and their theories, listening intently, the silence at the center.

Often he looked up at me, or turned to see where I was sitting. He wanted me near him. We joined our silences.

As the day went on, more of the people who came to Galvamand were armed: troops of men, some with nothing but sticks and cudgels but others with long knives, lances with new-forged heads, Ald swords taken from soldiers in the street battles two nights ago. During a long argument, I went out to breathe fresh air and look at the fountain. I went round to visit Gudit, and found him at the little stable forge hammering out a spearhead, while a young man stood waiting with a long shaft for the lance.

The talk in the high room at the front of the house when I returned was less of meeting and voting and the rule of law than of assault, attack, plans to slaughter the Alds, though they didn't say so openly. They spoke only of massing strength, of gathering the forces of the city together, of stockpiling weapons, of issuing an ultimatum.

I've thought often since of what I heard then and the language they used. I wonder if men find it easier than women do to consider people not as bodies, as lives, but as numbers, figures, toys of the mind to be pushed about a battleground of the mind. This disembodiment gives pleasure, exciting them and freeing them to act for the sake of acting, for the sake of manipulating the figures, the game pieces. Love of country, or honor, or freedom, then, may be names they give that pleasure to justify it to the gods and to the people who suffer and kill and die in the game. So those words – love, honor, freedom – are degraded from their true sense. Then people may come to hold them in contempt as meaningless, and poets must struggle to give them back their truth.

Late in the afternoon one of the leaders of these troops, a young man, hawk-faced and handsome, Retter Gelb of Gelbmand, urged his plan for the expulsion of the Alds from the city. Meeting some opposition among others there, he turned to the Waylord. 'Galva! Did you not hold the book of the oracle in your hand, did we not hear its voice, *Set free?* How can we set our people free so long as the Alds' very presence here enslaves us? Can the meaning of the words be clearer?'

'It might,' said the Waylord.

'If it's not clear, then consult the oracle again, Reader! Ask it if this isn't the moment to seize our liberty!'

'You may read for yourself,' the Waylord said mildly, and taking a book from his pocket, he held it out to Retter Gelb. The gesture was not threatening, but the young man started back and stood staring at the book.

He was young enough that, like many people of Ansul under the Alds, he had perhaps never touched a book, never seen a book except torn to fragments, thrown into a canal. Or it may have been fear of the uncanny, of the oracle, that came over him. He said at last, hoarsely, 'I can't read it.' And then, ashamed and trying to regain his challenging tone, he said, with a quick glance at me, 'You Galvas are the Readers.'

'Reading was a gift we all shared once,' the Waylord said, his voice no longer mild. 'Time, maybe, that we all relearn it. In any case, until we understand the answer we got, there's no use asking a new question.'

'What good is an answer we don't understand?'

'Isn't the water of the fountain clear enough for you?'

I had never seen him so angry, a cold, knife-edge anger. The young man drew back again; after a pause he bowed his head a little and said, 'Waylord, I beg your pardon.'

'Retter Gelb, I beg your patience,' he responded, still very coldly. 'Let the fountain run water a while before it runs blood.'

He set the book down on the table and stood up. It was a small book bound in dun-colored cloth. I didn't know if it was the book that had given us the oracle or some other.

Ista and Sosta were coming in with lamps.

'A good evening to you all, and a peaceful night,' the Waylord said, and taking up the book again, limped away from the crowd of people, back towards the shadowy corridors.

People left the house, then, bidding me a subdued good night. But many of them stayed to stand about on the maze in the courtyard, talking. There was a sense of unrest, unease, all through the city, a stir in the warm, windy, darkening air.

Gry came out of the house with Shetar on the leash and said to me, 'Let's walk over to Council Hill and see what's doing,' and I gladly joined her. Orrec, she said, was in the house, writing; he had mostly kept to their apartments that day. He didn't want to be part of the discussions and debates, she said, not being a citizen of Ansul, yet knowing whatever he said would be grasped at eagerly and given undue weight. 'It worries him,' she said, 'And this feeling that something is about to happen, some violence, something fatal that can never be undone . . .'

As we walked, people constantly greeted us, and saluted Gry and her lion, the first to face down Iddor and the redhats. She smiled and returned the greetings, but in a quick, shy way that did not lead to further talk. I said, 'Does it scare you – being a hero?'

'Yes,' she said. She laughed a little and shot me a glance. 'You too,' she said.

I nodded. I led us off Galva Street to a byway where we would meet nobody and could talk quietly as we walked.

'At least you're used to all these people. Oh, Memer, if you knew where I came from! One street of Ansul has more houses in it than there are in all the Uplands. I used to go months, years, never seeing a new face. I used to go all day never speaking a word. I didn't live with human beings. I lived with dogs, and horses, and wild creatures, and the hills. And Orrec . . . None of us knew how to live with other people. Except his mother. Melle. She came from the lowlands, from Derris Water. She was so lovely . . . I think his gift is from her. She used to tell us stories . . . But it's his father he's most like.'

'How is that?' I asked.

She pondered and spoke. 'Canoc was a beautiful, brave man. But he feared his gift, and so he hid his heart. Sometimes I see Orrec do that. Even now. It's hard to take responsibility.'

'It's hard to have it taken from you, too,' I said, thinking of the Waylord's life all the years I had known him.

We came back to the street at Goldsmiths' Bridge and went on up to the Council Square. There were a lot of people there, drifting and swirling about, mostly men, and many of them carrying weapons. Someone was haranguing the crowd from the terrace of the Council House, not too successfully, for people kept coming to listen and drifting away again. Over on the east side of the square was a solid line of both men and women, some afoot and some sitting down, keeping their place side by side and very much on the alert. I spoke to one of the women, a neighbor of ours, Marid; she told us they were there 'to keep the kids from getting into trouble'. Beyond them, down the hill, torches gave enough light that we could just make out the cordon of Ald soldiers guarding the barracks. These citizens had made themselves a barrier between the crowd and the soldiers, preventing random insults and forays against the Alds by young men looking for a fight or by idle stone-throwers. Anybody trying to provoke the soldiers into violence would have to break through that line of fellow citizens. It continued on across the square, in front of the stables, where I had sat and talked with Simme.

'You are a remarkable people,' Gry said to me as we went back across the square. 'I think you have peace in your bones.'

'I hope so,' I said. We were in the center of the square, where the great tent had been. The wreckage was gone now; there was no trace of it except the blackening of the pavement stones, a slight crunch of ash and cinders under the feet. We were walking where Desac had died, burnt alive in the fire he had set. I shuddered all over, and Shetar, at the same moment, set up a long, strange wail, stretching her head up. I remembered how she had taken against Desac, glared at him. I saw him alive, straight-backed and soldierly, arrogant, passionate, talking with the Waylord – 'We'll meet again, free men in a free city!' he had said. His shadow was all round us.

Returning, we crossed the bridge and paused at the railing from which we had seen a man thrown to his death. We looked down at the dark canal that reflected a glimmer or two of light from the houses on the bridge. Shetar growled a little, informing us that she did not want to go back down there and go swimming again. A band of boys ran past us, shouting a chant I had heard several times in the street that day, 'Alds out! Alds out! Alds out!'

'Let's go down to the Lero Stone,' I said, and we did; neither of us wanted to go inside on this strange night, with the city all awake and restless about us, and it was good to walk, too, after sitting still listening to people talk all day. We cut down by the Slant Bridge on Gelb Street to West Street and to the Stone. A good many people were there, quietly waiting and doing as I came to do: to touch the Stone and say the blessing of Lero, who holds the balance.

We started back up West Street. I said, not knowing that I was going to say it, 'Did you and Orrec never have children, Gry?'

'Yes. We had a daughter,' she answered in her quiet voice. 'She died of the fever in Mesum. She lived a halfyear.'

I could say nothing.

'She'd be seventeen now. How old are you, Memer?'

'Seventeen,' I said, finding it very hard to say.

'I thought so,' Gry said. She smiled at me. I saw her smile in the faint lamplight of the High Bridge. 'Her name was Melle,' she said.

I said the name and felt the touch of the little shadow.

Gry reached out her free hand to me, and we walked hand in hand.

'This is Ennu's day,' I said, as we came to the turning of Galva Street. 'Tomorrow will be a day of Lero. The balance will turn.'

◆ ◆ ◆

IN THE morning it seemed that the balance might have turned already: we heard early that there was a great crowd gathering in the Council Square, not yet offering violence, but noisy and determined, demanding that the Alds leave the city this same day. The Waylord conferred briefly with Orrec, and they came into the gallery together. Orrec looked tense and strained. He spoke to Gry for a moment, and she went to shut Shetar into the Master's room, while Gudit brought out both horses. Orrec mounted Branty. Gry mounted Star, and I ran with her, following Orrec through the crowds in Galva Street.

They willingly parted for us, calling out Orrec's name.

He rode to the line of citizens still holding firm in the square in front of the line of soldiers. There he asked both the citizens and the soldiers if he might speak with the Gand Ioratth. They let him through at once. He dismounted and ran down the steps towards the Ald barracks.

I held Branty's bridle now, there in the crowd, like a real groom. He didn't need much holding. He stood solidly, alert but not troubled by the hubbub all round, and I tried to imitate him. Star shook her head often, whuffing and shuffling when people pressed up too close, and I tried not to imitate her. I was glad, though, that the horses kept a little space around us, for the presence of so many people was overwhelming. I could not think clearly, and emotions ran through me – elation, dread, excitement – they ran through us all, like the wind through leaves on a tree before a storm. I held Branty's bridle and watched Gry's face, which was still and calm.

There was a deep roaring in the crowd nearer the steps of the Council House; everybody turned that way, but I could see nothing over the heads and shoulders. Gry touched my arm and indicated that I should mount Branty. 'I can't!' I said, but I couldn't hear myself, and she was making a hand stirrup for me, and a man near us said, 'Up you go, girl!' – and I was abruptly sitting in the saddle on Branty's back, bewildered. Gry swung up onto Star, right beside me. 'Look!' she said, and I looked.

People stood on the speakers' terrace: a woman in a dun-and-white striped gown, and Orrec in his black coat and kilt. They looked very small and bright to me, like images. The crowd was shouting and chanting. Some people were calling out, 'Tirio! Tirio!' A man near us shouted ragefully, 'Ald's whore! Gand's whore!' and immediately people turned on him, shouting at him with equal rage, while others tried to hush and separate them. I could not reach the stirrups with my feet and felt most insecure perched way up there on the saddle, but Branty stood like a rock, and I was at least safe from the pushing and trampling of the crowd. Gradually the noise died away; Orrec had raised his right hand. 'Let the maker speak,' people cried, and silence spread out slowly across the crowd, as the water of the fountain had spread out across the wide basin.

When he spoke at last his voice rang out, distant but clear and resonant.

'This is Lero's day,' he said. And said nothing further for a long time, for the whole crowd took up the deep, slow chant of 'Lero, Lero, Lero!' – and my breath caught and tears filled my eyes and I was chanting with them, 'Lero, Lero, Lero . . .' At last he raised his hand again, and the chant died away down the streets leading to the square.

'I who am not of Ansul and not of Asudar – will you let me speak again to you?'

'Yes!' the crowd roared, and, 'Speak! Let the maker speak!'

'Tirio Actamo, daughter of Ansul and wife of the Gand of the Alds, stands here with me. She and her husband ask me to say this to you: The soldiers of Asudar will not attack you, they will not interfere with you, they will not leave their barracks – such are the Gand Ioratth's orders, and his soldiers will obey. But he cannot order the soldiers to leave Ansul without the consent of his king in Medron. So he waits to hear from Medron. And he, and Tirio Actamo, and I, beg you to be patient, and to take your city back and claim your freedom in peace, not in blood. I who saw the ruler, betrayed and imprisoned, set free – I who with you saw water leap from the fountain that was dry two hundred years, and heard with you the voice that cried aloud from silence – I your guest – while we wait together for Lero to show us how the balance falls, and whether we are to destroy or to rebuild, to fall to war or walk in peace – while we wait, may I offer in return for your hospitality and the grace of the gods of Ansul a story, a story of war and peace, of slavery and freedom? Will you hear the *Chamhan*? Will you hear the tale of Hamneda when he was made a slave in Ambion?'

'Yes,' the crowd said, and now the sound was like a great, soft wind in grass. We could all feel the tension in us lessening, and we were grateful for it, grateful to the voice that freed us from dread and passion and unreason, if only for a little while, for the time it takes to tell a story.

Anywhere else in all the Western Shore, people would have known that story; even here, where the books had been destroyed, many in the crowd knew it, or at least knew the hero's name. But many had never read the story nor heard it told. And to hear it told aloud, among a great throng, openly, asserting our inheritance as our right and our heroes as our own – that was a great thing to us, a great gift Orrec gave us. He told it as if he himself had never known it before and discovered it as he spoke it, as if the betrayal of Hamneda by Eloc appalled him, as if he were chained and beaten with Hamneda, and wept with him at the torture and death of old Afer, and feared for the slaves who risked their lives to help him escape. He was no longer telling the *Chamhan* I had read, but his own tale in his own words, when he came to the confrontation in the Palace of Ambion, when Hamneda released the tyrant Ura from his chains, bidding him be gone from Ambion, and said to the rebels of the city, 'Freedom is a lion let loose, the sun rising: you cannot stop it here or there. Give liberty to have liberty! Set free to be free!'

Since then I have heard people maintain that that is what the voice of the oracle said on the steps of Galvamand: *Set free to be free.* Maybe it was so.

In any case, when they heard those words, the crowd in the Council Square made the sound a great crowd makes when it hears said what it wants to hear. When Orrec finished the tale they were not silent, but roared praise, and their mood was jubilant, as if they themselves had been freed from constraint or dread. They flooded up around Orrec on the terrace of the Council House, and Gry and I had no chance at all of getting to him.

We could, however, from our horseback height, see him and Tirio; and we saw the crowd begin to swirl around them and carry them slowly towards Galva Street. Gry hopped off Star and shortened my stirrups, then swung up again into her saddle. 'Hold with your knees and never mind the reins,' she called, and we set off, surrounded by our own swirl of praise and jokes and shouting, on my first horseback ride – out of the square, across the three bridges of Galva Street, to Galvamand.

The people parted and made way for us, so that we soon caught up to Orrec and Tirio. Dismounting at our stable gate, I ran back to the house in time to see Tirio's meeting with the Waylord in the gallery. He stood up, seeing her, and she ran forward with her hands held out, saying his name, 'Sulter!' They embraced and held each other, both in tears. They had been friends when they were young, maybe lovers, I don't know; they had known each other in youth and wealth and happiness and then been separated for years of shame and pain. He was crippled. She had been beaten, her hair torn out. I remembered how he had said to me, long ago, tenderly, 'There's a good deal to weep about, Memer.' I cried then too, for them, for the grief of the world.

Orrec came beside me, as I stood there inside the doorway trying to hide my tears. His face still had the bewildered brightness of one who has been acclaimed, taken out of himself by the power of the crowd; but he put his arm round my shoulders and said softly, 'Hello, horse thief.'

◆ ◆ ◆

IT SEEMED as if Orrec and Lero had tipped the balance. That day and the days following, there was still tremendous unrest in the city, but it was less rageful, less threatening. There was a lot of angry talk, but fewer weapons were brandished. The Council House was opened for debate on the planning of an election.

People kept coming to Galvamand to talk in the gallery and to dance the maze – I saw it at last, I saw women dance the maze. After a day or two, Ista went out among them, scowling, with a dishcloth in her hand, and said, 'You've got it all wrong. You turn here, when you sing 'Eho!' and then you turn there.' And she showed them how to dance the blessing properly. After that she went back to the kitchen.

She was working very hard, and so were Bomi and I and even Sosta. People kept bringing gifts to the house, gifts of food, knowing how strained our hospitality must be with the endless flow of guests. Ista had brought herself to accept them, not as gifts exactly, or honor, or tribute, but as what was due the Waylord and his house – as debts owing and repaid. So her mind worked, like many minds in Ansul. If we have peace in our bones, we have commerce in them too.

Ialba went back with Tirio to help her care for Ioratth, whose burns were severe and slow to heal. The next day Tirio sent three women from the barracks to help us keep the house. They were city women who had been taken and kept as slaves for the use of the soldiers, like Tirio. As she won the Gand's favor, she had been able to bring them out of utter subjugation to a more decent servitude. One of them, who had been taken and used by the soldiers as a girl of ten or eleven, was crippled and a little mad, but if we set her at any task of cleaning where she could work alone, she worked hard and contentedly. The others had both been of respectable households, knew how to keep a house, and were of great assistance to us.

Ista was inclined at first to treat them coldly and tried to keep them from talking to Sosta and me – look at what they'd been, after all, no doubt it wasn't their fault, but they were no fit company for young girls of a good house, and so on. They and I paid no attention to that. One of them had a man friend she'd known as a slave; he moved right in and took a hand with the heavy work. Gudit got on pretty well with him, because he had been a cartwright, and could plan how to build a carriage out of the broken-down bits of carts and wagons Gudit had been hoarding for years.

So in a few days there was a great increase of people, of life, in the house, and I liked it. There were more voices and not so many shadows. There was a little more order, a little less dust. Many hands touched the god-niches now in passing worship, not just mine.

But these days I saw very little of the Waylord. Only in public, among others.

And I had not been to the secret room since the night the oracle spoke through me.

My life had been suddenly and wholly changed. I lived in the streets, not in books, and talked to many people all day long instead of to one man alone in the evening, and my heart was full of Orrec and Gry, so that sometimes I didn't even think of him. If I felt shame for that, I could excuse myself: I'd been important to him when I was the only person close to him, but now he no longer needed me. He was truly the Waylord again. He had the whole city to keep him company. He had no time for me.

And I had no time to go to the secret room, nights, as I had done for so many years. I was busy all day, tired at night. I kissed my little Ennu and fell asleep. The books in that room had kept me alive while my city was dead, but now it was coming back to life, and I had no need of them. No time, no need.

If I was afraid to go there, afraid of the room, of the books, I didn't let myself know it.

✦ 15 ✦

In those days of early summer, it was as if we had forgotten the Alds, as if it didn't matter that they were still in the city. Armed citizen volunteers kept a close watch night and day on the barracks and the Council House stables, having formed a kind of militia and doing guard duty in relays, but in the Council House itself all the talk was about Ansul, not the Alds. There were daily meetings, large and tumultuous but led by people experienced in government, determined to restore Ansul's power and polity.

Per Actamo was at the center of these plans and meetings. He wasn't yet thirty, but he took to leadership as one born to it. His vigor and intelligence kept the older men from too quickly dropping back into 'the way we always did it'. He questioned the way we always did it, and asked if it mightn't be done better; and the constitution of the Council began to take shape freed of many useless traditional perquisites and rulings. I went often to hear him and the others speak in the open meetings, for they were exciting, full of hope. Per was at Galvamand daily to take counsel with the Waylord. Sulsem Cam came with his son Sulter Cam, usually to argue that everything should be done the way we always did it; but his wife Ennulo supported Per's proposals. So did the Waylord, though more indirectly, always striving to bring about a consensus and not to become locked in a mere debate of opinions.

They were already laying plans for the election day, when one sunny morning, in an hour, the news was all over the city: An Ald army is coming through the Isma Hills.

At first it was only a rumor that could be discounted, some shepherd's tale of seeing Ald soldiers, but then a boatman coming into the city down the Sundis confirmed it. A troop of soldiers had been seen marching on the east side of the Isma Hills. They were probably already in the pass above the springs of the river.

Then there was panic. People ran past the house crying, 'They're coming! The Alds!' Crowds at the Council Square and in the streets swelled ceaselessly. Weapons were brought out again. Men rushed to the old city wall that runs along outside the East Canal and the gate where the road from the hills comes in. The wall had been half destroyed when the Alds took the city, but the citizens made barricades across the road and at the Isma Bridge.

The people who came to Galvamand that day were frightened, looking for guidance. Too many remembered the fall of the city seventeen years ago. Per and others who might have spoken to them were at the Council House. The Waylord kept calming them, and they listened to him; but soon he called me and talked to me in the corridor alone.

'Memer,' he said, 'I need you. Orrec can't get through the crowd; they'll stop him and want him to tell them what to do. Can you get through the lines – to Tirio, to Ioratth – and find out what they know about this force of soldiers, and whether the Gand has changed his orders to his troops? And bring word back to me?'

'Yes. Have you any word for them?' I asked.

He looked at me then just as he used to look at me when I happened to get the words of some translation from the Aritan exactly right, not surprised, but deeply pleased, admiring. 'You'll know what to say,' he said.

I put on my boy's tunic and tied back my hair. People knew me now, and I didn't want to be recognised and stopped with questions. So I went as Mem the half-breed.

I got along Galva Street all right for a while, dodging and shoving, but after the Goldsmiths' Bridge it was hopeless – the crowd was solid. I ran down the stairs we'd taken that evening, remembering the clatter of hoofs and the shouting and the smell of smoke. I ran along the canal to the Embankments, crossed there, and went back down the east bank to where I could cut across to the exercise grounds and the hippodrome. They were empty, deserted, but I saw the line of Ald soldiers on guard, up on the long, low swell of Council Hill behind the stables. All I could do was climb the hill towards them, my heart beating harder and harder.

The soldiers stood and said nothing. They watched me. A couple of crossbows were aimed at me.

I got to within ten feet of them, stopped, and tried to catch my breath.

They looked more foreign to me, those men, than they had ever looked in all the years I'd seen Ald soldiers, my whole life. Their faces were sallow, their short, pale sheep hair curled out under their helmets, their eyes were pale. They stared at me without expression, without a word.

'Is there a boy named Simme in the Gand's stables?' I said. My voice came out very thin.

None of the six or seven men nearest me in the line moved or spoke for so long I thought they were not going to answer at all. Then the one right in front of me, who had no crossbow, but a sword in his belt and his hand on the hilt, said, 'What if there is, youngster?'

'Simme knows me,' I said.

He looked his question: *So?*

'I have a message from my master the Waylord to

the Gand Ioratth. I can't get through the crowds. I can't get through the lines. It's urgent. Simme can vouch for me. Tell him it's Mem.'

The soldiers looked at one another. They conferred a little. 'Let the kid through,' one said, but the others said no, and finally the swordsman nearest me said, 'I'll take him in.'

So I followed him on round the long back of the stables. Not every moment of this time is clear in my memory. I was so set on my goal that how I reached it seemed unimportant, details swallowed in the overriding urgency. I do remember some things clearly. I remember Simme coming into the small room where the swordsman had brought me to his officer. Simme saluted the officer and stood stiffly. 'Do you know this boy?' the officer asked. Simme's eyes shifted to me. His head did not turn. His face changed entirely. It went soft, like Sosta's face when she looked at Orrec. His lips quivered. He said, 'Yes sir.'

'Well?'

'He's Mem. He's a groom.'

'Whose groom?'

'He belongs to the Maker and the Lion Woman.

He came here with them. He lives at the Demon House.'

'Very good,' the officer said.

Simme stood still. His gaze came back to me, beseeching. He looked white and not so pimply. He looked tired, the way so many people of Ansul had looked, all my life. He looked hungry.

'You have a message from Caspro the Maker for the Gand Ioratth,' the officer said to me.

I nodded. The name of Caspro the Maker might be a safer password than that of Galva the Waylord.

'Say it to me.'

'I can't. It's for the Gand. Or for Tirio Actamo.'

'Obatth!' the officer said. After a moment I realised he was swearing. He looked me over again. 'You're an Ald,' he said.

I said nothing.

'What are they saying out there about an Ald force coming over the pass?'

'They say there is one.'

'How large a force?'

I shrugged.

'Obatth!' he said again. He was a short, worn-faced man, not young, and he too looked hungry.

'Listen. I can't get through to the barracks. The city people are holding the line between us. If you can get through, go ahead. Take a message for me too. Tell the Gand we've got ninety men here and all the horses. Plenty of fodder but short of food. Both of you go. You heard the message, Cadet?'

'Yes sir,' Simme said. I could see his chest fill with a deep breath. He saluted again, wheeled round, and strode out. I followed him, and the officer followed me.

The officer got us through the cordon, and then I got us through the line of citizens that faced them. I looked for a face I knew. Marid wasn't there, but her sister Remi was, and I talked her easily enough into letting us pass. 'A message from the Waylord to the Lady Tirio' was what did it.

Once out in the crowd of citizens in the open square, we were on our own. Fortunately Simme had no uniform except the blue knot on his shoulder. Once somebody said, 'Are those kids Alds?' – seeing our hair – but we wriggled away into the crowd. We pushed and shoved and got cursed at clear round the east end of the stables, across the steps below the Council Square, and then we had to face the line of citizens again, near the barracks. Again I found a face I knew, Chamer, one of Gudit's old friends, but how I talked us through I don't remember. Chamer spoke with the Ald guard facing him, quite a discussion, I do remember that. Then we were through both lines, and a guard was taking us across the parade ground to the barracks, shouting as he went for Simme's father.

I saw his father come running. Simme stopped and stood still and tried to salute him, but his father took him in his arms.

'Victory is well, Father,' Simme said. He was crying. 'I exercised her as much as I could.'

'Good,' his father said, still holding him. 'Well done.'

Other men and officers came pouring out of the barracks, and we gathered quite an escort walking past the long buildings and outbuildings. Whenever an officer stopped me, Simme and his father were there to affirm that I came from the Demon House, where the Maker Orrec Caspro was, with a message from him. Then we went into the last building of the row, and the soldiers and officers dropped back. I saw Simme watching me as I was sent forward alone.

I went past a door guard into a long room with long windows overlooking the curve of the East Canal. Tirio Actamo came forward to meet me.

She did not know me at first, and I had to say my name. She took my hands, and then embraced me; and I wasn't far from crying myself, from sheer relief. But there was my message to be given.

'The Waylord sent me. He needs to know what the Gand knows about the army coming from Asudar.'

'Best you talk to Ioratth yourself, Memer,' Tirio said. Her face was still swollen and discolored and her head bandaged, but the bandage became her, like a little hat; nothing could make her ugly. And she had a sweet, easy way about her, she comforted one's heart just by speaking. So I was less scared than I might have been when she took me across the room to the bed on which the Gand Ioratth lay.

He was propped up on a lot of embroidered pillows. A red cloth had been hung from the ceiling over the head of the bed, so that coming close was like entering a tent. The Gand's legs and feet were out from under the covers, covered with raw burns and black-scabbed ones, painful-looking. He glared at me like a leashed hawk.

'Who's this? Are you Ald or Ansul, boy?'

'I am Memer Galva,' I said. 'I come to you from the Waylord, Sulter Galva.'

'Hah!' said the Gand. The glare became a gimlet. 'I've seen you.'

'I came with Orrec Caspro when he recited to you.'

'You're an Ald.'

'If I'd borne you a child, you might well take it for an Ald,' said Tirio, mild and ladylike.

He grimaced, absorbing this.

'What's your message then, if the Maker sent you?'

'The Waylord sent me,' I said.

'If Ansul has a leader, Ioratth, it is Galva the Waylord,' Tirio said. 'Orrec Caspro is a guest of his house. It might be for the best if you and he were in communication.'

He grunted. 'Why did he send you?' he demanded of me.

'To ask if you know why soldiers are coming from

Asudar, and how many, and if you'll change your orders to your troops when they come.'

'Is that all?' said the Gand. He looked at Tirio. 'By God, this is a cool young sprout! One of your family, no doubt.'

'No, my lord. Memer is a daughter of the house of Galvamand.'

'Daughter!' the Gand said. The gimlet became a glare, and finally a blink. 'So she is,' he said, almost resignedly. He moved in discomfort, and winced, and rubbed his head with its frizz of half-burnt hair. 'And you think I should send her back to Galva with a list of my strategies and intentions, do you?'

'Memer,' Tirio asked, 'is the city going to attack the barracks?'

'If they see an army coming down the East Road, I think they will,' I said. I had heard it urged again and again that morning – wipe out the soldiers here before these reinforcements arrive! Take the city back before they take it back!

'It's not an army,' Ioratth said almost peevishly. 'It's only a messenger from the Gand of Gands. I sent him one two weeks ago.'

'I think the people of the city had better know

that,' said Tirio, as mildly as ever, and I added, 'Quickly!'

'What, you think my sheep are in revolt, do you?' His tone was caustic, sarcastic, a sarcasm directed at himself, perhaps.

'Yes, they are,' I said.

'Turned lions, have they?' he said in the same way, with another glance at me. He brooded a minute and then said, 'If it's that bad, I wish it was an army coming . . . For all I know it is. But I doubt it.'

'It would be well to know, my lord,' said Tirio.

'I have no way to know! We're cooped up here. Surely the idiots fortifying the bridge down there could send some scouts up the road on horseback to spy out the size of this army?'

'No doubt they have,' I said, stung. 'Maybe the soldiers killed them.'

'Well, we have to gamble till we know,' the Gand said. 'And I'll gamble that it's no army, but a messenger with a troop of fifteen or twenty guards. Tell your Waylord that. Tell him to keep his lion-sheep from stampeding, if he can. Tell him to come here. To the square. With Caspro the Maker, if he will. And I'll get myself carried out there, and we can talk to the people. Calm them down. I heard what Caspro did the other day, cooling them off with his tale of Ura and Hamneda. By God he's a clever man!'

I remembered how politely, even ornately, the Gand had spoken in public with Orrec and his officers. He was blunt and coarse now, no doubt because he was in pain, maybe also because he was talking to mere women. I tried to answer with stiff politeness, but fired up as I spoke. 'The Waylord is not at your bidding, sir. He keeps to his house. If you want his help keeping the peace, come to him yourself.'

'Sulter Galva is as lame as you are, Ioratth,' said Tirio.

'Is he? Is he?'

'From torture,' I said, 'when he was your son's prisoner.'

The old man had been riled by my insolence, but at that he looked at me, a long look, and then away. After a while he said, 'Very well then, I'll go there. Order up a litter, a chair, something. Tell them we want an open parley, there, at what d'ye call it, Galvamand. No use throwing it all away . . . There's been enough . . .' He did not finish his sentence. He lay back on his pillows, his face colorless and grim.

To arrange a parley was going to require some parleying, given the jittery confusion in the city. Ioratth was talking with several of his officers, giving them instructions, when we heard a trumpet call, sweet and high, far off, eastward, across the canal. It was promptly answered by a trumpet from the barracks here.

Within a few minutes the Ald force was reported in sight: a troop, as the Gand had hoped, of twenty or so, riding out of the hills with banners. We could hear the swelling noise of the crowds up on the Council Hill and in the streets leading to the East Canal. But as no army followed the mounted troop, the crowd noise at least grew no louder.

From the southeast window of the barracks house we could see the River Gate and the Isma Bridge. Tirio and I watched the troop arrive, halt outside the half-ruined wall, and talk with the citizens who had been guarding and fortifying the bridge. It took a while. At last, one Ald was allowed through the gate, on foot. Escorted by thirty or forty citizens, he crossed the bridge and came straight along the

Eastway towards the cordon guarding the barracks. I saw that he carried a wand of white wood, which I knew from history books was the envoy's token.

'Here's your messenger, my lord,' Tirio said to the Gand.

And before long the blue-cloaked officer came striding in, holding the wand, a troop of soldiers escorting him now, and saluted the Gand. 'From the Gand of Gands and Son of the Sun, High Priest and King of Asudar, the Lord Acray, a message to the Gand of Ansul, the Lord Ioratth,' he said, in the rolling, measured voice the Alds used for public speaking.

The old Gand got himself up higher on his pillows, gritting his teeth, made a kind of hunch for a bow, and said, 'The messenger of the Son of the Sun, our most honored Lord Acray, is welcome. Dismissed, Polle,' he said to the captain of the escort troop. He looked around at Tirio and me and Ialba who was there too, and said, 'Out.'

I felt like snarling like Shetar, but I followed Tirio meekly.

'He'll tell us what the man says as soon as he's

gone,' she said to me. 'Now that we have a little time for it, are you hungry?'

I was both hungry and thirsty after my difficult journey through my city. She brought out what they had to offer: water, a small piece of black bread dried hard, a couple of dried black figs. 'Siege rations,' Ialba said with a smile. I ate them with the care and attention poverty's gift deserves, wasting not a crumb.

We heard the messenger depart, and soon enough Ioratth shouted, 'Come!'

Are we dogs? I thought. But I came, with Tirio and Ialba.

Ioratth was sitting up straight, and his sallow, seamed face looked feverish. 'By God, by God, Tirio, I think we're off the hook,' he said. 'God be praised! Listen. I want you both to go to the palace or the Demon House, wherever there's some kind of chief, somebody in charge of the mob, and tell them this: No army has come from Asudar. No army will come from Asudar, so long as the city keeps the peace. Tell them that the Gand of Gands offers to his subjects of Ansul full relief from tribute, to be replaced by taxation paid to the treasury in Medron

as a protectorate state of Asudar. The Son of the
Sun has honored me with the title of Prince-Legate
to the Protectorate. In good time I'll invite the chief
men of Ansul to take counsel with me and hear our
orders concerning the government of the city and the
terms of trade with Asudar. A number of soldiers
will remain here as my personal guard and to protect
the city from its own unruly elements and from
invasion from Sundraman or elsewhere. The greater
part of our troops will return to Medron – when it's
certain that Ansul is in compliance with our orders.
Now, is there anybody in this damned city capable
of answering that, and acting on it?'

'I can take the message to the Waylord,' I said.

'Do it. Better than dragging me through the
streets in a cart. Do it and come back with an
acceptance. Come back with some men to talk to.
Why do they send me children, girls, by God!'

'Because women and girls are citizens here, not
dogs and slaves,' I said. 'And if you knew how to
write, you could send your so-called orders to the
Waylord yourself and read his answers yourself!' I
was shaking with fury.

The Gand gave one sharp glance at me and made a dismissive gesture. 'Tirio, will you go?' he said.

'I'll go with Memer,' she said. 'I think that would be best.'

Indeed it was best. All I'd heard, all I could hear of the Gand's message was that we were ordered to pay taxes to Asudar, submit to be a protectorate not a free state, and do whatever the Alds told us to do.

I had to listen to what Tirio said to the Waylord, when we got back to Galvamand, and what he said to the people, and what people said about it, all day long, before I was able to understand that in fact Asudar was offering us our freedom – at a price – and that my people saw it clearly and truly as a victory.

Maybe they could see it so clearly because it did have a price on it, in money and trade agreements, matters my people understand.

Maybe I had so much trouble seeing it because nobody died bravely for it. No heroes fighting on Mount Sul. No more fiery speeches in the square. Only two middle-aged men, both crippled, sending messages across a city, cautious and wary, working out an agreement. And wrangles in the Council

House. And a lot of talking and arguing and complaining in the marketplaces.

And the fountain running in the forecourt of the House of the Oracle.

And the temples of Ansul, the little houses of the gods and spirits, the shrines at every street corner and on every bridge, rebuilt, set up again, brought out of hiding, cleaned, carved anew, decorated with flowers. Lero's Stone was so covered with offerings sometimes you could not see it. On Iene's Feast, the solstice, men and boys brought garlands of oak and willow into the city in procession through the streets and hung them over the house doors, and women danced in the marketplaces and the square and sang Iene's songs. The older women taught the girls, like me, who did not know the dance steps or the songs.

All that summer people kept coming to the city from the rest of Ansul. Often they followed after the troops of Ald soldiers who were being withdrawn from the northern towns and gathered here before they were sent back east over the hills to Asudar. Citizens came to find out what was happening in the capital, and to take part in the elections; merchants and traders followed. In early autumn the Waylord

of Tomer came to stay with the Waylord of Ansul.
Ista lived in a passion of anxiety for two weeks,
making sure he was entertained in all ways as
befitted the honor of the House of Galva.

By then the Council was meeting regularly, and
Galvamand was no longer the center of political
planning and decision making. It was just the
Waylord's house, where a lot of talk took place
about trade, about hay transport and cattle markets
and what you could get in Medron or Dur for dried
apricots or olives in brine. The first election held by
the newly elected Council had been that of the
Waylord of Ansul, voted unanimously to Sulter
Galva; and with the post they allotted funds for
entertainment and upkeep of the house. Not lavish
funds, but wealth untold to us who ran the
household, and a heartening sign of the difference
between paying tribute as a subject state of Asudar
and paying taxes as a protectorate.

I had been utterly wrong about the Gand's
message. I had misjudged it, and him. I had wanted
to refuse patronisation, manipulation, compromise –
politics. I had wanted to fling off every bond, to defy
the tyrant. I had wanted to hate the Alds, drive them

away, destroy them . . . my vow, my promise, made when I was eight years old, that I had sworn by all the gods and by my mother's soul.

I had broken that promise. I had to break it. *Broken mend broken.*

◆　◆　◆

THE MESSENGER of the High Gand returned to Medron a few days after I carried the message to Ioratth. They had an escort of more than a hundred soldiers, under the command of Simme's father, and Simme rode beside him, going home. I had asked Ialba and Tirio to tell me what they could find out about them, and that is what they told me. I never saw Simme after he and I went through the lines together.

That troop escorting the messenger back to Medron also carried a prisoner in one of the provision carts: Iddor, son of Ioratth. He was in chains, we heard, in slave's clothing, with his hair and beard grown long, a sign of shame and disgrace to the Alds.

Tirio told us that Ioratth had not set eyes on his son since his betrayal, had not let anyone ask what should be done with him, would not let his name be spoken. He had, however, ordered that the priests be released from prison, even those who had been captured with his son. Presuming on this leniency, the priests had tried to intercede on Iddor's behalf, with a tale that they and Iddor had hidden Ioratth in the torture chamber only to save him from the vengeance of the rebel mob. Ioratth told them to be silent and be gone.

Since he had been through the fire, both burnt and spared, his soldiers saw their Gand as clearly favored by their Burning God, as holy as any priest. Realising their disadvantage, most of the priests chose to go back to Asudar with this first contingent of the army. So Ioratth's captains, left to their own judgment, decided the best thing to do with their embarrassing prisoner, his son, was send him off too, and let the High Gand decide what to do with him.

I was disappointed by this ignominious, uncertain outcome. I wanted to know Iddor would be punished as he deserved. The Alds loathed treachery, I knew, and were shocked by the betrayal of a father by a son. Would he be tortured, as he had tortured Sulter Galva? Would he be buried alive, the

way so many people in Ansul had been, taken down
to the mudflats south of the city and trampled into
the wet, salt mud until they suffocated?

Did I want him to be tortured and buried alive?

What did I want? Why was I so unhappy
through all this bright summer, the first summer of
our freedom? Why did I feel that nothing was
settled, nothing won?

◆ ◆ ◆

ORREC WAS speaking in the Harbor Market. It
was a golden autumn afternoon, windless. Sul stood
white across the dark-blue straits. Everybody in the
city was there to hear the maker. He told some of
the *Chamhan*, and they called for more and wouldn't
let him go. I was too far away to hear well, and was
restless. I left the crowd. I walked up West Street
alone. Nobody was in the streets. Everybody was
there behind me, together, in the marketplace,
listening. I touched the Sill Stone and went into my
house, clear through it, past the Waylord's rooms, to
the back, to the dark corridors. I wrote the words in
the air before the wall and the door opened and I

went into the room where the books and the shadows are.

I had not been there for months. It was as it had always been: the clear even light from the high skylights, the quiet air, the books in their patient, potent rows, and if I listened, the faint murmur of water in the cave down at the shadow end. No books lay out on the table. There was no sign of any presence there. But I knew the room was full of presences.

I'd intended to read in Orrec's book; but when I stood at the shelves my hand went to the book I had been working on last spring, the night before Gry and Orrec came, a text in Aritan, the *Elegies*. They are short poems of mourning and praise for people who died a thousand years ago. The names of the authors are mostly not given, and all we know of the people named in the poems is what the poet says.

One of them reads, 'Sullas who kept the house well, so that the patterned pavements shone, now keeps the house of silence. I listen for her step.'

Another, the one I'd been trying to understand when I stopped reading, is about a horse trainer; the first line is, 'Surely where he is, they are around him, the long-maned shadows.'

I sat down at the table, at my old place, with that book and the wordbook of Aritan, with its notes in the margins written by many hands over the centuries, and tried to make out what the next lines meant.

When I'd understood the poem as well as I could, and had it in my memory, the light from the skylights was fading. Lero's Day, the equinox, was past, the days were getting short. I closed the book and sat on at the table, not lighting the lamp, just sitting there feeling for the first time in a long time a sense of peace, of being in the right place. I let that feeling come all through me and penetrate me and settle in me. As it did, I was able to think, slowly and clearly, not so much in words as in knowing what matters and seeing what has to be done, which is the way I think. I hadn't been able to think that way for months.

That's why when I got up to leave the room, I took with me a book from it, a thing I had never done before. I took *Rostan*, the one I called Shining

Red when I was a little child building walls and bear's dens with the books.

I had heard Orrec speak of it longingly, not long ago, as a lost work of the Maker Regali. The Waylord had said nothing in reply.

He had never said anything to Orrec about the books in the secret room. So far as I knew, he and I alone knew of the room itself.

That the oracle spoke through books, people knew vaguely, and now they'd actually heard its voice; but they didn't ask to know more about the mystery, they didn't want to pry into it, they let it be. After all, for years, books themselves had been accursed and forbidden, dangerous things even to know about. And though we of Ansul live comfortably among the shadows of our dead, we're not a people with much taste for the uncanny. Sulter Galva the Reader was held in some awe, as was I; but people much preferred to deal with Sulter Galva the Waylord. The oracle had done its work, we'd been set free, and now we could get back to business.

But my business was a little different. That's what I'd seen at last, sitting at the reading table, with a closed book in my hands.

✦ 16 ✦

Orrec, Gry and Shetar had returned from the Harbor Market late in the afternoon, Orrec to collapse and sleep for a while as he always did when he could after a public performance. He was reviving now, roaming about barefoot and disheveled, when I came to the Master's rooms. He said, 'Hello, horse thief,' and Gry said, 'There you are! We were just talking about taking a walk in the old park before it gets too dark to see.'

Shetar did not understand separate words, such as 'walk', as many dogs can do; but she often was aware of intentions before people knew they were intending anything. She was already standing up, and now she paced over with her graceful slouch to the door and sat down to wait for us. The plumed tip of her tail twitched back and forth. I scratched her around the ears and she leaned her head into my hand and purred a little.

'I brought this for you, Orrec,' I said, and held out the tall book with its gold-printed red cover. He came over, slouching a bit himself and yawning, to take it. When he saw it was a book his mouth snapped shut and his face went taut. When he saw what book it was, he stood motionless, and it was a long moment before he drew breath.

'Oh, Memer,' he said. 'What have you given me?'

I said, 'What I have to give.'

He looked up from the book then to my face. His eyes were luminous. It gave me great joy to give him joy.

Gry came to his side and looked at the book; he showed her what it was, handling it with a lover's care, reading the first line half aloud. 'I knew,' he said, 'I knew they must be here – some of the books of the great library – But this—!' He looked at me again. 'Was this – Are there books here in the house, Memer?'

I hesitated. Gry, as quickly aware of feeling and intention as Shetar, laid her hand on his arm and said, 'Wait, Orrec.'

I had to think, and quickly, what indeed my intention was, what right I had and what responsibility. Was this book mine to give? And if it was, what of the other books? And the other lovers of books?

What I saw was that I could not lie to Orrec. And that answered the question of my responsibility. As for the right, I had to claim it.

'Yes,' I said. 'There are books here. But I don't think I can take you to the place where they are. I'll ask the Waylord. But I think it's closed, except to us. To my people. I think our guardians keep it hidden. The spirits of the house, the ancestors. And the ones who were here before us. The ones who told us to stay here.'

Orrec and Gry had no trouble understanding this. They too had gifts of their lineage. They knew the burdens and chances laid on us by the shadows in our blood and bone, and by the spirits of the place we live in.

'Orrec, let me tell him I gave you the book,' I said. 'I didn't ask him if I could.' Orrec looked concerned, and I said, 'It'll be all right. But I need to talk to him.'

'Of course.'

'He never spoke of the books to you, because it was dangerous to know,' I said. I felt I must defend the Waylord's silence. 'For so long, he had to hide them all. From everybody. The Alds could never find them, here. So they were safe, and people weren't in danger for having them. But people knew. They brought books here in secret, at night – hidden in packages of candles or old clothes – in firewood – in a hay bale – they risked their lives bringing books here, where they knew we could keep them safe. Families who'd hidden their books, like the Cams and the Gelbs, and people we didn't know, just people who'd found a book or kept it or saved it from the Alds. They knew to bring it here to Galvamand. But now, now we don't have to hide any more – do we? Can you – could you ever read to the people, Orrec? Instead of reciting? To let them know, to let them see that books aren't demons, that our history, our hearts, our freedom's written in them?'

He looked at me with a slow, joyful smile that

became almost a laugh. 'I think it's you that should read to them, Memer,' he said.

'*Warrawarrroo!*' Shetar said, losing patience at last.

Gry and I left Orrec with his treasure. We let Shetar lead us out and guide us in the twilight up to Denios' Fountain. There she roamed about through the fallen leaves and rustling shrubbery, hunting mice, while we talked, sitting on the old marble bench by the fountain. Lights were coming on down in the houses of the city. Far out in the straits, under the last dim purple of sunset, we saw the glimmer of the boats of night fishermen. Sul was a pure cone of darkness against the dying light. An owl swooped past near us, and I said, 'The good omen to you.'

'And to you,' Gry said. 'You know, in Trundlede they call owls bad luck? They're a gloomy, down-hearted lot there. Too much forest, too much rain.'

'You've travelled all over the world,' I said dreamily.

'Oh, no, not yet. We've never been to Sundraman. Or the capes of Manva or Melune. And among the City States we've seen only Sentas and Pagadi, and we came only through a corner of Vadalva . . . And even if you know a land well, there's always a town or a hill you haven't seen. I don't think we'll run out of world.'

'When do you think you'll go on?'

'Well, until just now, I'd have guessed that Orrec might be thinking of moving on to Sundraman before the winter, or in the spring. He wants to see what kind of poetry they have there, before we go back to Mesun. But now . . . I doubt he'll go till he knows every book you can show him.'

'Are you sorry?'

'Sorry? Why? You've given him a great happiness, and I love to see him happy. It doesn't come easy to him. Orrec has a difficult heart . . . You know what he can do with a crowd of people, how easy it seems to come to him and how they love him – and doing it, he's carried away by it – but afterward, he feels cast down and false. It isn't me at all, he says, it's the sacred wind blows through me, and it empties me and leaves me like dry grass . . . But if he can write, and read, and follow his own heart in silence, he's a happy man.'

'That's why I love him,' I said. 'I'm like that.'

'I know,' she said, and put her arm around me.

'But you yourself might want to be going on, Gry. Not just sitting here all year with a lot of books and politics.'

She laughed. 'I like it here. I like Ansul. But if we stay through the winter, and I think now we will, I might find somebody who needs a hand training horses.'

'*Surely where he is, they are around him, the long-maned shadows,*' I said. I said the rest of the poem for her when she asked.

'Yes. That poet got it right,' she said. 'I like that.'

'Gudit is hoping to get some horses for the Waylord to use.'

'I might train a colt for him. It stands to reason . . . But, anyhow, we'll go on, eventually. And sooner or later we'll go back to Urdile, to take what Orrec's learned to the scholars in Mesun. He'll be busy copying that book, and anything you give him, from now on.'

'I could help him copy.'

'He'll wear you out if you offer.'

'I like doing it. I learn the book while I copy it.'

She was silent for a little and then said, 'If we did

go back to Urdile, next spring or summer, whenever
– would you think of coming with us?'

'Coming with you,' I repeated.

Sometimes, back in early summer, I had made a
daydream of the caravan wagon which stood now in
our stables: a daydream of Star and Branty pulling it
across some long gold plain where the poplars cast
shadows, or over a road in the hills, and Orrec
driving it, and Gry and Shetar walking with me
along the road behind. It had been just a fancy to
cheer me, to take my mind away from anxiety, in the
time of the fire and the crowds and the fear.

Now she made it real. That road lay before me.

I said, 'I would go with you anywhere, Gry.'

She leaned her head against mine for a moment.
'We might do that, then,' she said.

I thought, trying to see what it is that matters and
what I have to do. I said finally, 'I would come back
here.'

She listened.

'I couldn't leave him and not come back.'

She nodded.

'But more than that. I belong to Galvamand. I
think I am the Reader. Not he. It's passed along.' I

was speaking out of my own thoughts and I realised she could hardly know what I meant. I tried to explain. 'There is a voice here, and it must speak through one who can – who can ask, who can read. He taught me. He gave me that. He kept it for me and passed it to me. It's not his to carry, but mine. And I have to come back to it. To stay here.'

Again she nodded, gravely, consenting fully.

'But Orrec could teach me, too,' I said, and then, sure I had gone too far and asked too much, I shrank into myself.

'That would complete his happiness,' Gry answered. She said it serenely and as a matter of course. 'To have the books he longed for, and you to read them with – oh, you may not have to worry about leaving Galvamand, Memer! The problem may be getting him to leave . . . But I think you'd like it, the way we travel, stopping to stay a while in a town or a village, and finding the makers and musicians there. And they'll speak and sing for us, and Orrec for them. They'll bring out the books they have to show him, and the little boys who can recite 'Hamneda's Vow', and the old women who know old songs and tales . . . And then we always go back to Mesun. It's a fine city, all towers on hills. I know Orrec would like to take you there, because he's said so to me. To meet the scholars he knows there, and read with them. You could take them the learning of Ansul, and bring their learning back with you to Galvamand . . . But the best part is, I'd have you with me all that time.'

I bent my head to kiss her hard, strong little hand, and she kissed my hair.

Shetar came bounding past us, a wild thing in the darkening night.

'It must be supper time,' Gry said and stood up. Shetar came to her at once, and we went down to the house. Orrec was of course lost in *Rostan*, and had to be dragged from it bodily, and we three were late to table, arriving about the time Ista finally took her place.

We ate in the dining room now, not in the pantry, for we were generally twelve or more at table, what with the increase to the household, and Sosta's new husband, and guests. I haven't told of Sosta's wedding. We cleaned the great courtyard for it, taking out all the broken stone and rubbish that had been left there since the house was looted and burned, replanting the marble flower boxes and training the trumpet vines that wreathed the walls, sweeping the tessellated pavement of red and yellow stone. The celebration was on a hot afternoon of late summer, a day of Deori. All the friends of both households came. Ista set out a splendid feast, and people danced while the moon crossed the sky above the courtyard. And Ista said, watching the dancers, 'It's like the good times, the old times! Almost.'

This night, we had no guests but Per Actamo, who was as often at our house as his own. He had been elected to the Council, and was valued for his connection with the Gand Ioratth, now the Prince-Legate, through his cousin Tirio Actamo. Tirio herself played a peculiarly difficult part – once slave-concubine to the tyrant, now wife of the legate – victim of the enemy yet his conqueror. There were people in Ansul who still called her whore and shameless, and more who adored her, calling her Lady Freedom. She bore it all with steady mildness, as if there were no such thing as a divided loyalty. Most people ended up believing her to be nothing more than an ill-used, well-bred, sweet-natured woman making the best of her strange fortune. She was that, but she was more. Per was a man of lively intelligence and ambition, and he took counsel with Tirio as often as he did with the Waylord.

He brought a message from her, which he told us after dinner, in the Waylord's rooms. Thanks to a gift sent by the Waylord of Essangan we had wine after dinner these days, a few drops of the golden brandy-wine of those vineyards, like fire and honey. One after another we offered our glass to the god-niche and drank the blessing. Then we sat down.

'My cousin has persuaded the Prince-Legate of Asudar to request to visit the Waylord of Ansul, at last,' said Per. 'So I am the bearer of that request, couched in the usual incivilities of the Alds. But I think it's meant civilly.'

'I grant it civilly,' the Waylord said with a bit of a grin.

'Frankly, Sulter, can you stand the sight of him?'

'I hold nothing against Ioratth,' the Waylord said. 'He's a soldier, he followed his orders. A religious man, he obeyed his priests. Till they betrayed him. Who he is himself, I have no idea. I'll be interested to learn. That your cousin holds him dear is strongly in his favor.'

'We can always talk poetry with him,' said Orrec. 'He has an excellent ear.'

'But he can't read,' I said.

The Waylord looked up at me. A girl among grown women and men, I still had the privilege of listening without being expected to talk, and mostly silence was my preference. But I had realised recently that when I did speak, the Waylord listened attentively.

Per Actamo was also looking at me with his bright, dark eyes. Per was fond of me, teased me, pretended to be awed by my learning, often seemed to forget he was thirty and I seventeen and talked to me as to an equal, and sometimes flirted with me without knowing, I think, that he was doing it. He was kind and handsome and I'd always been a little in love with him. I'd often thought that I'd marry Per some day. I thought I could, if I wanted to. But I wasn't ready for all that yet. I didn't want to be a woman yet. I'd had great love given me as Galva's daughter and heir, but I'd never yet had what Gry and Orrec offered me – freedom, the freedom of a child, a younger sister. And I longed for it.

Per asked me now, 'Do you want to teach the Gand how to read, Memer?'

His teasing and the Waylord's attention put me on my mettle. 'Would an Ald let a woman teach him anything? But if the Gand's going to deal with people in Ansul, he'd better learn not to be afraid of books.'

'Maybe this isn't the best house in which to prove that particular point,' said Per. 'There's at least one book here that would put the fear of the gods into anybody.'

'They said the last priests went back with the troops that left today,' said Gry. The connection of her thought was clear to us all.

'Ioratth kept his house priests,' Per said. 'Three or four of them. To say the prayers and lead the ceremonies. And drive out demons when necessary, I suppose. He doesn't find as many demons here as his son did, though.'

'It takes one to find one,' said Gry.

'"The god in the heart sees the god in the stones,"' Orrec murmured, a line of Regali, though he said it in our own language.

The Waylord didn't hear him. He was still brooding, and now he asked me, as if he had been following the idea since Per had jokingly said it, 'Would you teach the Gand Ioratth how to read, if he consented to learn, Memer?'

'I'd teach anybody who wanted to learn,' I said. 'As you taught me.'

The talk passed on to other things. After arranging that the visit to Galvamand by the Prince-Legate and his consort would take place in four days, Per took his leave. Orrec was yawning hugely, and he and Gry soon went off to sleep. I rose to see that the Waylord had what he needed before I too went to bed.

'Stay a minute, Memer,' he said.

I sat down willingly. Since I'd been back to the secret room and renewed that bond with all my past years there, I felt that things were as they used to be between him and me. Our bond, too, that I'd thought was weakened, held as strong and as easy as ever. He was linked now to many people other than me, and I to some people other than him; we no longer needed each other so urgently for strength and solace; but what difference did that make?

Hidden in solitude and poverty, or among people in a rich busy world, he and I were bound by all the shadows of our ancestry, and by the power we shared and the knowledge he'd given me, and by dear love and honor.

'Have you been to the room at all?' he asked me.

We were indeed bound very close.

'Today. For the first time.'

'Good. Every night I think I'll go there and read a little, but I can't drag myself. Ah, it was easier in Ista's old days, I'll admit. I could spend all day talking grain prices and half the night reading Regali, then.'

'I gave *Rostan* to Orrec,' I said.

He looked up, not following at once, and I went on, 'I took it out of the room. I thought it was time.'

'Time,' he repeated. He looked away, thinking, and at last said only, 'Yes.'

'Is it true, as I think, that only we can enter the room?'

'Yes,' he said again, almost absently.

'Then shouldn't we bring the books out of hiding? The ordinary books. As we kept them in hiding. For the same reason. So that people would have them.'

'And it's time,' he said. 'Yes. I suppose you're right. Though . . .' He brooded a little longer. 'Come, Memer. Let's go there,' he said, and pushed himself up from his chair. I took up the small lamp and followed him back through the ruined corridors to the wall that seems to be the back wall of the house, the wall that has no door in it. There he wrote in the air the letters that spell the word 'open' in the language of our ancestors who came from the Sunrise. The door opened, and we went through. I turned and closed it and it became the wall.

I lighted the big lamp on the reading table. The room bloomed with its soft light, and the gold on the spines of books glimmered a little here and there.

He touched the god-niche and murmured the blessing, and then stood looking about the room. He sat down at the table, rubbing a stiff knee. 'What were you reading?' he asked.

'The *Elegies*.' I brought the book from the shelf and laid it before him.

'How far have you got?'

'"The Horse Trainer".'

He opened the book and found the poem. 'Can you say it?'

I recited the ten lines of Aritan.

'And?'

I said my reading of it, as I had to Gry. He nodded. 'Very satisfactory,' he said, with a suppressed smile.

I sat down at the table opposite him, and after a little silence he said, 'You know, Memer, Orrec Caspro came just in time. He can teach you. You were about to discover that you can teach me.'

'Oh no! I mostly just guess at the *Elegies*. I still can't read Regali.'

'But now you have a teacher who can.'

'Then – you're not displeased – it was right to give him *Rostan?*'

'Yes,' he said, with a deep breath. 'I think so. How can we know what's right, when we can't understand the powers we have? I am a blind man asked to read the message given him by a god.'

He turned over the pages of the book on the table and closed it softly. He looked down towards the end of the room where the light of the lamps died away. 'I told Iddor I was the Reader. What is reading when you don't know the language? You are the Reader, Memer. Of that at least I have no doubt. Do you doubt it?'

The question was abrupt. I answered it without hesitation: 'No.'

'Good. Good. And that being so, this is your room, your domain. Blind as I was, I kept it in trust for you. And for all those who brought their treasure to us here, the books . . . What shall we do with them, Memer?'

'Make a library,' I said. 'Like the old one here.'

He nodded. 'It seems to be the will of the house itself. We merely obey it.'

That was how it seemed to me too. But I still had some questions.

'Waylord, that day . . . The day the Fountain ran.'

'The Fountain,' he said. 'Yes.'

'The miracle,' I said.

With that same hint of a smile, he said, 'No.'

I was perhaps surprised, perhaps not.

His smile grew broader and merrier. 'The Lord of the Springs showed me the means, some while ago,' he said. 'I'll show you, when you like.'

I nodded. That was not where my mind was.

'Does it grieve you or shock you, Memer, that a miracle may be taken into our own hands, as it were?'

'No,' I said. 'Not that one. But the other . . .'

He watched me and waited.

'You weren't lame,' I said.

He looked down at his hands, his legs. His face was grave now. 'So they tell me,' he said.

'You don't remember?'

'I remember coming to this room in fear and anguish. As soon as I entered, it came to me that I should let the fountain run, and I hurried to do that, not reasoning why. As if obeying. And next, it came to me that I should take a book from the shelf. And I did that. And there was need for haste, so I . . . could it be that I ran? I don't know. It must be that those who silenced me when they needed my silence, needed me then to waken your voice.'

I looked down the room, to the shadow end. So did he.

'You didn't ask the . . . ?'

'There wasn't time to consult the oracle. And it wouldn't have answered me. It speaks to you, Memer, not me.'

I didn't want to hear what he was telling me, even though I had said that I was the Reader. My heart protested in fear, in humiliation. 'It doesn't speak to me!' I said. 'It uses me!'

He nodded briefly. 'As I was used.'

'It wasn't even my voice – was it? I don't know! I don't understand it. I'm ashamed, I'm afraid! I don't ever want to go into that darkness again.'

He said nothing for a long time, and finally spoke gently. 'They use us, yes, but they do not use us ill . . . If you must go into the dark, Memer, think, it's only a mother, a grandmother, trying to tell us something we don't yet understand. Speaking a language you don't yet know well, but it can be learned. So I told myself, when I had to enter there.'

I thought about that for a while, and it began to give me comfort. It made the darkness of the cave less uncanny, to imagine that my mother's spirit was there, with all the other mothers of my race, and they wouldn't seek to frighten me.

But I had one more question.

'The book – the one you had in your hand – is it on the oracle shelves?'

His silence now was different; he was finding

difficulty in answering. At last he said, 'No. I took the first book I saw.'

He got up, limped to a bookcase nearby, the closest to the door, and took a little volume from a shelf at eye level. I recognised the dun-colored, unlettered binding. He brought it back and held it out to me in silence. I was afraid to take it but I took it, and after a minute I opened it.

I recognised it then. It was a primer, a reading book for children, *Tales of the Beasts*. I had read it when I was first learning to read, years ago, here, in the secret room.

I turned the pages, my fingers stiff and awkward. I saw the small woodcuts of rabbits and ravens and wild boars. I read the last line of a story, 'So the Lion returned home to the desert and told the beasts of the desert that the Mouse was the bravest of all creatures.'

I looked up at the Waylord, and he looked back at me. His face and his slight gesture said: *I do not know.*

I looked at the little book that had set us free. I thought of Denios' words, and said them aloud:

"'There is a god in every leaf; you hold what is sacred in your open hand.'"

After a while, I added, 'And there are no demons.'

'No,' the Waylord said. 'Only us. We do the demon work.' And again he looked down at his crippled hands.

We were silent. I heard the faint sound of the water running in the dark.

'Come,' he said, 'it's late, the dream senders are all around us. Let's let them have their way.'

I held the small lamp in my left hand and with my right hand wrote the bright letters on the air. We went through the door, and along the dark corridors. Passing his room I bade him sleep well, and he stooped to kiss my forehead, and so we parted with the blessing for the night.

THE END

Also by Ursula le Guin

◆ TALES FROM EARTHSEA ◆

'The magic of Earthsea remains as potent, as wise and as necessary as anyone could dream.'
Neil Gaiman

Here, collected together for the first time, are five magical tales of Earthsea, the fantastical realm created by a master storyteller that has held readers enthralled for more than three decades.

'The Finder', a novella set a few hundred years before *A Wizard of Earthsea*, when the Archipelago was dark and troubled, reveals how the famous school on Roke was started.

In 'The Bones of the Earth' the wizards who first taught Ged demonstate how humility, if great enough, can rein in an earthquake.

Sometimes wizards can pursue alternative careers – and 'Darkrose and Diamond' is also a delightful story of young courtship.

Return to the time when Ged was Archmage of Earthsea in 'On the High Marsh', a story about the love of power and the power of love.

And 'Dragonfly', showing how a determined woman can break the glass ceiling of male magedom, provides a bridge – a dragon bridge – between *Tehanu* and *The Other Wind.*

This enchanting collection is rounded off with an essay about Earthsea's history, people, languages, literature and magic.

'Le Guin makes a triumphant return ... the publication of this collection is a major event in fantasy literature.'
Publishers Weekly

• THE OTHER WIND •

The bestselling saga that started with *A Wizard of Earthsea* continues in this triumphant, potent and fantastical tale of magic, love and dragons.

Every night the sorcerer Alder dreams of his wife, who died young and wants so much to return to him that she kissed him across the low stone wall that separates our world from the land of the dead. The dead pull Alder to them, seeking to free themselves through him and invade Earthsea.

In desperation, Alder turns to Sparrowhawk, the former Archmage, and is told to seek out Tenar, Tehanu and the young King Lebannen. With these three and the amber-eyed Irian, a dragon able to take the shape of a woman, Alder journeys to the Immanent Grove on Roke. For the incursion of the dead is not the only danger threatening Earthsea: the dragons are back.

And after centuries of peace, they come to claim what they believe is rightfully theirs.

'I adored *The Other Wind*. Real mythmaking, done by a master of the craft .... The magic of Earthsea remains as potent, as wise and as necessary as anyone could dream.'

Neil Gaiman, author of *Coraline* and *The Sandman*.

· GIFTS ·

Orrec is the son of the Brantor of Caspromant; Gry the daughter of the Brantors of Barre and Rodd. They have grown up together in neighbouring domains, running half-wild across the Uplands.

The people of the domains are like their land: harsh and fierce and prideful; ever at war with one or other of their neighbours, raiding cattle, capturing serfs, enlarging their holdings. It is only the gifts that keep a fragile peace.

The gifts are powers: the Barres can call animals. The women of Cordemant can blind or make deaf, or take away speech. Olm can set a fire burning. Brantor Ogge of Drummant has the gift of slow wasting. But the Caspro gift is both best and worst: it is the gift of undoing.

Gry's gift runs true, but she will not use it to call animals for the hunt. Orrec too has a problem, for his gift of undoing is wild: he cannot control it – and that is the most dangerous gift of all . . .

GIFTS is Ursula Le Guin at her legendary best: an exciting, moving story beautifully told.

'Le Guin writing for children is more thought-provoking than most people writing for adults. In this book, she looks at power, love and social prejudice, seen through the eyes of two teenagers . . . a brilliant exploration of society at its worst and at its best, with a tender and hopeful ending' *Publishing News*

'Thoughtful, wise and exciting storytelling' *Books for Keeps*